Praise for Ellie Alex

"Delectable." v

"Delicious." —*RT Book Reviews*

"Quirky . . . intriguing . . . [with] recipes to make your stomach growl." —*Reader to Reader*

"This debut culinary mystery is a light soufflé of a book (with recipes) that makes a perfect mix for fans of Jenn McKinlay, Leslie Budewitz, or Jessica Beck."
—*Library Journal* on *Meet Your Baker*

"Marvelous." —*Fresh Fiction*

"Scrumptious . . . will delight fans of cozy mysteries with culinary delights." —*Night Owl Reviews*

"Clever plots, likable characters, and good food . . . Still hungry? Not to worry, because desserts abound in . . . this delectable series."
—*Mystery Scene* on *A Batter of Life and Death*

ith] *Meet Your Baker,* Alexander weaves a tasty tale eit, family ties, delicious pastries, and murder."
—Edith Maxwell, author of *A Tine to Live, A Tine to Die*

satisfy both dedicated foodies and ardent mysers alike."
—Jessie Crockett, author of *Drizzled with Death*

Also
by Ellie Alexander

Meet Your Baker

A Batter of Life and Death

On Thin Icing

Caught Bread Handed

Fudge and Jury

A Crime of Passion Fruit

Another One Bites the Crust

Till Death Do Us Tart

Live and Let Pie

Ellie Alexander

St. Martin's Paperbacks

LIVE AND LET PIE

For information address St. Martin's Press, 175 Fifth Avenue, New York, NY 10010.

ISBN: 978-1-250-15939-7

Printed in the United States of America

St. Martin's Paperbacks edition / January 2019

St. Martin's Paperbacks are published by St. Martin's Press, 175 Fifth Avenue, New York, NY 10010.

10 9 8 7 6 5 4 3 2 1

Chapter One

They say that you can't go back, that it's better to keep the past in the rearview mirror. That may be true, but lately it felt like my past was creeping into everything I touched. Not that it was necessarily a bad thing. It had started with my mom's gorgeous midsummer wedding. Seeing her marry her longtime love, the Professor (Ashland's resident detective and Shakespeare scholar), had filled my heart with happiness, but it had also opened up memories of loss that I thought I had buried long ago—the permanent loss of my father.

When my dad died in my formative years, it forever altered the course of my future. Mom and I had cocooned ourselves in, sharing the burden of grief, and pouring our energies into Torte, our family bakeshop. We weren't merely mother and daughter. We were best friends. She was my rock, my confidante, and my steadfast supporter. She had nudged me (well, maybe more like forced me) to follow my dreams of attending culinary school. Without her gentle yet firm guidance I might have never left my hometown of Ashland, Oregon. Now I had come full circle. After years of traversing the seas on a boutique cruise ship I had returned to Ashland and was content to have found my way home.

The only problem was that my husband, Carlos, was still out to sea. Like Odysseus, he had been sailing vast oceans lured by the siren song of steel-blue waters while I had chosen to plant my feet firmly on Ashland's hallowed ground. Being apart from him had left a wound in my heart. A wound that, while painful, had forced me out of my comfort zone. It had given me the gift of distance and the opportunity to be alone with myself, maybe for the first time as an adult. I'd spent many months reflecting on my choices, and I was beginning to understand how my father's early death had influenced my decisions for better and for worse. I hadn't realized how much I had isolated myself during my years on the ship. Maybe it was what I needed. Or maybe I could have done it differently. Regardless, I had learned valuable lessons and returning to Ashland had cemented my need for stronger and deeper connections. With each passing day my circle of friends and family expanded. It was almost as if I could feel myself branching out, acknowledging the risk of reinjuring old wounds, armed with the knowledge that love and loss go hand in hand.

When Carlos and his son Ramiro were in Ashland for Mom's wedding he had professed his desire to be a part of the new life I was carving out. I was torn. As much as I missed Carlos, I wasn't convinced that he belonged on land. Some people are born to wander. I couldn't quite picture Carlos thriving in our small, tight-knit community. Wanderlust ran deep through his Spanish blood. He made fast friends at every port of call and thrived on the thrill of ever-changing adventures. Ashland was bucolic, quiet, and quaint. Not that we were without culture. In fact, quite the opposite. As home to the famed Oregon Shakespeare Festival, our sun-drenched town nestled in the Siskiyou Mountains saw travelers from all over the globe who came to take in a production of *Sleeping Beauty* under the stars or dine at one of dozens of award-winning restaurants. But there was a difference between catering to adventure seekers and actually seeking adventure. I wasn't sure what Carlos was going to decide, but I knew that Ashland was exactly where I was meant to be.

"Stop daydreaming, Jules." I shook myself from my thoughts and reached for a tennis shoe. At the moment I was due at an interview. But thanks to a demonstration of tempering chocolate gone completely wrong, I had had to come home to change out of chocolate-splattered clothes.

Kitchen flubs can happen to the best chefs—I had had my fair share of disasters over the years—but today's took the cake. I wasn't entirely to blame. Torte was undergoing a major expansion. We had recently modeled the basement, which was now home to our baking operations. I was still getting used to the new setup in the kitchen and had forgotten that I had asked Sterling and Andy to move a stack of boxes from upstairs. My chocolate-tempering demonstration had gone without a hitch until I backed into one of the boxes, slipped on the floor, and ended up covered in melted chocolate.

I knew that my team was going to tease me relentlessly for weeks to come.

Oh well, such is the life of a pastry chef. You have to be able to laugh at yourself. At least I'd given my staff something to chuckle about. They had been working around the clock and in less than desirable conditions during the remodel.

The next phase of our growth was under way and involved punching stairs through to the coffee bar and dining area above. Our contractor had run into a couple of challenges (one being that our architect's wife had been accused of attempting to poison me) that had set us back a few weeks. Dust and the constant sound of hammering and drilling don't exactly mix with the artisan pastries and coffees we serve at Torte. I couldn't wait for construction to wrap and to get back to the business of baking.

In the interim, I had been lining up interviews for potential new hires. We had always run a tight ship at Torte with a small but mighty staff. Our physical expansion and Mom's desire to cut back a bit meant that we needed to ramp up our team. I was excited about the possibility, but I wanted to make sure whoever we hired would be a match. The wrong person could completely change the recipe we had created with our young and highly capable staff.

Sterling, a closet poet with soul-piercing eyes and a gentle heart, was responsible for the majority of our savory items—daily soups, grilled paninis, fresh chopped salads, and hearty pastas. Bethany and Stephanie were my pastry stars. They couldn't be more different in appearance or attitude. Steph's goth style and aloof attitude, paired with purple hair and a tendency to stare at her feet while speaking, gave off the impression that she didn't care. Nothing could be further from the truth.

Working with her had taught me never to judge a book by its cover. Stephanie was devoutly dedicated to the bakeshop and spent her spare time (when she wasn't studying for her coursework at SOU) watching baking tutorials on the Pastry Channel and poring through cookbooks. Bethany was bubbly and upbeat. Her cheery, positive attitude brought a lightness to the kitchen. Her baking skills were equally vibrant. She had a natural sense of how to balance sugary confections so that they didn't end up cloyingly sweet. Finishing out the team was Andy, our resident barista and all-around good guy. Andy's coffee creations had become a thing of legend. Locals and visitors lined up for his foamy lattes and flavor-infused cold brews.

The trick would be finding new staff with skills complementary to our current crew. It was a big task, but I was up for the challenge. Ashland is a college town, home of Southern Oregon University, so there was never a shortage of energetic and eager help. Fingers crossed, I would find some gems in the candidates that I had lined up to interview.

Armed with a list of interview questions and a clean T-shirt, I tied my long blond hair into a ponytail and left my apartment. My apartment sat above Elevation, an outdoor store on the plaza. The minute I stepped outside the sound of laughter and cheers greeted me. I walked down the stairs to find one of the staff members from Elevation balancing on a slack line that had been strung up in front of the store. A small crowd had gathered to watch him as he held his arms out in a T and danced across the line on his tiptoes.

I joined in the applause when he made it to the opposite end of the rope and took a bow. "Today only, you can go home with your own slack line for the low price of $99. And come watch bigger and better stunts at Lithia Park this afternoon at four. We'll be showing off our best balancing acts and giving everyone a chance to walk the line." I overheard his sales pitch as I turned to the left toward Torte.

The plaza, Ashland's downtown core, was awash with colorful activity. Each storefront was constructed to resemble Tudor architecture. Seasonal summer displays, from butterfly gardens to racks of costumes and wigs, beckoned shoppers inside.

A group of tourists loaded with shopping totes stopped to admire a window display at the jewelry shop, where sparkling diamond-studded tiaras and crowns of rose gold reflected the sunlight. I chuckled at the banner above the glittery gems that read: WHERE WOMEN GET *IN* TROUBLE AND MEN GET *OUT* OF TROUBLE.

One of the tourists pointed to the clever line as I walked past. "So true, honey," she said with a wink to one of her friends. "Let's go get into some trouble. I see a pair of platinum earrings that will make my husband's eyes spin."

I smiled as I walked on toward Torte, which sat at the far end of the block. Across the street, near the bubbling Lithia fountains, a musician blew on a didgeridoo. The trumpetlike sound echoed throughout the crowded sidewalks. It was nearly impossible not to feel happy in Ashland. Maybe that was due to our Mediterranean climate, the long stretches of sun, the fact that mountains swept to the sky in every direction, the sepia-toned hills to the east, and the dark green forests to the west. Or maybe it was due to our eclectic community of artists—drawn to the southernmost corner of Oregon for its picturesque vistas and star-cluttered skies. Ashland was a haven for creative types—writers, painters, sculptors, dancers, actors, visual artists, and technology wizards all landed in our hamlet, meshing together seamlessly. And then there were the tourists. I was convinced that one of the reasons Ashland exuded such a laid-back and happy vibe was because at any given time vacationers filled our charming downtown streets, popping into shops and restaurants for an unhurried afternoon and lingering over late-night cocktails after the evening show.

Yep, you're one lucky woman, Jules, I said to myself as I arrived at Torte and pushed open the front door.

Inside, the familiar throb of hammering and the hum of the espresso machine greeted me. Our makeshift dining room consisted of crammed-together chairs and a handful of our dining tables. Usually the front of the bakeshop was open with bright, airy window booths, a collection of two- and four-person tables, our pastry counter, and the coffee bar, but during construction we had temporarily reconfigured the space. It was snug to say the very least.

The entire back half of the shop had been taped off with thick clear plastic. We had removed most of the tables, taken out the old pastry case, and set up a small counter for the short term that housed our pastry trays and espresso machine.

Andy waved from behind the counter, where he was pulling shots of dark, aromatic espresso. I breathed in the scent and said hello to a couple of regulars who were sitting within earshot of the coffee bar. "It's looking good in here, Jules," one of them said, raising an iced matcha latte. The green tea and foamy milk made for a lovely glass.

I glanced around the tight space. Every spare inch of countertop contained trays of cookies, hand pies, and crusty loaves of bread. The plastic tarp flapped in rhythm with the work crew's power tools. Customers squished into booths and tables, and light dusty footprints led from the front door to the construction zone. "Thanks, I think. Hopefully we're in the home stretch. It's . . . uh . . . cozy in here."

"Don't give it a thought, dear. No one cares. Torte is meant to be cozy." The woman pointed to her honey-lavender scone. "As long as you keep making baked goods that taste like this, we'll eat out of garbage cans, won't we, Wendy?"

Her friend Wendy flashed me a thumbs-up as she took a bite of her pesto-egg croissant sandwich, smothered with melted provolone cheese and stuffed with thick-sliced bacon.

"Let's hope it doesn't come to that." I grinned and left them to their breakfast. "How's it going?" I asked Andy.

He wore a red Southern Oregon University football T-shirt, revealing tan, muscular forearms. Practice for the new season began in a few weeks, meaning that Andy would have to take off early for daily doubles. Yet another reason I needed to hire extra staff—stat. "Great, boss!" he yelled over the sound of a jackhammer. "Another quiet morning in coffee paradise."

"Right." I rolled my eyes.

Andy grinned. His impish attitude was one of the many things that endeared him to customers, particularly with the teen and twenty-something set. There was often a long line at the espresso bar that I knew had as much to do with Andy's boyish good looks and charm as it did with his droolworthy espresso concoctions. "You don't look like a dark chocolate mocha anymore," he teased.

"Ha-ha." I held up the file folder with the resumes. "Somehow I figured that being coated in chocolate might not make a good first impression for our potential candidates."

"Or maybe they'd feel so sorry for you they'd take the job on the spot." Andy snapped his finger. "Speaking of interviews, there's a woman waiting for you downstairs. She's here early for her interview and I didn't know where else to put her and she was trying to get a look at my machine." He caressed the top of the espresso machine. "Not cool, not cool. Hands off the machinery. I sent her outside and downstairs."

At that moment Bethany came through the front door with a tray of lemon drop cupcakes just as two women were leaving. Bethany balanced the tray with one arm as the women ducked under the tray, narrowly avoiding a collision. Visions of lemony buttercream splattering on the floor and windows danced through my head.

"Nice reflexes." Andy applauded. "Skills. That's how you do it, boss."

A splotchy blush crept up Bethany's fair, freckled cheeks. I had suspected for a while that she had developed feelings for Andy. I couldn't tell if he was oblivious to the fact that she turned bright red anytime she was around him, or if he simply wasn't interested and figured the kindest thing to do was to play dumb in order to spare her any embarrassment. "Thanks." She set the tray on the counter. "There's a woman waiting for you downstairs, Jules."

"Already told her. You're too late, Beth." Andy shot Bethany a wink and poured foam in the shape of a heart in one of our signature Torte mugs.

When my parents had opened the bakeshop three decades ago, they had wanted to create a gathering space where everyone who walked through the front door was treated like royalty. Torte's cherry-red-and-teal walls, corrugated metal siding, and focus on handmade artisan coffees and pastries had done just that. Now it was my responsibility to make sure that we stayed true to their vision through the new changes and growth. My goal was to ensure that the Torte our customers knew and loved would feel the same. From our delicate Torte logo with its fleur-de-lis design to our fire-engine-red aprons and diner-style coffee mugs, my mission was to keep the essence of the bakeshop strong and steady while expanding our square footage. It was also my responsibility to keep them safe. The construction could not be over soon enough. Between my chocolate catastrophe and Bethany's near miss with the tray of cupcakes, we were flirting with disaster. Adding even more people to our cramped working conditions was only going to make things worse. But I didn't have a choice. We were desperate for help.

I left as Andy gave Bethany a high five for her cupcake-saving skills. Then I stepped outside and inhaled the fresh mountain air before heading downstairs for my first interview. The woman waiting for me was one of ten interviews. I was confident that I would find someone (and hopefully multiple someones) who would be the perfect blend for the bakeshop. Things were about to change at Torte. There was no denying that fact.

Chapter Two

After drinking in the sweet jasmine-scented summer air I turned toward the exterior stairs leading to the basement. What had once been an abandoned, mildew-ridden underground space that felt like a dungeon had been transformed into a bright baking hub. For the time being we had to access the kitchen from the outside. It wasn't an ideal setup. The building's original brick steps had been cleaned and resurfaced in the initial phase of construction, but having to traverse the old stairwell, past tourists and customers who tended to gather at the corner of the sidewalk, and back inside Torte's front door all while carrying trays of strawberry-rhubarb pies and lemon meringue tarts was a challenge to say the very least.

The gurgling sound of Ashland Creek greeted me as I descended into the basement. Inside, to the right of the stairs, our new baking operations were the thing of dreams for any pastry chef. There were large industrial racks that could be wheeled and moved as needed. Shiny white countertops and sturdy, waterproof faux-barn-wood floors made the kitchen feel large and open, as did the specialized workstations. There was a section for decorating with neat tubs and drawers of spatulas, pastry bags, piping tools and tips, food coloring, and sprinkles. Our massive mixers sat in a neat row nearby. The walk-in fridge was strategically located near the ovens for quick, easy access. And the pièce de résistance was the exposed brick oven at the far end of the kitchen.

Additionally, there was extra seating for overflow from upstairs. A few tables, chairs, and a comfy couch surrounded a second atomic style mid-century modern fireplace. Customers could nosh on a marionberry and cream cheese scone and watch my team in action in the kitchen. The basement wasn't open to customers yet. Stacks of boxes, extra chairs and tables from upstairs were temporarily taking up every square inch of available space.

A young woman with a pile of dreadlocks sat on one side of the couch. The other side was piled with cookbooks and boxes of artwork and succulent plants that would be displayed behind the coffee and pastry counter upstairs.

"Are you here for the interview?" I asked. "Sorry it's such a mess down here."

"Yeah. No worries." She fluffed her layered tie-dyed peasant skirt.

"Great. I'm Jules." I held up the file folder. "Let me go check in with my kitchen staff for a minute, and then I'll be right with you."

"Cool." She flashed me a peace sign. Anywhere other than Ashland her appearance and mannerisms might have mistaken her for someone auditioning for a part in *Hair*. In Ashland she was part of the norm. While our small town was a haven for retirees and professionals it also had a distinct counterculture segment of "travelers" or modern-day hippies passing through on their way up and down the West Coast.

I peered into the kitchen where Sterling was searing sausages on the stove.

"Hey, Jules." He wiped grease splatter from the pristine countertops with the edge of a dishrag. "Did you see that your first interview is here?"

I glanced over my shoulder. The woman was gnawing her fingernails. She must be nervous, I thought to myself. I wanted to ask him about his first impression but didn't want to risk having a potential new staff member overhear us. I guess that was one downside to an open-concept kitchen. "Yeah. I just wanted to make sure everything is good in here before I get started."

He flipped a beautifully charred sausage with a pair of tongs. "Everything's under control. Bethany ran a tray of cupcakes up a minute ago. She's doing a special lunch brownie—blood orange and dark chocolate."

"That sounds divine." I walked closer to the stove. "And your sausages smell incredible. I'm almost willing to burn my tongue for a taste."

"That doesn't sound like wise advice from a seasoned chef." Sterling curled his bottom lip. His ice-blue eyes lit up. "Do you see what's happening to me? I'm stuck with Bethany and Steph down here and am starting to talk in puns."

"You'll live." I patted his shoulder. "What's your plan for the sausages? And where is Stephanie?"

"She's finishing the wholesale deliveries." Sterling

carefully cut through one of the sausages to test whether it was done. "Is that too pink?" he asked.

I used a fork to pull back the beautifully crisp casing. Pork gets a bad rap when it comes to safety. People panic about seeing the color pink, which tends to lead to overcooking the delicious, tender, lean meat. Sausages often pull pink due to salt (which helps meats retain their natural color) and spices like paprika. "It looks good to me, but there's only one way to tell," I said to Sterling.

"Meat thermometer?" he asked, opening the drawer to the left of the stove.

"You got it."

I watched as he tested the meat.

"One hundred and sixty-five degrees." He held up the thermometer.

"Like I said, perfect." I tried to wink but was sure that my face had contorted in a goofy squint instead.

"Show-off," Sterling teased. He placed the thermometer in the sink and showed me his stack of ingredients. "I was thinking of doing an old-school-style sausage roll. Stephanie made Italian loaves. I was going to grill them with some garlic-infused olive oil and then do some caramelized onions and charred peppers. Add that to the sausage with a creamy beer cheese sauce and spicy brown mustard."

"Can it be lunchtime right now?" I placed my hand over my stomach to stop it from gurgling.

"You like it?" Sterling's angular cheekbones softened as he smiled. He was an innately talented chef but hadn't yet developed the confidence required to run a kitchen on his own. I hoped that as we gave him more responsibility and independence he would learn to trust his instincts.

"I love it." I lowered my voice. "Please save me one. I have a full day of interviews lined up and I have a feeling I'm going to need some sustenance to get through them."

"Deal." He flipped a sausage. "Oh, by the way, nice shirt. We all still think you should have stuck with the chocolate look. Bethany was talking about creating a Jules chocolate special in your honor." His ice-blue eyes flooded with enjoyment.

"Whatever." I pretended to be offended.

Bethany and Steph came downstairs together. Stephanie held two large empty boxes. The tips of her purple hair had been dyed black. It reminded me of our black-and-white dipped cookies.

"How did deliveries go?" I asked.

"Fine." She set the boxes next to one of the bread racks and tucked her hair behind her ears. "The Green Goblin wants a few dozen cupcakes for trivia night. I told them I would have to check with you."

Bethany washed her hands and moved to the decorating station. She began filling a piping bag with French buttercream. "I made extra for the lunch rush. I can use those for the Goblin as long as they aren't picky about flavor and then I'll double my brownie recipe."

Stephanie wrapped an apron around her waist. "I don't think they care."

"Great. I'll leave you to it and go start interviews. I'll be right over there most of the afternoon if you need me." I pointed to the seating area. Then I found a notebook and pencil. We always kept paper on hand in the kitchen. You never knew when inspiration for a new recipe or cake design might strike.

"Sorry to keep you waiting," I said to the young woman with dreadlocks as I pulled a chair up next to the couch.

She sat up and planted her hiking boots on the floor. "No worries." Fumbling through an oversized hemp bag, she reached inside and handed me a wrinkled piece of paper. "Here's my resume. I'm Sequoia, by the way."

"Nice to meet you, Sequoia." I shook her hand. Her name didn't surprise me. Ashland's eclectic community attracted a variety of personalities. Judging by Sequoia's appearance, I had definitely pegged her correctly as one of Ashland's travelers, a younger crowd that had a deep connection to nature and could often be found busking in Lithia Park on warm summer afternoons. One of the things that I appreciated most about our town was that every group—professors, actors, doctors, students, and hospitality staff—lived harmoniously. Ashland's open-hearted spirit naturally led people from all walks of life to land here.

"Tell me about yourself and your baking background." I flipped open the notebook and waited for Sequoia to speak.

She wrapped her finger around one of her dreadlocks. I was happy to see that her hands were well groomed. Her fingernails were trimmed and had been painted with pastel tie-dye polish that matched her skirt. "Uh, well, I've got a bunch of experience with coffee. I've worked a lot of places. I spent the past few years traveling, really getting a sense of the world, you know? I've worked at coffee stands in Santa Monica, Santa Cruz, Austin, Dallas, and at coffee carts in Portland and one in Seattle. I also spent time as an apprentice at a San Francisco roasting company."

I opened the file folder and pulled out her resume. "You're interested in the barista position, correct?" Her resume highlighted her barista training. "I see that you attended a three-day barista course in San Francisco."

"Yeah, the roaster I worked for sent me to that. I learned espresso extraction, drink preparation, milk texturing, cupping, latte art, cold drink prep. Everything."

I was impressed. The institute where Sequoia had received her training had a reputation for turning out some of the best baristas on the West Coast.

"What brought you to Ashland?" I continued.

Her gold-flecked eyes stared up at the sunlight streaming in through the window. "I've got people here and I like the vibe. Ashland is super chill, you know?"

"I do know." I smiled internally and jotted down a few thoughts. My first concern about Sequoia was whether or not she would stick around. I didn't have the time to train someone new only to have them leave a few months later. My second concern was whether she was too chill for our team.

As if sensing my hesitation, she sat up straighter and smoothed her peasant skirt. "My parents own a coffeehouse in Vermont. I grew up in the business and part of me misses it, but the West Coast is more my speed, you know?"

I had a feeling every sentence was going to end with "you know."

"What sort of things did you do in your family's coffeehouse?"

She answered with a lengthy list of tasks, including cleaning the grease trap (one of the most dreaded jobs in any coffee shop), that left me surprised and potentially willing to give her a chance.

"You want me to show you what I've got?"

I scrunched my brow. "What you've got?"

"My skills, you know? I can make you a latte right now."

"Well." I hesitated. I hadn't intended to have job candidates perform on the spot.

"The espresso machine is upstairs, right?" Sequoia stood. "Let me give it a go."

"Okay, I guess." I followed her upstairs. The crowd had thinned out. It would be busy again for the lunch rush soon, but there was often a lull between morning breakfast service and the noontime blitz.

Andy was packaging a customer's pastry order to go at the register.

"This is Sequoia. Andy, she's going to do a demo on the espresso machine for me."

For the first time maybe ever, Andy's buoyant grin hardened. He looked from me to Sequoia and then back to me. "What's that, boss?" His eyes were filled with distrust.

"Sequoia is going to make a latte for me as part of her interview." I tried to mouth "Relax" but his eyes were lasered on Sequoia. He didn't blink as he handed the customer a box of pastries and then stood protectively in front of the espresso machine.

"You know how to use this baby?" he asked, not attempting to hide the skepticism in his tone. "This is a state-of-the-art machine. This isn't your grandma's coffeepot."

Sequoia rolled up the sleeves on her loose hemp blouse. "I'm very familiar with La Pavoni. That's the two-group model."

Andy didn't budge. He ran his hands along the top of the sleek red Italian machine.

"Whoa, I've heard of people loving coffee, but not a machine." She turned to me in hopes that I would agree.

Andy glared at her.

I stepped between them. "Andy is a master and the espresso bar is his domain." I gave him a nudge. "But let's give Sequoia a chance to test it out."

"Boss, this isn't a machine for novices," Andy protested, moving to the far end of the counter.

Sequoia seized the opportunity and immediately began changing the dials.

"Don't touch that. I have everything set for a perfect ratio." Andy took off his baseball hat and punched it into his palm.

"I know what I'm doing." Sequoia shot him a look. Then she expertly ground beans and tamped them with one hand. With the other she began steaming milk.

Andy buried his face in his hat. "I can't watch this. I can't. It's too painful."

"Look," I said in a low voice, dragging him away from the espresso machine. "I don't know if she's going to be a fit for us, but when she suggested making a coffee, I figured it wasn't a bad idea. Watching her work should give us a good sense of her skills. And, she has been professionally trained. She attended the International Coffee Institute in San Francisco."

"But, Jules, she's going to ruin everything." Andy never called me "Jules." Since the first day we met, he had called me "boss."

"I promise, it will be fine. She's been classically trained."

He scowled. "Really? She doesn't look it." He paused and lunged over the counter. "Don't do that. You're going to steam the milk too high."

Sequoia rolled her eyes. "Like I said, I know what I'm doing. Are you familiar with the history of La Pavoni? Their machines date back to the early nineteen-hundreds." She rattled off facts about the manufacturer and our particular model. Andy listened with his arms folded across his chest.

I was surprised by his possessive behavior. One of my top priorities in hiring more staff was support for him.

A customer came in for a lunch order, so I shoved him over to take care of her. Meanwhile, Sequoia moved with a fluid ease. She reminded me of a dancer the way she stretched her arms out to pour the creamy milk. With a slight flick of the wrist she created a peace sign in the top of my foam. Then she folded her arms across her chest. "Tell me what you think."

Andy had finished taking the customer's order and peered over my shoulder.

"Foam is decent. It could use some finesse," he muttered under his breath.

I took a sip of Sequoia's drink. The ratio of coffee and milk was perfect. There was a nice layer of fluffy foam and a rich, dark espresso flavor. "It's really good."

She gave Andy a triumphant smile.

He snatched the coffee mug from me, nearly spilling the latte. "Let me try it." He took a drink and swished the latte around in his mouth, as if he was tasting a fine wine. Then he held the mug to the light. He stuck his finger into the foam to measure the depth. When he finally finished his assessment, he handed Sequoia the mug and shrugged. "It was okay."

Sequoia wasn't fazed.

I glanced at the clock. My next interviewee would be arriving soon. "Let me walk you out," I said to Sequoia.

Andy gave her a three-finger wave and began resetting the machine.

"What's his story?" Sequoia stopped at the front door. "He's uptight."

"Not usually. In fact, never." I glanced at Andy.

"Thanks for the chance," she said. "I take it, it's a no?"

"I didn't say that." I opened the door and motioned outside. "I'm going to be doing more interviews. I'll talk to Andy. I think he's just nervous because he's been a one-man show up until now, but he needs help and so do I."

"Cool. I'm around and I can start anytime. The sooner the better. I'm trying to get into a permanent place here and having a job will help." She unfolded her billowy sleeves.

I waited for a group of teenagers to skateboard past us. "To be honest, my main concern is about your commitment level. From your resume it's clear that you've jumped around a lot, and I'm looking for someone long-term."

"That's me. I want to be here long-term. I have to be." She didn't elaborate.

"Great. I'll be in touch."

I watched her walk away. There was something about her energy that drew me in. Her coffee had been delicious. She clearly wasn't exaggerating about her barista experience. Now the only question was how to make sure Andy wouldn't kill me if I hired her.

Chapter Three

The rest of the day brought more interviews. There were so many qualified applicants I had no idea how I was going to decide. The top of my list included Marty, an older, jovial gentleman with a thick handlebar mustache and an equally thick waistline. He had been a baker in San Francisco for years before his wife became ill. They had moved to the Rogue Valley to be close to family and medical care. She had recently passed away, leaving him ready for a new challenge and eager to develop connections in the area. He had been retired for ten years but seemed energetic and ready for a fresh start.

Also in the running was Rosa, a native Spanish-speaker with a soft-spoken personality. She was about my age with excellent references. She came highly recommended from my friend Chef Garrison, who raved about her work ethic and her pan de coco, a popular sweet bread filled with brown sugar and coconut that originated in the Philippines. Rosa had met Chef Garrison while working at a small family-owned bed-and-breakfast in Jacksonville. She waited tables and helped with breakfast preparations. The owners had recently sold the inn and Rosa would soon be without a job. I liked her immediately.

Despite Andy's attitude, Sequoia was in front of the pack in terms of baristas. Everyone else I had interviewed struggled with the machine. Plus none of the other candidates had the level of training and experience that Sequoia did.

"You look like you could use a serious dose of caffeine," Andy commented when I returned upstairs with a stack of resumes.

"Hit me with the strongest stuff you've got." I smiled.

"I thought you'd never ask, boss." Andy wiggled his fingers with a devilish grin. "I know just the thing." He began grinding an assortment of beans. "Listen, I want to say sorry for earlier. I don't know what my problem is. I guess it's just weird to think about Torte changing. When your mom hired me in high school I never really thought that I would end up staying so long and having a chance to kind of do my own thing here. It's been pretty amazing."

"Absolutely." I set the resumes on the counter and glanced around the room. The bakeshop was sparsely populated with a few regulars nursing cups of coffee and focused on their laptops. "I get it, Andy. Probably more than anyone. I'm nervous about the changes too."

He fiddled with a paper cup. "It's stupid. I guess it's just that Torte has become my second home."

I wanted to wrap him in a hug, but instead placed my hand over my heart. "Andy, I know. That means the world to me. Mom and I had a long talk about our goals for the expansion and our top priority is to make sure that the new staff we hire blend in. I know at first glance

Sequoia looks alternative, but you can't argue with her skills and her training."

The scent of coffee enveloped me as syrupy espresso dripped into a shot glass.

"It's cool. Don't sweat it." Andy poured one shot into a twelve-ounce cup and then another. "But, the deal is that I'm still in charge of this beast, right?"

"Right." I gave him a serious nod. "Absolutely. You are the main man when it comes to Torte's coffee."

He poured a third shot into the cup.

"Three shots?"

"Nope." Reaching for a fourth, he smirked. "Four. I call this the ER 411."

"You really are mad about hiring someone new, aren't you?"

"Nah. I'm over it, but this will get your blood pumping." He finished off the heavily caffeinated drink with Irish cream. "You'll bust through those resumes in no time with this."

I took the drink. It smelled divine, but I had a feeling if I polished off half of it I would be buzzing for days. "Thanks. I think."

Andy turned up the overhead music. I cradled the coffee cup, placed the file of resumes under one arm, and ducked under the plastic tarp to check on progress. The resumes could wait for a minute. I wanted to see how the renovations were going and take a little break from thinking about whom to hire.

The crew had already left for the day, but from the look of things they had definitely made some gains. An iron railing had been installed to the roughed-in stairs. Mom and I had gone back and forth about carpeting the stairs versus using the versatile, waterproof laminate flooring we had installed in the basement. We ultimately decided on the laminate. Carpet might have had a sound-dampening effect but since we would constantly be bringing trays of pastries, soups, and sandwiches up and down the stairs, laminate was much more practical.

I placed my coffee cup on the floor and tested the top of the railing. It felt solid. There were still sections of Sheetrock that needed to be patched, trim for the windows and door frames was still missing, the flooring for the stairs needed to be installed, and then the new coffee counter and pastry case would be put in place. I hated to get my hopes up, but it was starting to look like we were nearing the finish line.

There was no time like the present to give them a try, so I grabbed my coffee and balanced it and the resumes in one hand, staying next to the far-left exposed-brick wall and making sure to watch for any protruding nails as I descended into the basement. Having internal access between the kitchen and upstairs was going to be a game changer.

I took the stack of resumes and Andy's 411 and set them on the table near the couch. Then I went to get the scoop from everyone on any first impressions they might have had on our candidate pool.

Sterling was scrubbing the sink with a scouring pad. The kitchen smelled of lavender and lemon cleaner and a faint hint of applewood smoke. Bethany and Steph had packed away their decorating supplies for the night and were updating the whiteboard with tomorrow's deliveries and special orders.

"Okay, lay it on me, guys. Did you get a glimpse of any of the candidates? First impressions? Thoughts?"

Before anyone could answer, Mom peeked out from behind one of the rolling carts.

"Want some company?" Mom's walnut eyes flickered with the delight of surprising me. She wore a pair of white capris with matching white clogs that had two bright cherries imprinted on them.

"Hey, what are you doing here?" I was thrilled to see her.

Mom hadn't been a fixture at Torte of late. Since she and the Professor had returned from a sun-swept honeymoon in Greece, they had been on a mission to find their dream house. She had stopped by a few times to check on renovations and shower our staff with gifts from their trip. She had brought Bethany an oversized scarf handcrafted of silk. The wrap was designed with a print of the Greek god Poseidon in creamy yellows and sea blues. It looked beautiful against Bethany's skin. She had worn it nearly every day since Mom had returned. For Stephanie Mom brought an old-world recipe book of Greek pastries. Andy received sample bags of Greek coffee, and Sterling a handmade olivewood mortar and pestle.

She and the Professor had chosen a Greek tapestry picturing the tree of life with stylish blue-and-green leaves and hovering birds for me. "Won't this look wonderful hanging from the wall of your new home?" she had asked with a sly smile.

Her house hunting had a direct impact on me, as she had been not-so-subtly hinting for a while that it would be wonderful if I would consider moving into my childhood home. She and the Professor hadn't found their dream house yet, but I was confident they would soon. Selfishly, I hoped their house hunting would be successful because I missed having Mom around the bakeshop.

She pointed to the Torte apron tied around her narrow waist. "I needed a break from house hunting and I was lured in by Sterling's lunch special. I figured if I was already here, I might as well get my hands in some dough." An antique ring sparkled on her finger.

"You better be careful with that," I cautioned. "You don't want to lose it in the dough."

Her eyes lit up when she laughed. "I said that to Doug earlier. It's been a long time since I wore a wedding ring." She reached for the simple silver necklace around her neck where she wore her original wedding ring. "I overheard some bits and pieces of your interviews but not enough to have any first impressions."

Sterling dried his hands on a towel and untied the apron that he wore folded halfway around his waist. "Me, too. The older guy seemed to have good energy."

"Marty," I offered. "I liked him too. He's a top contender. A former bread maker from the Bay Area."

Steph and Bethany took a break from reviewing the schedule. "I don't think Andy liked any of the baristas, especially the hippie chick. He was flipping out the whole time she was here."

"I know." I sighed. "Unfortunately, Sequoia—the hippie chick—is highly qualified and made me an amazing latte."

"Then hire her," Stephanie said without emotion.

"She's on the top of my list," I said. Then I glanced

around the spotless kitchen. The white countertops gleamed. The mixers had been returned to their places and looked like mirrors reflecting the light from above. "Why don't you all take off?" I suggested. "I'm going to go over the resumes one last time and can finish up in here later."

No one put up a fight. "See you tomorrow, Jules," Sterling said as he, Steph, and Bethany headed for the exterior stairs. "Try not to wrestle with the chocolate tonight."

Mom's brow furrowed. "Wrestle with chocolate?"

"Don't ask."

She untied her apron. I noticed the slightest tightness in her jaw as she stretched her fingers after tossing her apron in the laundry bin.

"How are you feeling?" I asked. She had been diagnosed with early arthritis. So far it hadn't slowed her pace, but I didn't want her to overextend herself.

"Fine." She laced her fingers together. "There's some tightness, but honestly I think kneading the bread dough this afternoon was perfect therapy."

I raised one brow. "Is that what your doctor said?"

"Now you sound like Doug."

"Good. The Professor is one of the wisest people on the planet. You should listen to him." I walked toward the seating area and plopped on the empty side of the couch.

She waved me off and sat in the chair opposite me. "What's the drink? It has a wonderful scent."

"Andy's special. He calls it the 411. I think he's trying to knock me out with this one. It's pretty much caffeine meets caffeine."

"That sounds . . ." Mom paused for a moment. "Intense?"

"Yeah. It is." I took a gulp. "But it's so good I can't stop drinking it."

"Juliet." Mom shook her head. "What am I going to do with you?"

"Help me make a decision on whom to hire." I handed her a resume.

"You say that as if you were asking me to pull a tooth." Her walnut-brown eyes seemed to pierce through me. "When you were talking to the staff it sounded to me like you already know what you want to do."

"Yeah, but I'm not sure. What if I make a mistake? What if whoever we hire doesn't fit in?"

"Let's start there," Mom said in a calm tone. "Remember, you can't make a wrong choice. If we give one of the candidates a try and they end up not being a fit, so be it. We can't know that without trying. Taking on new staff always comes with unknown questions. A one-page resume and thirty-minute interview can only tell us so much. I say go with your gut."

She had a special way of framing things and a naturally grounded presence. Even with the caffeine pulsing through my veins, I felt calmer. "Right, but what about Andy? His reaction to Sequoia was visceral."

"That comes with the territory." Mom glanced upstairs. "Did you know that when I hired Andy I wasn't sure that he would last more than a couple of weeks?"

"Really?" I sipped the coffee, trying to pace myself.

"Don't get me wrong, I loved him from the moment I met him. His energy, his warmth, his humor. But I wasn't sure that he was ready for the responsibility. I took a chance on him, and we didn't have a smooth start. You should have seen him behind the coffee bar in those early weeks. His cheeks were constantly the color of red peppers. He would sweat profusely trying to keep up with the line. He never bantered with the customers. He had to concentrate on watching the machine. Customers complained that the milk was too cold or scalding hot. His workstation was a mess. There were grounds everywhere and stacks of shot glasses."

"Are you kidding? Why didn't you ever tell me this?" I shifted my body position. My back felt tight. As a baker I was used to being on my feet all day. Sitting for ten interviews ironically had left me feeling stiffer than a shift in the kitchen.

"There was no need. I could see his potential. He was an eager learner and a hard worker. I couldn't ask for anything more. I knew that with time and practice he would improve. Look at him now. You wouldn't even recognize him as the bumbling barista I hired." She smiled. Her skin was naturally tanned from summer hikes with the Professor. Marriage had been good for her. The honey highlights in her short bob framed her face and gave her a healthy glow. Mom didn't rattle easily. She had always possessed an internal calmness and strength. That had only deepened since the wedding.

I had a hard time reconciling the Andy she was describing with the skilled barista I knew.

"Maybe Andy needs a little reminder about how far he's come." Mom handed me Sequoia's resume. "And reassurance that he will remain our lead barista until he decides to move on. Do you think we can afford to give him a raise? A small increase in compensation for his services training new staff, along with a new title."

"I like it. Maybe lead barista?"

"He's earned it."

Andy appeared at the top of the stairs. He held a box of pastries and bread. "Hey, Mrs. The Professor! I didn't know you were down there."

"Shhh. Don't tell." Mom pressed her finger to her lips.

Andy gave her a salute. "I'm heading out. Everything's done up here. I boxed up the extra pastries. I'll leave them on the counter, okay?"

"Thanks, that would be appreciated." Mom smiled. We had a practice of donating any extra baked goods to the community shelter.

"What about the rest of the team?" I asked Mom when Andy was out of earshot. "Do you think we should give everyone a little raise?"

She looked thoughtful. "Stephanie and Andy have been here the longest. Bethany just started and since she has some profit share I think she's in a good position. Sterling has taken over quite a few kitchen duties. It might be a good idea to see if we can afford a little something more for him too."

"Let me run some numbers." Torte had had a banner year. Sales were up by nearly fifty percent, thanks in large part to our growing wholesale accounts, custom wedding cake designs, and some high-end catering accounts (like Lance's elaborate season-opening bash). Paired with the revenue we would be bringing in from Uva (the winery where I was a one-third owner) I thought we could probably swing a bump in pay to our existing staff. Not that the bakery business is extremely lucrative, but since Mom and Dad opened Torte they had been committed to paying their employees a livable wage with benefits like free food and drink, a share of tips, and flexible hours.

I didn't want to get over our heads, but we wouldn't be where we were today without long hours and tremendous effort put in by our current staff. If things were changing, I wanted to find a way to make sure the changes were for the good.

Chapter Four

I put in a late night reviewing spreadsheets, looking over projected work in the months ahead, and budgeting for construction costs. We had received a grant to bring the basement up to code and ensure that it wouldn't flood again, but the remainder of the expansion would be paid off through a long-term loan. Even with loan payments we were now able to produce so much more product and take on accounts that we would have had to turn down in our old kitchen that, at least in theory, small raises penciled out on paper.

The next morning, I called the team together before we opened the doors for the morning rush. Andy passed around cups of French press with a dollop of homemade almond-infused whipping cream. I sliced into a layered egg and ham strata loaded with Italian bread crumbs, gouda cheese, fresh chives, sundried tomatoes, and red onions. I had arrived at Torte early to bake the special fluffy egg dish for my staff.

"Can someone say food coma?" Bethany lifted her slice to her nose and inhaled. "I don't think I even need to eat this. I just gained a pound smelling this wonderful eggy goodness." She set her plate on the counter and began snapping pictures on her cell. "Is this going to be on the specials board today? Because I'm pretty sure the second I post a picture of this beauty we're going to have a line around the block."

I smiled. "Yes. I have a strata supply waiting downstairs."

"Strata supply, nice one, boss." Andy raised his coffee cup.

"What's the occasion?" Sterling asked. He studied my face. "Is this like our last meal or something?"

"Or something." I flicked his shoulder. "No. It's the opposite. I wanted to take a minute to thank you profusely for your help and flexibility through this construction project. You guys are amazing." The words caught in my throat. I hadn't anticipated being emotional. "Sorry." I cleared my throat. "This is a celebratory breakfast. The expansion is almost complete, and I think I've found three new hires that are going to make our lives easier."

I gauged their reactions. Stephanie, as usual, stared at her plate, not making eye contact. Bethany nodded enthusiastically. Sterling watched Andy, who tried to put on his game face. "This is a small token of my thanks. I'd like to meet with each of you individually this morning to talk about new roles that Mom and I have outlined. With new staff coming on, I'm going to be calling on the four of you for training and to take on some new responsibilities."

Sterling stabbed his strata. "Whatever you need, Jules. You know we have your back. It is going to be weird having a bunch of new people in here."

Everyone agreed.

"True, but that's all the more reason why I want you each to feel empowered. I'm going to be leaning on you to help train the new staff. And, I'm going to want your feedback on how the transition is going. If someone isn't a match, I want to know that. The sooner the better."

"What's the big deal?" Bethany asked. "I think it's going to be great to get some more energy in here."

I shot her a look of thanks. I could always count on her for bringing a positive attitude.

"Jules, it's not like any of us are pissed. It's just going be strange for a while. But we're cool." Sterling stared at me.

"Thanks." I placed three resumes on the counter. "These are the staff that we've chosen. They will be on a ninety-day probationary period. So again, if you feel like they aren't working out—obviously after giving them a chance to get acclimated—it's important that you come to me."

"We got it." Sterling motioned for me to continue.

Was I overthinking this?

"Sequoia will be working the coffee counter with Andy. Marty will be downstairs in the kitchen. Marty is a retired professional baker. His specialty was bread, so I think he'll be a great asset to the team, especially since you two prefer pastry work." I addressed Bethany and Steph.

They nodded.

"Rosa is a native Spanish speaker. She's going to be a floater. I'll have her work on catering accounts, corporate orders, and help with whatever is needed during the morning and noontime rush. I'm planning to start her on the pastry counter because I have the sense she'll be really good with customers given her experience working at a bed-and-breakfast."

"Hey, what are you saying?" Andy pretended to stab himself in the heart.

"I'm saying that you need extra hands up here. You can't be running back and forth between crafting espressos and ringing up orders."

"Isn't that what Sequoia is for?" Andy's tone was light, but I knew there was more to his words.

"Yes, but I see Sequoia keeping her focus on coffee production and not as much on customer interaction. That's where you and Rosa will come in."

He shrugged. "Sure thing."

We finished our strata and French press. My inspirational pep talk hadn't gone exactly as I had planned, but at least we could move forward. The team split up to start the morning prep. I called Andy into the office first. A fine layer of dust coated the desk and filing cabinet. I tried to wipe it with a towel, but that just illuminated patchy streaks on everything.

"Sorry. It's pretty dusty in here," I said to Andy, motioning for him to sit in a folding chair.

He pointed to his khaki shorts and T-shirt with a silhouette of the state of Oregon. In the bottom corner was a star pointing to Ashland's position on the map. "Yeah, I wouldn't want to get dust on these. High fashion."

I smiled. "After our conversation yesterday, I wanted to check in and see how you're doing."

"I'm good, boss. I'm always good." His words didn't

match his demeanor. His right foot bounced on the floor as he spoke.

"Funny. I mean, you're okay with giving Sequoia a test run?"

"Yeah. No problem." His foot continued to bounce. Was he more upset than he was letting on?

"Good. I have some other news. Mom and I discussed a promotion."

He sat up. "What?"

"We'd like to officially make you head barista and offer you a raise."

Andy fist shot in the air. "No way. Awesome. This changes everything. Wow, I mean, this could not come at a better time."

I hadn't expected Andy to react so strongly to the news. I didn't want to disappoint him with the dollar amount of his raise. "It's not huge, but you deserve it, and like I said earlier, I'm really going to be leaning on you to train Sequoia on how things run at Torte and get her up to speed."

His body language shifted completely. "You got it, boss. Thank you so much. You have no idea how great this is for me right now." He jumped to his feet and gave me a salute. "Head barista reporting for duty."

"Congratulations, Andy."

I smiled to myself as he returned to the coffee bar. Hopefully the raise and new role would appease him. I did wonder whether something might be going on in Andy's personal life. Was he having financial difficulties? I was going to have to figure out a way to broach the subject, but for the moment I would let him revel in his new role as our lead barista.

 Ellie Alexander

Sterling and Stephanie reacted positively. Even Steph cracked a real smile when she heard about the raise. Torte returned to homeostasis. Soon the scent of applewood smoke and baking bread wafted upstairs. I met with the work crew to discuss the ramp they would be installing at the front of the bakeshop for accessibility. Torte was like hallowed ground in my humble opinion. We were a safe space for anyone entering our doors, and we wanted to make it as easy as possible for our clients to access the bakeshop. The construction foreman took me outside to show me how they would grade Torte's front entrance so that a wheelchair could easily maneuver through the front door.

We were in the final stretch. Once the last finish work was complete inside the crew would install the ramp and we would officially be ready to open the basement space and say good-bye to dust and the sound of jackhammers forever. I did a little happy dance.

"Juliet!" I heard a woman's voice call from across the street.

I froze and turned to see a petite woman in her sixties waving. It was Pam, the owner of Nightingales Inn, one of Ashland's oldest bed-and-breakfasts, located in a gorgeous restored Victorian mansion just around the corner from Torte.

Pam propped an oversized tote bag on her arm and crossed the street. She had long strawberry hair and a heart-shaped face. A bright yellow and blue sailboat necklace hung from her neck. A matching yellow-and-blue striped beach towel was tucked into her bag.

"You caught me in the act," I said, feeling my cheeks warm.

"I liked your dance. It's a good day for dancing." Pam mimicked my dance moves.

"Or a swim," I said, pointing to her beach bag.

"Oh this?" Pam patted the top of the towel. "I'm off to the lake and thought I would stop by Torte for one of your delicious picnic lunches."

"How's the inn?" I asked, stepping to the side to let a group of teenage girls enter the bakeshop. I had a feeling these were some of Andy's coffee groupies.

"Wonderful. We've been booked all summer. Today we have guests from Japan, L.A., and Canada. It made for a lively breakfast conversation."

"I bet." Nightingales was known for Pam's breakfasts. She didn't skimp when it came to hospitality. Every morning she prepared a hot breakfast at the inn complete with savory potatoes and red peppers, sticky buns, and granola with fresh fruit. She often stopped by Torte for boxes of dessert for her evening literary salons where she invited guests and locals to nibble on pastries, sip chilled wine, and mingle with a visiting author.

Pam's face hardened when a woman in a business suit marched past us. The woman gave Pam a curt nod and continued on without saying a word.

"Who's that?" I asked, watching the woman push her way through a crowd of tourists gathered in front of Puck's Pub where a street performer dressed like a medieval knight was showcasing his sword-wielding techniques with a fake metal sword.

"Stella Pryor." Pam shook her head in disgust. "Don't even get me started on that woman, Juliet. I'm so mad at her I could scream. I could honestly scream right here in the middle of the plaza."

"Really?" I was surprised to hear the disdain in Pam's tone. Pam was typically upbeat. Andy referred to her as Ashland's cheerleader. Pam knew everyone in town and made a point to get to know newbies, sharing tickets to the theater, welcoming them to lunch at the inn, and hosting wonderful garden parties.

She looked around us as if she was concerned that someone might be listening. "Have you heard that she's trying to get her grubby hands on Edgar's property? She already owns half of Ashland. I have no idea why she wants Edgar's place."

"No, and I'm not sure I know who Edgar is, to be honest."

"Come with me, I'll show you." Pam adjusted her tote and pulled me toward Main Street without waiting for my response. She led me up two blocks. Nightingales sat on the next corner. It towered over the street surrounded by hundred-year-old pines. Cement steps led up to the creamy yellow Victorian, with another sweeping set of steps leading to the front porch. The historic house had been painstakingly restored to its original beauty. Bright white trim lined the sash windows. A stone pathway wrapped from the front to a miniature English garden in the back. Flowers spilled from ceramic pots and sunlight danced off a stained-glass window cut in the shape of a hexagon on the third floor. Visits to Nightingales as a kid had always made me feel like I was stepping into the pages of a fairy tale. The inn's intricately carved wooden archways and massive dining room table that sat twelve to fourteen guests rivaled that of any castle I'd read about in books. Pam had adorned the living room with black-and-white photos of her ancestors and the inn's original owners. There was a friendly ghost said to haunt the upstairs bedrooms. I had been convinced that the ghost's identity was hidden in one of the photos.

I remembered playing tag behind the giant pine trees at one of Pam's many summer garden parties. She and my parents had been friends long before I was born. Her parties were the stuff of legend. China platters would line the dining room table, overflowing with roasted pork loin infused with rosemary and garlic, braised chicken and leeks, brown butter mashed potatoes, fennel and tomato salad, and cornmeal rolls. There were terrines of butternut squash soup and smoked-salmon chowder. And then there were the desserts. Pam displayed desserts in glass cake stands on bistro tables tucked throughout the garden. It was as if the desserts had sprouted among the blooming white baneberry bushes.

A flash of a memory of my father surged through me. I could hear his voice through the sturdy trees and see him kneeling next to a pot of rosemary and lavender in the back gardens. "Juliet! Come quick."

I remember the smell of honeysuckle and weaving through grown-ups sipping wine.

My father's impish eyes met mine when I darted past my mom and Pam who were dancing along with the band.

"Juliet, look what I've found." My father waved me over.

I crouched next to him. "What?"

He pointed to the pot. "Look closely. What do you see?"

I studied the flower pot with its leafy greens and pops of colorful flowers. "What? The flowers?"

"No, look closer." He ran his fingers along one of the leaves. "Do you see it?"

The leaf appeared to shimmer with tiny flecks of something sparkly. "What is it? Gold?"

"Fairy dust." My father's eyes twinkled with delight. "Do you know what that means?"

"No." I shook my head, rubbing the leaf with my fingers.

"It means that a fairy lives here. Do you know what Shakespeare said about fairies?"

I stared at the golden residue on my fingertips. "No."

"'Hand in hand, with fairy grace, Will we sing and bless this place.'"

"What does that mean?"

He stood and kissed the top of my head. "It means that the fairies are here. If you close your eyes and listen, you can hear them sing."

For the rest of the party I sat with my eyes shut tight, listening to the sound of singing fairies. Anytime after that when my father and I happened to pass by Nightingales, we would pause, close our eyes, and listen for the fairies. He believed in magic and created a world for me to believe, too.

"Nightingales is here," Pam's voice pulled me back into the moment.

"Right." I blinked back a tear and shook my head to try to ground myself.

I wasn't sure why Pam was giving me a geography lesson on the inn's location. I'd been inside dozens of times.

Pam pointed to her left where there was a huge open lot. A small, rundown house that looked as if it was slipping off its foundation sat at the edge of the lot. Wild deer used the empty lot as their grazing grounds. "This is Edgar's property."

"Okay. And how does Stella play in? Is she a real estate agent?"

"Worse. Much worse." Pam's voice turned almost shrill. "She's a developer. A greedy developer who could care less about preserving Ashland architecture. You are aware that property is at a premium in Ashland?"

I nodded. Ashland had enacted strict urban growth boundaries decades ago in order to protect the integrity of our small town and the wild mountainous spaces around us.

"Look at this lot." Pam's finger shook as she pointed. "It's nearly flat. That's unheard of in Ashland."

That was also true. Much of the town was built on the hillside, which meant that in nearly any direction you ventured you had to trek uphill one way—or sometimes both.

"It's a prime location. Two blocks from the plaza. Level. Half a city block."

"And Stella wants to develop it?" I added.

Pam tucked her finger around a loop in her beach bag. "Yes. She wants to build upscale tiny houses. Can you imagine that, Juliet? Tiny houses. One of our neighbors said that the plans include fifteen houses. That will be terrible. Absolutely terrible. It's already impossible to find street parking here. How in the world could anyone think they could cram fifteen tiny houses in this space?"

I could see why Pam was upset. The driveway to the back of Nightingales Inn paralleled one side of the open lot. Pam's property butted up against the northernmost edge of the lot closer to Edgar's house—or perhaps a better term would have been *shack*.

Pam noticed me staring. "I've been pestering the city for years to have Edgar's place condemned. Don't get me wrong, I'd love to see that eyesore torn down, but adding fifteen tiny houses to this neighborhood isn't the answer. Nightingales was built in 1880. We spent years restoring it to its original beauty. Our guests expect a certain level of elegance. It's part of the Ashland experience. That will be completely destroyed by a bunch of ugly, modern boxes."

Before I could respond, Pam continued, her face beginning to flush. "I called an emergency meeting with our neighbors. Everyone is up in arms. The city can't do this to us."

Most of Pam's neighbors were also B and B owners. Like its urban growth boundary restrictions, Ashland was equally rigid about zoning for vacation rentals. Since the city relied heavily on tourist dollars, hotels took precedence. Short-term vacation rentals were only allowed on major arterials streets. The section of Main Street where Nightingales was located housed dozens of bed-and-breakfasts, most in old converted historic houses.

"Sorry to hear that," I said. "Is there anything I can do to help?"

"Can you poison Stella or Edgar with one your pastries for me?" Pam laughed. She stared at me for a second. "Oh, don't give me that look, Juliet. I would never do something like that. I'm just venting, but I would appreciate your help."

"Sure. Anything."

"Can you keep your ears open? Everyone gossips at Torte. If you hear anything about Edgar's property coming up for sale, will you call me right away?"

"Of course." Although I wasn't sure that I would have much luck.

Pam blew me a kiss with her hand. "You're a doll. I should let you get back to work and pick up my lunch order."

We returned to the bakeshop, but I gave the empty lot one last stare. I hated that there was drama in our idyllic village and hoped for Pam's sake that the situation would sort itself out soon.

Chapter Five

The next few days had me running up and down our newly installed stairs. I kept watch over the new hires in the kitchen and at the espresso bar. Our test run seemed to be going smoothly, although I refused to say that aloud for fear that Andy might launch into a dozen reasons why Sequoia wasn't going to be a long-term match. For the moment, I took it as a small miracle that they were able to work side by side. In my observations I had noticed that they said very little to one another as they pulled shots and steamed milk. Andy kept his head turned toward waiting customers, chatting them up, and sending a not-so-subtle message that he was dealing with Sequoia's presence but wasn't happy about it.

By the end of the first week, I felt like we were hitting a good rhythm. I couldn't believe how much more we were able to produce and accomplish with three extra sets of hands. So much so that I was kicking myself for not hiring extra help sooner. When Mom called to ask me if I had time to go look at a house on Emigrant Lake, I could actually say yes without feeling guilty. She and the Professor had decided that rather than move into one of their houses they would buy something new together. I thought it was a brilliant idea—starting new and fresh instead of trying to fit into an old life.

She picked me up at Torte late in the afternoon on a Saturday. Emigrant Lake was a short drive just outside of town. Mom looked refreshed when I hopped into the passenger seat and tossed my things in the back. "You packed snacks?" I asked.

"The property we're going to see is on the hillside near the old cemetery. I thought it might be nice after we look at the house to take the long route and walk around the lake, through the graveyard, and have a little picnic by the lake if you have time?"

"That sounds great." Emigrant Lake was one of my favorite places in the Rogue Valley. I had many childhood memories of spending summer days on the water slides and lounging on the dock. The lake was a popular spot for water lovers of all kinds—swimmers, divers, rowers, and families with young children who splashed in the shallow water along the lake's banks.

"How goes the house hunting?" I asked as Mom steered the car out of the plaza.

"Not great." She sighed. "Doug and I can't seem to agree on what we want."

"Really?" This news surprised me. Mom and the Professor were usually so in synch.

"Oh no, I shouldn't have said it like that. I don't mean that we are arguing, but everything we see is a contender. At last count I think we've toured twenty properties. There are only a couple that we've crossed off the list. There are so many good options. Too many good options."

We passed new construction at the north end of the plaza. "Like that," Mom said, pointing to the three-story structure. "Those are going to be modern open-concept condos with balconies and a rooftop garden."

"That could be cool," I said. "It's a great location. You could walk to everything."

"Exactly." Mom tucked her hair behind her ears. "That's the problem. Doug and I can envision ourselves in a modern condo and in an historic Victorian up in the forest. We can't decide."

"I don't think you should stress about it," I reassured her. "When you find the right house, you'll know it."

Her cheeks creased when she smiled. "I'm sure you're right, honey. I suppose I thought it would be easy, but after being in the same home for over thirty years, I'm not sure what I want next. Maybe something smaller like a condo would be fun, but maybe a cabin up in the woods would be equally enjoyable."

"It's understandable. Have you made a decision about your house yet?"

She took her eyes off the road for a minute. "Have *you* made any decisions about the house yet?"

When Mom and the Professor decided to purchase something new together they had taken me out to dinner and asked if I had any interest in moving into my childhood home. The conversation had taken me by complete surprise. The truth was that I hadn't ever thought about it. I had imagined that Mom would stay in the house for many years to come, so when the Professor slid an envelope across the table to me and Mom sat beaming next to him, I wasn't sure how to respond.

"What is this?" I had asked.

"Open it." The Professor nodded at the creamy envelope.

Inside was the deed to Mom's house. "I don't understand."

Mom nudged the Professor. He cleared his throat. "Juliet, your mother and I want you to have the house."

"Oh no. I couldn't. That's very generous of you both, but no, I couldn't take the house."

"Doug, I told you she'd say no." Mom sounded disappointed.

The Professor looked thoughtful for a moment. "Juliet, I'm reminded of this quote: 'The best journey always takes us home.'"

"That can't be Shakespeare?"

"No, but I do ask that you think about those wise words and consider our offer for a while before you make a decision."

I agreed. They were wonderful. They didn't try to pressure me, or nudge me in a particular direction, but rather made it clear that if I wanted the house, it was mine. I refused that very kind and generous offer. But ever since, I'd been dreaming about the house.

My tiny apartment above Elevation, the outdoor store, had served me well. It had been the perfect landing spot while trying to regain my footing on solid ground. I loved that it was a short walk to Torte and to Lithia Park, but lately I'd been feeling ready to put down more permanent roots. I knew that Ashland was home. I wasn't going anywhere anytime soon. If ever. And, having more space would be nice. I didn't think it was an exaggeration to say that if I stretched my arms as far as they could reach, I could probably touch each wall in the living room. The apartment's tiny galley kitchen had been great for cooking quick and easy meals, but if I ever wanted to have friends over for a dinner party or to hang out there was no place to put them.

The question I had been ruminating on was whether or not I could see myself in my childhood home. The house was wonderful. It was tucked in the hillside above Southern Oregon University on Mountain Avenue, surrounded by sequoia, aspen, and pine trees. Its giant windows looked out into the forest. As a kid I always thought that we lived in a tree house. Yet the house was still easily within walking distance of the plaza. It was a two-story Craftsman with a large living room, a beautiful kitchen with an eat-in nook, and a formal dining room with French doors that led to an outdoor deck with stunning views of Grizzly Peak to the east. I hadn't said a word to anyone about the idea, but I could already hear Lance's voice in my head, saying, "Darling, it's simply perfect. The pine trees, the views, the charm."

Maybe there was a reason I was hearing his words.

Mom cleared her throat. "Are you daydreaming again?"

It was a constant joke between us. She was convinced that I had inherited my father's tendency to drift off with my own thoughts.

"Maybe." I chuckled.

"So does that mean you're thinking about the house?"

"Yeah. I am, but I don't want you to wait for me. If you're ready to list it and get it on the market, I understand."

"Juliet, stop. We wouldn't have offered it to you if we didn't want you to have it."

"I'm not 'having' it, Mom. If I end up there, I'll buy it from you."

She pursed her lips. "We'll see about that, young lady."

"There's no question about it. I'm going to buy something here in Ashland anyway. What's the difference?"

"The difference is that Doug and I would love to see you in the house. It would be wonderful to keep it in the family. Doug is the one who brought up the conversation initially. Not me."

I reached over and patted her forearm. "You found a good man."

She winked. "I know."

"But there's no chance that I'm not buying it from you."

"Time will tell." She pointed to the sky. "Oh, look at that hawk."

I knew that she was intentionally changing the subject. That was fine. I needed more time to sit with the idea. I didn't want to rush into anything, yet the thought of baking a farmers breakfast in my mom's kitchen or sipping a glass of wine outside on the deck in the evening, taking in the golden glow of the hills, was definitely appealing.

We zoomed along Highway 66, passing goat farms, an equestrian sanctuary, old farmhouses, and gently rolling green hills. The turnoff to the lake took us onto a gravel road. Ahead there was a huge retaining rock wall, holding back the lake waters.

Mom steered the car past stacks of bright white crew boats, a boat ramp and dock. We followed the road to the playground, picnic area, waterslides, and swim cove.

I spotted two fishermen casting from the opposite hillside. To our left were orchards of trees with picnic tables and shady benches tucked in the grove.

We arrived at the lake house. Only a handful of private homes dotted this side of the lake. The house we were here to view was a mid-century single-level ranch. From the front the house didn't look like much. It was painted forest green to blend into the natural environment. I knew that everything would be oriented to the back. An open-house sign was propped on the stone pathway that led to a charcoal-gray front door.

"Shall we take a peek?" Mom asked as a teal-blue convertible zoomed into the parking space next to us. A woman got out of the car and approached us. I recognized her immediately. It was Stella Pryor, the real estate developer with whom Pam was furious for trying to build a tiny-house development next to Nightingales.

"Are you here for the open house?" Stella slammed her car door shut.

I wondered how she had managed to keep her long, dark hair tied in a tight ponytail with the top down on her convertible.

"Yes, I'm Helen." Mom stepped forward and extended her hand. "My real estate agent told me that there was an open house today and suggested I stop by and take a look. Are you the owner?"

"No," the woman scoffed. She reached into her handbag and pulled out a business card with her face on it. "I'm sure you recognize me, I'm Stella Pryor."

Mom looked at the card and handed it to me. It was hard to tell how old Stella was through the layers of makeup caked on her face.

She rolled her eyes. "I'm Stella of Steller Development. We are Ashland's premier developer. We have dozens of projects in the works."

"Ah. I see." Mom handed Stella back her card.

"Keep it. A word of warning, if I can get the city to pull its head out of the sand and agree to zoning updates that are decades overdue, the house that you're about to look at is going to be bulldozed."

"Oh." Mom looked at me.

Before we could ask more, Stella flipped around and marched toward the front door.

"She's um . . ." I tried to think of the right word.

"Intense? Type A? Off-putting?" Mom offered.

"All of the above." I chuckled, and then I told her about my conversation with Pam and how furious Pam was about a potential tiny-house development going up on the property adjacent to Nightingales.

"That doesn't sound like Pam," Mom said, with a touch of concern in her voice. "I'll have to stop by Nightingales and check in with her. I know that she's been busy with the constant rotation of guests for the high season. I'll have to see if there's anything I can do to help."

We headed inside. The house didn't disappoint, with white-birch floors, an open fireplace connecting the living room and dining room, soaring ceilings, and tons of natural light. I hoped that Stella wouldn't succeed in her quest to convince the city to update its zoning policies. It would be a shame to see the house bulldozed. Its vast windows offered a one-hundred-and-eighty-degree view of the lake. I could picture the Professor relaxing in a comfy chair in front of the woodstove, reading a book of poetry, or Mom whisking up a soufflé in the chef's kitchen, complete with granite countertops and an eight-burner gas stove. The house was nestled in the foothills of Grizzly Peak with private lake views and numerous stone patios for outdoor entertaining.

Stella wasn't the only one interested in the property. The open house had drawn a number of people. Mom and I caught each other's eye multiple times while we toured the property. "Look at this bathtub, Juliet," Mom whispered, pointing to a clawfoot tub in front of a wall of windows that looked out over the lake.

"Amazing," I whispered back. I waited until we were back in the car before asking her opinion. "What did you think?"

She grinned. "I loved it. What did you think?"

"It's incredible. I can totally see you and the Professor there. Are you going to bring him back to see it again?"

"Absolutely." She nodded and steered the car back the way we came. "I was thinking I should call our agent right now."

"Go for it."

"The only downside is that this location is pretty far out of town."

"What? Like ten minutes?" Everything in Ashland was within a ten-minute drive. And aside from the occasional backup on Main Street during the height of the tourist season, the only time traffic came to a stop was when a herd of black-tailed deer were crossing the street.

"True. But we couldn't walk from here to the plaza."

"Yes, that's fair, but is that one of your top priorities? You've lived within walking distance of everything in

Ashland for a long time; maybe it would be good to have a different view." I paused and swept my hand toward the blue waters of Emigrant Lake. "How can you beat a view like this?"

"You have an answer for everything, don't you?" She patted my arm playfully.

"No. I promise, I have no ulterior motive in trying to sell you on this house, but I saw the way your eyes lit up from the moment we walked through the front door. Why don't you at least give the Professor a call and see if he can come take a quick look."

She glanced to the back. "What about our picnic?" We had pulled into the parking lot above the swim cove. Kids zipped down the blue waterslides and splashed in the shallow swimming area. Families and couples had spread out blankets and folding chairs on the grassy lawn among the picnic tables.

"It can wait. I'd love to get a nice long walk in. I haven't walked the cemetery trail in years. I'll walk along the trail and through the cemetery and meet you here for a picnic later."

"If you're sure?" She hesitated.

"I'm sure. You saw the crowd in there. If this is the house, you don't want to lose it."

That motivated her. She reached for her phone and called the Professor. I applied sunscreen, grabbed a floppy hat, bottle of water, and headed for the trail. I had to walk along the gravel road for a stretch. Once I rounded the corner where the crew boats were stacked I saw two guys carrying kayaks down to the water. This side of the lake was quieter. Red sandy soil revealed the erosion level. Forested hills rose on either side of the lake. In the winter they would be dusted with snow. Waves lapped on the shoreline as a motorboat sped to the middle of the lake. A group of teenagers dove off the dock and a handful of families floated in the lake on bright-colored rafts and inner tubes.

The path that wound above the reservoir to the old cemetery wasn't an official city hiking trail. It could have been an old deer trail, or perhaps a path that had been worn from years of foot traffic. It paralleled the lake for a little over a mile and then connected with the hillside cemetery. The cemetery had once been where Emigrant Lake now sat. It was moved in the 1960s when the old town was flooded.

Underneath the lake's vast waters sat the remains of an old town, now submerged. The town, Klamath Junction, was one of the region's original settlements. It wasn't a booming gold town, rather a small plot with a few houses, a service station, a dance hall, and a cemetery. In school we had learned about the Mill family, who had originally settled the claim.

Emigrant Lake was created in 1924 and then expanded in the 1960s, flooding Klamath Junction. The town and its inhabitants were relocated, and the cemetery was moved up the hillside.

There were rumors that the lake was haunted by the ghost of George Mill, a family member of one of Klamath Junction's original homesteaders, who went missing right before the town was flooded. According to local legend, George was so attached to his family's property and distraught over the town's impending destruction that he barricaded himself in and awaited his fate. When I was growing up, kids would dare one another to visit the cemetery on Halloween in hopes of waking ancient ghosts. They would dare each other to dive into the lake's frigid waters in search of buried treasure and ghosts.

I chuckled at the memory. I never agreed to a single late-night session at the cemetery or diving for treasure. Both thoughts had creeped me out as a child. To be honest, they still did.

I was glad that I had hiking boots on as I trekked through dried grass and bramble that reached my knees. A bee buzzed in my ear and a groundhog darted between my feet. The smell of murky lake waters and grilling barbecues at the waterslide area wafted through the air, as did the sound of children jumping off the docks. I crested the hill and paused to catch my breath.

Snake holes lined the dirt path. In a crop of trees on the hillside kids had built a fort out of driftwood. Honey-colored hills stretched in every direction. An osprey circled above. In the distance I could make out the crest of a rowboat and hear the shouts of the crew team as they cut through the waters. A large group of kids on inflatable rafts had gathered around the dock. They were taking turns trying to land on a doughnut-shaped floatie, pushing farther and farther from the dock's edge each time. Two younger girls swam in rhythm toward the middle of the lake. Their mom floated on a raft nearby, sipping lemonade and reading a book.

One of the girls stopped, began treading water, and adjusted her goggles. I watched as she did a perfect surface dive and disappeared. Her mom didn't look up from her book. The girl's friend treaded water, as if waiting for her to resurface. I glanced at my watch. My pulse quickened. I've never liked diving in water where I can't see the bottom. From my vantage point a hundred feet above, the lake looked as dark as a midnight sky.

Sweat formed on my brow as I watched for the girl. She'd been underwater for at least a minute. How long could she hold her breath? Emigrant Lake was known for having forests of reedy plants beneath the surface. Could she have gotten tangled up in them?

I was about to call down to her mom, when her head bobbed on the surface. I let out a sigh of relief. Except it was short-lived. The next thing I knew, the girl held something up in one hand and her friend let out a blood-curdling scream.

Chapter Six

Without thinking, I flew down the hill. I didn't care that thorns stuck in my thighs. The girl's screams echoed in the vast lake canyon. What had happened? By the time I made it to the shore, the mom had scooped both girls onto her inflatable raft and was paddling it with one hand. The group of kids who had been diving off the docks had cleared the water and were dragging their inflatables with them. There weren't lifeguards posted on this side of the lake. I wondered if I should run to the other side near the waterslides and get help.

A teenage boy sprinted into the lake. As soon as he was waist-deep in the water, he plunged his head in and began kicking so fast that a spray of whitewater spewed behind him. The girls both continued to sob, but their screams subsided a bit. When the teenager made it to the raft he kicked behind it and the mom paddled with one hand.

I wiped sweat from my face. When I looked at the back of my hand it was spotted with blood. A small gash on the side of my left cheek oozed. I must have cut it on a branch. I was breathless and confused but had had enough experience in crisis situations to try and assess the scene. I started with the kids who had been playing on the docks.

"Do any of you know what happened?" I asked.

"No, we heard screams so we got out of the water," a girl who looked to be about thirteen answered. "We thought maybe there was a shark or something."

"A shark?" I couldn't help but laugh. "In Emigrant Lake?"

She nodded earnestly. "We learned about river sharks in my science class. Did you know that some sharks can swim in fresh water?"

I didn't have time to debate the reality of sharks in the lake. "Did anyone else see anything?"

One of the boys raised a tanned arm. "I think there might be something in the water. Those girls went crazy and then their mom yanked them onto that raft."

I could see that I wasn't going to get far with the group of young teens. "You all stay put. I'm going to see what I can find out, but in the meantime, I think it's good that you got out of the water."

I heard one of them say something to the effect of "because of the sharks" under their breath as I walked away. The raft was almost to the shore. I could see that the two girls were huddled together. They looked okay. I didn't see any obvious signs of trauma. What could have happened? Had they gotten spooked?

The teenager helped the mom drag the raft onto the rocky beach. I ran up to assist. "Is everything okay?"

The mom shook her head. She motioned to the girls. "Hannah, Ellen, hop off the raft. I want you both to go wrap up in towels. They're by our picnic spot. I'm going to talk to this nice lady for a minute and then I'll be right there."

The girls hopped off the raft. The girl who I had seen diving was ashen white. Her tiny body quaked. Was she in shock? Her reddish-blond hair was tied in two long ponytails. She gnawed on the tip of one her ponytails while her friend repeatedly tossed a pair of goggles up in the air.

"Do I need to call for help?" I asked.

The mom nodded. "Please. I don't have my cell phone."

"Is your daughter hurt? Did something happen out there?" I asked, reaching into my pocket for my phone.

"Hannah isn't my daughter. She's Ellen's best friend. They were taking turns diving near the site of the old town."

I pointed behind us. "Yeah, I saw them from up on the hill."

The teenager had pulled the raft completely out of the water. He was staring at the raft in a strange way, as if it was about to explode or something. I was distracted by his reaction but needed to focus on what the woman was telling me. I wanted to be able to relay everything clearly and concisely so that the first responders would know what they were coming into.

"Last week the girls found an old gumball machine about ten feet under the water. They're convinced they're going to find a chest of money. Apparently there's a rumor floating around that there's an old bank underwater. They've been begging me to come back so they can take turns diving. They sketched out a map of the lake and have been marking their dive spots. It's been so cute. Kind of like a treasure hunt." Her eyes drifted to her daughter. Ellen was shorter than Hannah with an adorable pageboy haircut and doelike eyes. She had taken her goggles and looped them over one ear. Then she used them like a slingshot, trying to knock a pinecone off a rock nearby.

The woman put her hand over her mouth. "I never should have let them dive. What was I thinking?"

I knew that the woman was shaken up, but I needed her to stay focused. "Did Hannah get hurt when she was diving?" I kept one hand on my phone, ready to punch in 911. Hannah continued to chew on the tip of her braid, but she didn't have any outward signs of harm. I didn't see any bruises or blood on her body.

"Huh?" The woman looked at me for a moment and then blinked rapidly. "Oh, right. No. She's fine. No, she's not fine. I think she's in shock, but she's not hurt."

"Good." I kept my tone calm, but internally I wanted to scream. The woman was having a hard time getting to the point. "Why is Hannah in shock? If I call for help, they'll want to know."

"Huh?" She stared at the girls, who had wrapped themselves in giant polka-dotted beach towels, and then back to the raft. "She found that."

I followed her gaze. Suddenly I knew why the teenage swimmer had been acting off too. Sitting in the middle of the raft was a skull. An undeniably human skull.

"Hannah found that skull in the water?" I asked.

The woman's mouth hung partway open. "Can you believe it? She said that she thought she had found a doll. She saw something that looked like a flowy shirt. She tugged a couple times and then yanked the skull free. She was running out of air so didn't look at it until she reached the surface. That's when she screamed."

I glanced behind us. The girls had linked their arms together. Ellen's head rested on Hannah's shoulder. "No wonder she's upset, but it can't be real, can it? It's probably part of an old Halloween costume. Teenagers always come to the lake and old cemetery on Halloween night."

"It looked pretty real to me." The woman bit her bottom lip.

"Do you want me to take a look?"

"Would you? Yeah, that would be good." She tried to smile. "I didn't get your name."

"I'm Jules." I offered my hand.

Her fingers were cold to the touch. "Susan."

We walked to the raft. The teenage boy who had swum out to help the girls stood next to the raft. His surfer-style swim trunks dripped with water.

"Hey." He flashed us a hang loose sign. "Is everything cool?"

I knelt closer to get a better look at the skull that was propped in the middle of the inflatable raft. "We wanted to take a closer look to see if this is real or if maybe it's just an old prank from Halloween."

The teenager grabbed a stick. "I think it's real." He used the stick to flip the skull over. On the back of the head there was a large indentation as if something had fractured the skull.

My stomach fluttered with nerves. "Okay. Good move using the stick. Let's not touch it."

"What do we do now then?" Susan's brown eyes

bulged out of their sockets. "We can't call 911, can we? Or should we?" Her hands trembled.

I stood up and placed my hand over hers. "It's okay. I'll call my friend Thomas. He's a detective. He'll know what to do." Unfortunately, I had seen death close-up in the past, and knew that the single most important thing we could do at the moment was remain calm. I could tell that Susan was precariously close to going into shock too.

"Can you take her to go sit with the girls?" I asked the teenager.

He sprang into action, guiding the visibly shaken mother over to be with her girls. He called over a few of his friends who distracted the girls with gummy worms while he told funny stories about how he once tried to use the candy worms as fish bait. I could have kissed him. Thank God I wasn't here alone.

I called Thomas. He answered on the second ring.

"To what do I owe the pleasure?" His familiar voice held a hint of playfulness. "Is there a pastry emergency at Torte? Because if there is, Jules, you know I'm your guy."

"Thomas, there's a—uh—situation."

He cleared his throat and his demeanor shifted. "What's going on?"

I explained what had happened. He told me to stay put and that he would be there as fast as he could. After we hung up, I remembered that Mom had called the Professor about touring the house. Obviously I wasn't thinking clearly either. I should have called him first. How much time had passed since I left Mom in the parking lot?

Next I called Mom.

"Are you still at the open house?"

"We are just leaving, why? You sound funny."

"Mom, I need you and the Professor to get down to the other side of the lake by the crew boats and dock right away."

"We've on our way. But why? Juliet, what's wrong?"

I gave her a brief recap of what had happened.

"We'll be there as fast as we can, honey," she said, hanging up the phone.

Knowing that help was on the way brought my heart rate down. Now I needed to check on the girls. They had a bit more color and were laughing with the group of teenagers. I knelt on the beach next to Susan.

"The police are on their way. They should be here any minute," I said in a whisper.

She kept her dark brown eyes lasered on the skull. "I just can't believe that poor Hannah found a human skull. What am I going to tell her mom?"

"You don't need to worry about that right now. First, we don't know for sure that it's real. It could be fake."

"But it's all bashed up," Susan said in low whisper.

"True, but that could have happened if kids were playing around and dropped it on a rock or something." Even as I tried to think of rational explanations for Hannah and Ellen's discovery I wasn't convinced. The way the skull had deteriorated in the water and the fracture lines made me think it likely was human remains. If the skull had been made of hard plastic, it was unlikely to have weathered with time. "When the police arrive, I'm sure they'll be able to determine if it's real or not. If it is, they'll walk you through everything. They have therapists on staff and are trained to handle crisis situations. They'll take good care of you and the girls."

"How do you know so much?" Susan picked up a small piece of agate and massaged it with her fingertips.

"The lead detective who is on his way is my stepfather." I didn't like calling the Professor my "step" father. It sounded cold.

"That makes me feel slightly better. I always thought I would be a model of calm in a crisis, but I can't stop shaking." She held out the piece of agate in her quaking fingers as evidence. "I'm so worried about Hannah and Ellen. Is this the kind of thing that will scar them for life? They're only ten."

I sat down on the sand. "I'm sure they'll be okay. Kids are resilient. I know it's upsetting, but I also know that our community will encircle them with love and support."

She brushed a tear from her eye. "Thanks. I'm not sure why I'm so emotional."

"Because your daughter and her friend just found a skull. I would be worried about you if you weren't emotional."

"What do you think happened? If it's real, could it be from the old graveyard, or do you think someone drowned in the lake and they never recovered the body?"

I had been wondering the same thing. Was it human nature to be curious about cause of death, or did I have an unhealthy obsession with mortality? My mind spun with possibilities. The skull appeared to be fully developed. Aside from the gash, there weren't any other obvious signs of trauma. Not that I was an expert in forensics by any means. I knew from listening to the

Professor and Thomas that the remains would have to be carefully examined by an expert medical examiner.

The rocky soil felt hot even in my boots. A warm wind kicked up, causing ripples on the water. It was as if the once peaceful lake was sending a message. Had something sinister occurred within its deep cold waters?

The sound of police sirens cut through the air. That was fast.

"My friend Thomas is here," I said to Susan, standing and brushing dirt from my pants. "I'll go meet him and bring him down."

She managed to nod okay.

I hurried to greet Thomas. I was surprised he had turned on his sirens. An old skull didn't seem like it would warrant that level of response. I jogged over uneven ground. When I reached the parking lot Thomas and his new partner Detective Kerry were already out of the car and headed straight for me.

As usual, Detective Kerry was dressed in a pencil skirt and silky tank top. She wore three-inch heels. I wondered how she was going to navigate the rocky terrain. As the thought flashed through my mind, her heel caught in the dirt. She wobbled on one leg, trying to reclaim her balance. Thomas caught her from behind.

I watched as his hand lingered on her waist for a moment. She turned and gave him a look of thanks. Then he took her hand in his to help her down the steep hillside.

"Thanks for coming," I said when they reached me.

"Where's the skull?" Thomas asked. He looked very official in his blue police shorts and shirt with a gold badge pinned to his chest. Unlike Detective Kerry, he wore a pair of low-top sturdy hiking boots.

"This way." I pointed them toward the beach next to the dock. "I should warn you that the two girls who found it are pretty freaked out."

"Understandable." Detective Kerry gave me a curt nod.

She and I hadn't exactly hit it off. She took her responsibilities extremely seriously. Not that she shouldn't, but Ashland's laid-back vibe meant that the Professor and Thomas tended to take a slightly more personal approach to police work. Rather than slapping handcuffs on one of the travelers panhandling on the plaza, they knew the street kids by name and directed them away from the plaza or offered to buy them a coffee or doughnut to help them move along. The technique worked. They were true community police officers. Detective Kerry had been slow to embrace their style, but I had started to notice a subtle shift in her brisk attitude. I had also noticed a growing rapport between her and Thomas.

"The girl who found the skull is Hannah. She's in the pigtails. Her friend Ellen with the short hair is next to her, and that's Ellen's mom, Susan," I said, pointing out everyone.

"Let's see the skull first," Thomas said, pulling a pair of disposable plastic gloves over his hands.

I showed them to the raft. Thomas carefully examined the skull. As did Kerry. "Well, what do you think?" I asked, after they each had had a chance to study the skull. "Is it real?"

Thomas placed the skull back on the raft. "We're not

medical examiners, but I'd say odds are very good that it's real."

"How old is it?"

"That's a question for the medical examiner." He shrugged. "I'll put in a call and then we can interview the girls."

"We'll take it from here." Detective Kerry dismissed me and walked over to the blanket where Hannah and Ellen sat next to Susan.

I half expected her to begin interrogating the girls as if they were in a holding cell. I wondered if anyone noticed my mouth hang open when she dropped to her knees and spoke to them in a quiet, calm tone. She almost sounded maternal. Thomas followed suit. He handed each girl a police badge sticker.

"You two are real heroes, you know? You've cracked a case for us, and what quick thinking. That was so brave of you to recover your discovery."

I noted that he hadn't used the word "skull" or "human remains."

"Most people might have panicked but not you," he continued. "You both deserve these badges. You are officially part of the Ashland Police Squad, right, Kerry?"

She nodded. "Absolutely."

The girls looked at each other and giggled. "I almost dropped it when I realized what it was," Hannah confessed.

"She did. It's true," Ellen concurred.

"But you didn't. That's the important thing," Detective Kerry said. "You acted like real partners. What a great team."

Hannah and Ellen perked up.

"Do you think you could show us where you were swimming earlier?" Thomas asked.

The news that they were heroes revived their spirits. I wasn't worried that either of them was at risk for going into shock. Ellen pulled Hannah to her feet. "Come on, let's go show them."

Susan raised her index finger. "Officers, do you think that's such a good idea?"

Detective Kerry and Thomas shared a look. Kerry followed after the girls who were already running toward the shallow waters of the shoreline.

"One thing we know from experience is that it's critical to take statements from witnesses immediately. We're going to be calling in a dive team to dredge the lake floor and want to pinpoint as close as possible the spot where the remains were found."

Susan listened to Thomas, but kept her eyes focused on the girls. Detective Kerry had recruited the teens and sent them to flag down a motorboat.

Thomas continued. "The girls will be in good hands, and quite honestly I think getting them back on the lake will be good for their emotional well-being. You know the old saying, you have to get back on the horse? I think it applies in this case."

"If you're sure." Susan didn't sound convinced. She had wrapped the towel so tightly around her shoulders that I thought she might cut off circulation to her arms.

"I can vouch for Thomas and his partner. They're Ashland's best. They wouldn't do anything to put the girls in harm's way." I picked up a piece of lava rock.

"Okay, maybe I should come with you?" She yanked the towel tighter.

"You bet." Thomas was about to lead her away when the Professor and Mom arrived.

"Good timing, Professor." Thomas let out an audible sigh and went to show the Professor the skull, which was still propped in the middle of the inflatable raft.

"What happened?" Mom asked.

I filled her in while we watched the Professor remove plastic gloves and a pair of reading glasses from his short-sleeved Hawaiian-style shirt. He examined the skull and then placed it in a plastic evidence bag.

The motorboat zipped off with the girls, Susan, Thomas, and Detective Kerry inside. The Professor strolled over to us with a look of concern clouding his face.

"Doug, is everything okay?" Mom asked.

He held up the bag containing the skeletal remains. "I don't know yet, but I fear that we've stumbled upon a very old murder scene."

Chapter Seven

"A murder?" The incredulous look on Mom's face matched my thoughts.

Doug gave her a solemn nod. "I do believe that something is rotten in the state of Denmark."

"Huh?" I had a feeling the Professor's reference was from *Hamlet,* although admittedly my Shakespeare was a bit rusty. The man was a walking encyclopedia of knowledge when it came to the Bard. He could quote sonnets at will and rattle off a soliloquy without pausing for a moment.

"Hamlet." He tucked his reading glasses into the front pocket of his shirt.

Mom nudged him. "Doug, in modern language, please."

"But of course, my love." He smiled and kissed her cheek. "It's too soon to know, but there are very clear signs of trauma on the skull. It's certainly possible that our poor departed soul had an accident. However, in very synchronistic timing, I had been reviewing an unsolved murder case just the other week. It was presumed that the body was dumped into the lake but was never recovered. And there's a saying in police work—no body, no case."

"You think the skull that Hannah found is from the same case?"

"Odds are in favor, I would say. From my initial observations this has been underwater for decades. This isn't from a recent accident or otherwise. The coroner will date it, but if I had to wager a guess I would assume that it's been underwater for decades."

I shuddered.

"Speaking of the coroner, if you'll excuse me I need to place a few calls." He walked away for privacy.

Mom sighed. "Well, that wasn't expected."

She linked her arm through mine. "Me either." I placed my head on her shoulder.

We stood in silence, watching the motorboat make large circles around the area where the girls had been swimming.

"I almost forgot, what about the house? Did the Professor like it?"

Mom smiled. "He loved it. We're thinking of putting in an offer."

"You are? That's great." I wrapped her in a hug.

"I don't want to get too attached. It sounds like there are a number of other interested parties, and now with this . . ." She trailed off.

"Oh no. I'm so sorry. I shouldn't have dragged you into this."

"No, no. This is Doug's job. He would have been called to the scene anyway. This absolutely takes precedence."

"Maybe you should call your real estate agent. You

could write up the offer and then bring it over for the Professor to sign. It looks like he might be a while here."

The side of her mouth tugged down. "No. I don't want to do this without Doug. This is the next step in our new life together and I want us to both be a part of it."

"Good point." A dive team arrived on the scene. Red, blue, and white police lights flickered on the water. The team moved with speedy precision. One part of the team readied the boat while two divers suited up in wet suits and prepped oxygen tanks.

"Should we stay, or do you want to go?" I asked.

She frowned. "I don't know about you, but I'm not really in the mood for a picnic anymore. It would feel strange."

"Agreed. Let's head back to Torte."

We drove in silence. The image of Hannah surfacing with a skull replayed in my mind. I hadn't lied to Susan about my sense that the girls would recover from the shock, but I was still flustered by the shift the afternoon had taken. When we got to the plaza, Mom found a parking space near Lithia Park. She turned to me. "That wasn't how I was expecting the afternoon to go."

"My thoughts exactly."

Her cell phone buzzed. I waited for her to read the text. She massaged her brow. "Uncanny timing. That was my agent. She wants me to go see a lot nearby that has a few offers pending."

"A lot? Are you and the Professor considering building a new house?"

"Not necessarily. Doug mentioned it in our initial meeting. He said that if the right lot in the right location came on the market, it might be worth exploring. I don't know anything about the process of building a house, but Doug has plenty of connections."

"Where's the lot?"

She pointed up Main Street. "Right around the corner."

Was she talking about the lot that Pam had shown me?

"Want to go take a quick peek? We can walk."

"Sure." I left my things in the car. "I think I've seen the lot you're talking about. Pam from Nightingales came by and she was telling me about it. Is there a smaller, old house on it?"

"Yeah. That's the one," Mom said, and we walked up the street to the lot with the cabin in desperate need of repair behind Nightingales.

"I know this lot," Mom commented.

A FOR SALE sign was posted near the property line and sidewalk. It hadn't been there the other day.

Two older gentlemen and a young woman in her early thirties were talking in front of the dilapidated shack. One of the men wore painter's overalls that were splattered with brick-red paint. The woman had massive piles of thick black curls that bounced as she spoke. She held a clipboard in one hand and appeared to be pointing something out to the men. It didn't look like she was having much success.

The other man, who was dressed like one of the travelers who spend their days busking on the plaza, noticed us. He shuffled over to us.

"Hey, you lookin' at the sign?"

Mom extended her hand. "Yes, I'm Helen and this is my daughter, Juliet. My real estate agent mentioned that the lot was just listed for sale. We own Torte, the bakeshop just down the street, and thought we would come take a quick look. We don't want to disturb you though."

The man made a grunting sound. "Name's Edgar. I own the lot."

He was a man of few words. There was an awkward pause while Mom and I waited for him to say more.

"Well, I can see that you're occupied," Mom said as she pointed to the young woman and man in painting gear who were now headed our way. "I'll have my agent give you a call and schedule a time to come take a better look."

Edgar stared at her. "Why? You're here now, aren't you? Take a look. There's not much to see."

Mom hesitated.

The woman with the bouncy curls sounded breathless when she reached us. "What's going on?" She directed her question at Edgar but was looking at us.

Edgar didn't reply.

"We were just taking a quick look at the lot," Mom replied. I could hear the confusion in her voice. "Are you the listing agent?"

"For the lot?" The woman thrust her thumb toward the grassy open space. "No. The lot isn't for sale. Did you tell them that, Edgar?"

Again Edgar said nothing.

"I'm Gretchen. I'm the new director of the homeless council." She pushed thick brown glasses up the bridge of her nose.

"Of course." Mom smiled. "I thought you looked familiar. I read the feature story that the *Ashland Daily Tidings* did on you. Welcome. I'm Helen, I own Torte."

"Torte!" Gretchen's large brown eyes lit up. "Torte! You guys have been so great to us. I haven't been in Ashland long. I took the job a few weeks ago and have been meaning to swing by the bakeshop and thank you for your support and ongoing donations. My predecessor absolutely raves about you. She said you've been donating your overstock for decades. That's absolutely wonderful. I can tell you without hesitation that Ashland's unhoused population is grateful to get to share in your artisan pastries and baked goods. You wouldn't believe some of the donations we receive." She paused and fluffed her curls. "Don't get me wrong, we will gladly accept any donations that come through our doors, but when I'm speaking with school and church groups about the transient population I like to put them in the person's shoes. We get a lot—I mean a lot—of things like canned creamed spinach in the food bank. And, again, the families we serve are happy to get whatever food they can, but when I'm educating the general public, I ask people to think about what it might be like to only eat one meal a day, or less. Then to think about what they might want to receive if they were in the same position. Getting one of your beautifully designed cupcakes or a loaf of specialty bread can be a real mood booster for this population. It can really change someone's outlook to receive a luxury food item like what you donate."

Mom's cheeks reddened. "That's nice to hear. We're always happy to help support the community in whatever way we can."

Gretchen clasped her hands in prayer. "The thanks is all mine. Sorry about the speech. I just get so passionate about this topic." She looked to Edgar who curled his lip and shrugged.

"Passion is a good thing," Mom replied.

"You must be Juliet," Gretchen said, turning her attention to me. "I've heard so much about you. Everyone likes to boast that Ashland has one of the best pastry chefs in the country."

"I don't know about that." Now it was my turn to blush.

Gretchen clapped her hands together. "What a lucky afternoon. We're blazing a new deal and now I get to meet the famed owners of Torte."

She sounded like she was about to say more, but the man in the overalls finally made his way to us. His gait was unsteady, and I noticed a subtle limp on his left side. "What's all the commotion?"

"This is Helen and Juliet; they own Torte," Gretchen introduced us. "This is Henry. He lives in the house at the crest of the hill, above Edgar." She turned and pointed to the house directly above the lot. It was a rust-brown color with orange trim. The roof was spotted with moss. A large cedar deck wrapped around the back of the house. It looked down into Edgar's house and the attached overgrown lot. The house needed some TLC, and from the sight of painter's tape around the window trim and the large ladder propped against the siding it looked as if it was about to get a new coat of paint.

"I know Torte. Fancy coffee. Isn't that right, Edgar?" Henry asked. His overalls were splattered with paint and a tool belt hung around his waist.

Edgar grunted something.

"I thought maybe you were the real estate lady. I'm

going to get back to my painting, since you ladies are bakers and can't give us any idea about property lines." Henry turned and began walking back over the uneven grass. I wondered if he needed a hand. "See you for a gin later, Edgar?"

"Yep." Edgar nodded.

"These two are the cutest," Gretchen said. "They've been neighbors—for what—Edgar? Thirty years?"

"Longer." He turned and snarled at Henry. "Can't get rid of the old geezer."

"You two!" Gretchen put her hand over her heart and looked at me. "The cutest, right? Anyway, they have a nightly drink. Gin and tonic, right, Edgar?"

"Gin."

Gretchen laughed. Edgar didn't crack a smile.

"You must be a walking encyclopedia of Ashland history," Mom said to Edgar with a smile.

"I've been around long enough to see that the more things change, the more nothing changes," Edgar said as he waved off a dragonfly buzzing around his head.

"I can imagine," Mom continued. "I've been in Ashland over thirty years and I'm always surprised by how much we've grown, and yet maintained a sense of a small community."

Edgar glanced behind him toward Henry's half-painted house. "Try sixty years."

I could tell that he was warming up to Mom. His shoulders relaxed as he continued. "My family was one of the first to settle at Klamath Junction. You've probably never heard of it."

"We've just come from the lake," Mom said, shooting me a look of curiosity. "What uncanny timing. Klamath

Junction is on the top of my mind because the police are searching the old town as we speak." She went on to explain how the girls had discovered the skull and how the site of the now submerged town was being searched by dive teams.

Edgar's face blanched. He lost his footing as he swatted at the dragonfly again.

Gretchen caught him by the elbow. "Are you okay?"

"Heat's getting to me." He nodded to us and shuffled off to his house.

Gretchen waited until he was out of earshot. "Don't let his crusty exterior fool you. That man has a heart of gold. And those two have been looking after each other for longer than I've been alive."

"Henry mentioned something about property lines. Has the lot already sold?"

Gretchen's jaw tightened ever so slightly. "Oh, that's nothing. They have to map out where the property line ends for the sale. That's all."

"So the lot is already sold?" Mom repeated.

"Yeah. Yeah." Gretchen sounded unsure. She glanced at her clipboard. "I should really get back to work. It was great meeting you both. I'll have to stop into Torte soon and try one of your wonderful pastries."

"Please do," Mom said. "We'd love to have you."

"Only you might want to hold off for a couple days." I realized I was still wearing the floppy hat from the hike. I took it off. "We're almost done with a major remodel. I can't wait to dust and have the bakeshop back in order."

Gretchen chuckled. "I know the feeling." She tapped

her clipboard. "We're in the middle of a huge new project and I'm starting to wonder if I've taken on too much."

"Sounds like you two have a lot in common." Mom winked.

"I'll be by soon," Gretchen called as she returned to Edgar's house.

Mom and I turned to head down the hill. "Was that odd, or was it just me?"

"That was odd," I concurred.

"I think I can cross the lot off our list. I get the sense that there might be drama involved in the sale."

"Me too."

I was glad that Mom had come to that conclusion on her own. There was definitely something brewing between Henry, Edgar, Pam, and Gretchen. We had enough drama for the moment with new staff, a remodel, and figuring out what was next for Uva. I was happy to leave whatever property dispute might be in the works alone and focus on the wonderful things that lay ahead for Torte.

Chapter Eight

For the next few days I did just that—focused on the wonderful changes at Torte. The construction crew put the finishing touches on the upstairs, poured the new accessibility ramp, and gave the bakeshop a final deep cleaning. With eager anticipation Mom and I gathered the team and the Professor for the big reveal the night before our grand reopening. I had sent everyone home while the construction crew packed up their power tools. While the crew used a Shop-Vac to clean the stairs I hung posters of coffee charts, lined the shelves above the coffee bar with vintage cookbooks and succulent plants, and put the dining room back together. I asked the construction workers to leave the plastic in place, so I could surprise my staff, and I recruited Andy to help make a special drink for the occasion.

My eyes welled with happy tears as Mom, the Professor, Andy, Steph, Rosa, Marty, Sterling, Bethany, and Sequoia gathered in the dining room.

"I just want to say thank you for your support through this process. I know that it's been challenging, but you guys are the best team in Ashland."

"In the Rogue Valley!" Andy chimed in.

"Yes, in the Rogue Valley." I looked to Mom. "Do you want to add anything?"

The Professor had his arm wrapped around her shoulder. She smiled at him and then said, "No, I want to see it. Let's tear down that plastic."

"Drum roll, boss!" Andy shouted as I reached for one corner of the thick plastic that shrouded our new and improved coffee bar, pastry counter, and ice cream case.

Sterling stood at the opposite side of the plastic ready to tear down his end.

Bethany pounded the top of her thighs.

"Count it down, Mrs. The Professor," Andy said to Mom, holding three fingers in the air.

Mom and the Professor grinned at each other. "Okay, here goes. Three . . . two . . . one!"

Sterling and I ripped down the plastic in unison. Everyone cheered. The renovation had turned out better than I could have expected. We had nearly tripled our working counter space. Three brand-new pastry cases stretched from the top of the stairwell. There was a small cooler that would eventually house hand-churned concretes (like a frozen custard) and a passageway for staff to get in and out of the workspace. The far end of the long counter housed the espresso machine and coffee bar. We had repurposed the original kitchen butcher-block island (which had been the first piece of furniture that my parents bought when they opened Torte). It sat opposite the coffee counter and would serve as a space for lids, straws, napkins, cream, sugar, spices, house-made simple syrups, and anything else our customers might want to dress up their coffee.

The dining room had remained basically intact. There were still window booths and a variety of tables in the front, but we had also been able to add a number of two-person tables along the wall across from the coffee counter and pastry cases. I couldn't believe how large the space looked. Our signature chalkboard awaited a new quote and fun designs from Torte's youngest customers.

"This calls for a toast," Mom exclaimed, looking up to the wine rack for a bottle of something celebratory to open.

We stock a variety of wines and a small rotation of local craft beers for our evening crowd and for our Sunday Suppers, which had been on hold during renovations. I was eager to start planning our next one.

Andy held both of his arms up in the air. "Hold it right there, Mrs. The Professor. Jules and I have got you covered."

He squeezed behind the coffee bar and returned with a tray of clear twelve-ounce glasses. Each was filled with a scoop of our vanilla bean ice cream that had been drowned in shots of hot espresso and dusted with dark chocolate shavings and chopped hazelnuts.

"Affogatos, everyone." He beamed as he passed around the delectable Italian coffee dessert. "In Italian *affogato* means drowned. Get ready to be drowned in deliciousness."

The memory of Hannah and Ellen diving in the lake flashed in my mind. No one noticed that I shuddered internally at the mention of drowning as I took a sip.

"Did you flood these with espresso shots or strong-brewed coffee?" Sequoia asked, studying the creamy, melting ice cream. She sounded like she was genuinely interested in learning his technique, but Andy interpreted her question differently.

"Espresso," he snapped. "It's an Italian specialty, so obviously espresso is the only choice."

"Noted." Sequoia rolled her eyes.

I wondered if I should mention that I'd had affogatos made both ways while in Italy.

Mom swept in and patted Andy's muscular shoulder. "You have outdone yourself once again. These are divine."

He was appeased by her compliment. However, I noticed that he gave Sequoia a lingering glare. I couldn't let the tension between them simmer. Things hadn't improved between them. They hadn't gotten worse either. But Andy continued to be short and icy to Sequoia. I didn't want our food to suffer. Carlos believed that the feeling we infuse into food is as important as the food itself.

I could hear his voice in my head. "The food, it knows, Julieta. We must cook with love. It comes through in the flavor. The customers, they will know if the chef is angry when he is in the kitchen."

The question was how and when to intervene with Andy and Sequoia. It had only been a short time. In a dream world, they would find a working rhythm without any intervention from me. It was looking less likely that that would happen. I was going to have to keep a close eye on them, and if things didn't improve by the end of the week, it would be time to come up with Plan B.

Everyone drank the creamy affogatos and familiarized themselves with the changes to the space. I had a chance to speak with the Professor alone while Mom went over her vision for the pastry displays.

"Any updates on the skull recovered from Emigrant Lake?" I asked.

The Professor sipped his coffee. A dot of vanilla ice cream landed on his reddish beard. He reached into his breast pocket and dabbed it with a linen handkerchief. "Indeed. The dive team recovered the rest of the remains as well as what could be a possible murder weapon. We're waiting for final lab results, but we're relatively confident that we're going to be able to identify the body."

"Really?"

"As a matter of fact, I had recently been reviewing old unsolved cases, preparing for my eventual retirement."

"Are you getting closer?"

He was noncommittal. "Time will tell. In any event, I am convinced that the remains are those of George Mill."

"The George Mill? The one who supposedly stayed on his family homestead when Klamath Junction was flooded?"

"The one and the same. The Mill family (George's grandparents) was the original family who founded Klamath Junction. They were originally from Tennessee. They came to Oregon at the turn of the last century and staked their claim at what we now know as Emigrant Lake. The lake was originally created in 1926. Have you ever seen the old photos on display at the Southern Oregon Historical Society?"

"Maybe a long time ago, on a school field trip."

"It's worth a trip to Medford. Klamath Junction in its heyday was a small plot with two service stations, a garage, cemetery, dance hall, and family homes."

"And then they expanded the lake at some point, right? That's when the town disappeared underwater?"

"Correct." The Professor paused and took another sip of his affogato. "The lake was expanded in 1960. They moved the cemetery to higher ground, but the town is still standing—under hundreds of thousands of gallons of water of course."

I shuddered. Thinking about Hannah and Ellen finding George's body.

"What's the story with George Mill?" I asked. "I assume that discovering his remains clears up the rumor that he stayed on the homestead while the town was flooded."

"I'm afraid so. He went missing around the time the lake was expanded. Rumors at the time claimed that he refused to leave the family homestead. It was assumed that he drowned. His skeletal remains paint a different picture, as does what I've been able to uncover about his past thus far."

"How so?" My interest was piqued.

"George was cantankerous. There's a documented history of altercations with neighbors and poor, unsuspecting hikers who ventured onto his property."

"Like what?" I was so wrapped up in our conversation that I barely noticed as Mom and the team headed for the basement. I probably should have joined them but wanted to hear the rest of the story.

"For starters, he shot at anyone who came within a hundred feet of his property."

"Yikes."

The Professor nodded. "The Mill family had vast real estate holdings. I've been scouring through old records on microfiche and learned that he had some undisclosed business partners. I have Thomas and Detective Kerry pulling every story and article they can find on the Mill family. George had an ongoing battle with the county about restructuring the lake. He refused to sell, and at one point had threatened to chain himself to his cabin."

"Whoa."

"Here's where it gets interesting." The Professor leaned closer and lowered his voice. Not that it was necessary. We were the only two people left upstairs. "Right before the expansion of the lake it was rumored that George had cut a deal to sell the property to an undisclosed buyer. Which doesn't add up, since it was public knowledge that Klamath Junction as it was known was about to be devoured by lake waters."

"Weird."

"Indeed. The local paper ran a story about the Mill family and their pioneering spirit. A photo of George with his two sisters on the porch of the original family homestead ran the day before they opened the dam and let the waters flow into Emigrant Lake. The next day he was reported missing and has never been seen since."

"And you think there was foul play involved?"

The Professor finished his drink and set it on the counter. "This is between you and me, but there is most certainly damage to the skull that was recovered. Damage from some kind of a fatal blow. If it turns out to be a match with George Mill, I think we can say without hesitation that we have just uncovered an unsolved murder."

My breath caught in my chest for a moment. The Professor's words made the image of the skull looping through my head suddenly have a personal attachment.

"How do you even begin investigating a crime that took place over fifty years ago?" I asked.

He sighed. "That, my dear, is the question."

Everyone returned from the basement. The happy mood broke the dark pall that had fallen over me. The Professor gave me a kind smile. "We'll continue this conversation later. Thank you as always for your care and concern. It is one of your most endearing qualities, and one that I know you inherited from your mother."

I gave him a hug. Our relationship was changing and deepening. One unexpected gift of Mom and the Professor's marriage was that I felt like I had a father figure again. He had served that role already, but now that it was official something had shifted between us. The only holdup that I couldn't get past was that I had always known him affectionately, like everyone else in Ashland, as "the Professor." He had mentioned on more than one occasion that perhaps I might want to call him "Doug." Calling my stepfather "the Professor" did seem silly, but "Doug" just didn't roll off my tongue.

I had taken to not calling him by anything, which seemed even stranger. Eventually I was going to have to figure something out. For the moment, I was consumed with the thought of an unsolved murder. I hoped that the old case wouldn't be too stressful for the Professor as he was trying to scale back, and I also hoped that he could solve George's murder and bring closure to Hannah and Ellen and any of George's remaining family.

Once everyone left, I took the opportunity to clear my head. There's nothing like an empty kitchen in my opinion. Baking is my form of meditation. I locked the front and headed downstairs to the gleaming kitchen. For tomorrow's grand reopening bash, I wanted to make a signature Torte dish—raspberry bars.

At Torte we source only the freshest local ingredients. Through the years, we had developed long-term relationships with regional farmers, who delivered their handpicked crops to our front door every few days. Raspberries were in season. Two flats had been dropped off earlier in the day. I turned on some Latin music and allowed my thoughts to drift to Carlos as I sifted flour, baking powder, and salt.

Carlos and I had been circling through the same conversation in what seemed to be an endless loop.

"Julieta, *mi querida,* you must give me a chance." I could hear his pleading tone echo in my head as I creamed butter and brown sugar in the mixer.

"You cannot know if I will miss the sea if you don't allow me to come to you."

"But what if you're miserable here?" I argued.

"How can I be miserable if I am with you?" His voice was husky. "It will be a new adventure. With you in Ashland, and for Ramiro too. What are you afraid of, *mi querida*?"

I didn't have a response. He was right. There was no way to know if Carlos would be at home in Ashland without giving him a chance. I didn't admit it to him, but I was afraid. Afraid of what might happen to us and afraid that Carlos might disrupt the idyllic life I had created for myself here. It wasn't fair to Carlos or healthy for me to keep dragging things out between us. I needed to make a decision once and for all. Was I going to allow Carlos back into my life? Or was it time to say goodbye for good?

I tried to center my thoughts on the present as I squeezed fresh lemon juice into the creamed butter and sugar. Next, I sifted in the flour and mixed it until it resembled coarse cornmeal. I pressed the crumbly crust into greased glass pans. Then I slid them in the ovens to bake for fifteen minutes.

With the first layer baking, I started on the next layer. For this I whisked eggs, brown sugar, flour, and vanilla. This would create a gellike center for the bars.

The timer dinged on the oven. I removed the pans and placed them on the countertop to cool. Then I stirred in chopped walnuts and coconut in the eggs and brown sugar. Once the crust had cooled, I arranged fresh raspberries on top and covered everything with the runny mixture. I returned the pans to the oven to bake for another thirty minutes. They could cool overnight. In the morning we would cut them in two-inch squares. The shortbread-style crust with its almost frothy, nutty coconut layer and pops of tart, juicy berries should be delicious.

I cleaned up after myself. It was time to call it a night. My stomach flopped with eager butterflies as I exited the basement. Tomorrow we would open the new and improved Torte. I hoped that Ashland would embrace the changes we had made to the bakeshop.

Chapter Nine

The next morning Torte was a whirlwind of activity while we prepared to open for our first day of business with the connected spaces. We had plastered the plaza with posters about our grand reopening party. Everyone in town was invited to come see the new and improved Torte. We had spent days creating a special reopening menu complete with cherry-almond hand pies, chocolate-marshmallow cookies, banana cream cakes, hazelnut toffee, and grasshopper cheesecakes. To introduce the new staff, I asked each of them to make a dish that represented them. Rosa opted to make her signature pan de coco, Marty made dozens of loaves of his San Francisco sourdough with herb-infused butters, and Sequoia's offering was mehndi hand cookies, a spicy cutout cookie with henna designs made with black molasses frosting.

Vases of red roses and dainty white heliotrope were placed on the dining tables. Stephanie had sketched a drawing of the plaza and Lithia Park on the chalkboard. We had printed new menus and baked an assortment of wood-fired pizzas for tasting in the basement. Bethany agreed to snap photos and document the reopening on social media. Andy would be doing coffee cuppings throughout the day like wine tasting for coffee. He would brew a variety of our house blends and have customers inhale the scent before taking a long slurp and allowing the distinct flavors to slide down the tongue. And, finally, Sterling would give tours of the kitchen. It was going to be busy, but we were ready.

Customers buzzed with excitement when we opened the doors and our faithful coffee and pastry lovers flooded in.

"Jules, it's absolutely wonderful," Thomas's mom, who owned A Rose by Any Other Name, said as she handed me a bountiful bouquet of white lilies with red roses, and touches of teal carnations to match our color scheme. "A reopening gift. I know you ordered the vases, but I thought it might be nice to have a statement piece to put on the front counter."

"Thanks. That's so thoughtful of you." I breathed in the scent of the sweet lilies and placed them on the counter. "It's gorgeous."

"So is Torte," she gushed. "You and your mother have outdone yourselves. I think half of Ashland is downstairs trying to stake a claim in front of that cozy fireplace. That's going to be the coveted spot from here on out."

"I hope so. We're happy with the changes, but as you know it's been a huge undertaking."

She gave me a sympathetic nod. "Owning a small business is not for the faint of heart."

"Exactly."

"You don't need to worry though. Ashland has always embraced Torte. Just as Torte has embraced Ashland. I don't see that changing in the near future."

I appreciated her support.

"I won't keep you. Enjoy the celebration, and congratulations." She left me with a quick hug.

There was no denying the depth of Ashland's community spirit. Thomas's mom was one of dozens of other small-business owners and regulars who stopped me throughout the reopening party to compliment us on the renovations and declare their ongoing patronage. I overflowed with happiness. And the bakeshop overflowed with people. Everywhere I looked there were locals waiting in line for tastes of Andy's coffee special and nibbling on vanilla shortbread cut out in the Torte logo shape and iced with red and teal buttercream. I was about to go do a walk-through of the basement when I spotted Richard Lord muscle his way to the front of the coffee line.

Richard Lord owned the Merry Windsor, a Shakespeare-themed hotel across the street, and had been a thorn in my side ever since I had returned home. He looked ridiculous as usual in purple-and-green-checked golf pants and a lime-green golf shirt with a matching cap. He elbowed an elderly woman out of the way to grab a taster of cold brew.

Knocking it back like a shot of alcohol, he scanned the room until his eyes landed on me.

Great. The only thing that could put a damper on this day was a run-in with Richard Lord. I considered trying to make an escape to the basement, but the crowd was too thick.

Richard thudded in my direction. "Well, well, Ms. Juliet, the pastry princess of Ashland, prancing around with her loyal subjects lapping at her feet as usual."

"Hi, Richard. Glad you could make it," I said in the flattest affect possible.

"It's strange. I didn't get an invite." He stuffed a chocolate marshmallow cookie into his mouth in one bite. Chocolate crumbs fell everywhere.

"Everyone was invited. There were posters all over town."

"I'm surprised to see you spending money with reckless abandon, especially given the battle that we're going to have over ownership of Uva. If I were you, I would be counting every pretty penny." He grabbed another cookie, gave me a threatening stare, and headed to the basement.

I was familiar with Richard's intimidation tactics. He didn't scare me. However, I was dreading having a conversation with him about Uva's future. Carlos had negotiated the purchase of one of Ashland's first vineyards from the former owner, Jose. He had always dreamed of finding a plot of organic farmland to cultivate grapes and grow herbs and vegetables. His visions included farm-to-table dinners and a restaurant built upon the principles of sustainability. Had I known that Richard Lord would be part of the equation, I would have urged Carlos to abandon ship. Now I found myself in an unenviable position of being business partners with Mr. Lord. The only silver lining was that Lance had swept in and purchased a percent of the winery as well. If Richard wanted to go to battle he was going to have to armor up. I had numbers on my side.

On cue I heard Lance's singsong voice.

"Juliet, darling, over here!"

I turned to see him standing on his tiptoes, peering

over the crowd and waving with his fingers. He was dressed in a well-cut navy suit with a canary-yellow thin tie and a matching silk pocket square. He was accompanied by a man I recognized as OSF's company coordinator, Malcolm Heady. Malcom had been featured in the *Daily Tidings* lately because of his outreach to find affordable housing for members of the company. Resident actors at OSF receive complimentary housing for their first three years with the company. OSF is one of the Rogue Valley's largest employers. Malcolm's responsibility was to procure housing for the company. OSF contracted with a variety of private homeowners and professional property managers for real estate near the theater complex.

Ashland's rental market was extremely competitive, with a less than two percent vacancy rate. Things had reached a crisis point. The housing shortage and lack of affordable housing was impacting OSF. Highly sought-after actors, technical directors, and costume designers were turning down contracts with the festival due to the housing crunch.

According to the latest article in the newspaper, one of the reasons for skyrocketing prices was due to the state's legalization of marijuana. When legalization passed a few years ago, growers rushed into the Rogue Valley and bought up any available acreage. That in turn sent housing costs soaring. The valley had been flush with cash ever since, forcing minimum-wage workers to move farther and farther out of town. The city council had hosted a number of public meetings on the topic and had called for proposals from builders willing to invest in affordable housing. Malcolm had been at the forefront of the campaign, urging the city not to delay and warning that OSF could suffer huge future losses if the crisis wasn't addressed.

I waited for them to work their way over to me.

Lance kissed each of my cheeks. "Ashland's pastry queen has done it again. This is fabulous, darling."

I brushed off his compliment.

"Have you met Malcolm?" Lance slowly graced his hand in front of Malcolm as if they were on the stage.

Malcom was in his early thirties with wavy blond hair and a prominent square jawline. His facial features reminded me of a young Ted Kennedy.

"No. Great to meet you." I shook his hand. "I've been reading about you in the paper, and I have to say thanks. As a small-business owner, I'm worried about housing for my staff too. I heard from one of my employees that some retail and restaurant workers are driving over an hour one way. They're living out in Selma and way out near Dead Indian Road because they can't afford to live in Ashland, even with roommates."

Malcolm's jaw protruded as he spoke. "I'm glad to hear that you share my concerns. It's imperative that you as a small-business owner speak up. The city council has been dragging their feet on this issue and it's unacceptable. Unless something is done immediately to address the housing crisis Ashland is going to turn into a ghost town."

"A ghost town?" I said, looking around at the crowded dining room. That might be a stretch.

"Absolutely." He became more animated as he spoke. His hands flew in the air. He nearly knocked over a tray of green tea smoothies that Rosa was offering to guests.

"We can't sustain a town and certainly not an award-winning theater on retirees alone. How do we grow the next generation if they can't afford to live here? Did you know that two elementary schools have been shuttered within the last decade? That's not a statistic that the city wants tossed around, but the truth hurts. Young people and families have been priced out of this charming city and I fear that Ashland as we know and love it will be no more."

Lance nodded in agreement. "Malcolm is right. We lost out on a budding young starlet because she couldn't find anywhere to live and refused to drive from White City every day. We can't ask members of the company to sacrifice their time like that. They're already putting in ghastly theater hours. Can you imagine having to drive winding country roads after doing a performance of *Othello* that doesn't even wrap until close to midnight?"

"No." I hadn't thought about the impact on actors and members of the company.

"I've done my best to partner with as many home-owners as I can," Malcolm added. "I've literally knocked on doors and asked if anyone is willing to rent their property. We've gone so far as to house a couple of the interns in a tiny room above the Elizabethan."

"Really?" I was at a loss on how to respond. My first thought went to Mom's house. Maybe if I bought it I could offer up a couple rooms for rent. I certainly didn't need that much space myself and I spent most of my waking hours at Torte anyway.

Malcolm clapped Lance on the back. "Things are looking up though. It sounds like a lead I have on a lot might come through. If we can finalize the deal soon, we should break ground within the month and have an OSF housing development ready by the start of next season."

"An OSF housing development," I repeated.

"Yes, the idea is that we'll own the property, which is a good long-term investment for the company. The board has already signed off on the purchase. We've developed plans that will include a three-story modern apartment complex. They'll be two-bedroom units and the lot is literally five blocks from campus." He pointed in the direction of Edgar's property. This was the third person interested in purchasing the lot.

"Is there competition?" I asked, even though I already knew the answer.

Malcolm nodded. "Yes. The homeless council wants to purchase the lot for a permanent housing project. I'm in support of finding solutions for the homeless but not in this location. It's prime. The homeless council would be wise to look farther out of town—like that old abandoned farm off of Bear Creek." He paused. "I don't know if you know Stella Pryor?"

I nodded.

"She wants to put up a bunch of tiny high-end houses. Such a bizarre concept if you ask me. Luxury tiny houses? Anyway, I've been trying to talk sense into her. There's no way the city council goes for that. And there's no way the neighborhood does either. It's interesting because in some ways both the homeless council and Stella want the land for the same goal, but with very different visions. Both of them will have an uphill battle convincing the city council to change the statutes that allow for transitional housing. Things like building code violations and lack of full utilities."

He paused to catch his breath as Rosa circulated by with a tray of pink champagne sponge cakes layered with French pastry cream and raspberry puree. "Would you like a cake?" Her Spanish accent and the almost romantic cadence to her speech reminded me of Carlos.

"Oh, don't mind if I do," Lance said, helping himself to a tea-sized cake. "Enchanted." He gave Rosa a half bow then turned to me. "Who is this Latin beauty?"

Rosa blushed. She had good reason. Lance appraised her from head to toe. Coming from anyone but him, the gesture could have been interpreted as indecent, but Lance took his role as artist director seriously. He was constantly scouting new talent and seeking people with unique features for roles as extras onstage. Rosa was a natural beauty. She wore little to no makeup. Her long dark hair curled around her heart-shaped face, and her wide brown eyes held a deep intelligence.

"Don't pay any attention to him," I assured her. "He's incorrigible."

Lance gasped. "Moi? Please, darling. I simply must comment on elegance and fabulous bone structure when I see it." He flicked his wrist in the air. "Rosa, call me if you ever want a moment in the spotlight. I have *just* the dress for you. It would accentuate your womanly curves and that dainty waist." He let out an audible gasp.

Rosa stood speechless. She shot me a look that reminded me of a deer in headlights.

"I promise, he's harmless, but if left to his own devices he's going to try to convince you to audition for the theater." I nudged her toward a group of women who had just entered the bakeshop.

"No, thanks. I don't think I'm meant to be on the stage," Rosa said to Lance, and then quickly made her escape toward the women. I noticed Pam in the middle of the group. She spotted me too and headed our way.

"Lance, hands off my new staff. I'm trying to get them acclimated to Torte."

He pretended to be injured. "As am I."

I changed the subject. "Sorry, Malcolm. I think you were going to say something else about the lot."

"What?" Malcolm wasn't listening to me. He and Pam exchanged a frigid stare. Instead of joining our conversation, Pam pursed her lips at Malcolm, pivoted, and returned to the group of women she'd come in with.

Odd.

Malcom's eyes lingered in Pam's direction as he spoke. "The lot is situated on what we call 'Bed-and-Breakfast Row.' Those are established historical homes with high values. Can you imagine sticking a bunch of tiny homes there?"

Lance interrupted. "Enough talk about our problems. We're here to celebrate. Come, show us the basement." He turned to Malcolm. "I've already been privy to a first look, but I'm sure you'll be impressed with the clean design and blend of modern-meets-rustic touches that Juliet has created."

Malcom agreed, but not without a final plea, which almost felt like a demand given his severe tone. "I would appreciate your support on this issue as a small-business owner. Can I count on you as another voice and advocate for affordable housing?"

I glanced at Lance who rolled his eyes and shrugged. "What kind of support are you thinking of?" Not that I didn't want to help, but at the same time I had enough on my plate at Torte. Plus, I wasn't interested in getting involved in a huge battle with the city, Edgar, or anyone else vying for the empty lot.

"Your commitment is the only thing I need at the moment. I'll be in touch though. I'm working on crafting a formal letter to the city as well as staging some protests here in the plaza that should garner good press coverage. You put a starving actor on the street with a sign and call the media. Bam! Front-page feature. That will force the city to listen. If they want to keep OSF revenue here in Ashland, then they're going to have to meet our demands." He paused and glanced in Pam's direction again. She was chatting happily with her friends. "This is on the city's shoulders. They've allowed homeowners like Edgar Hannagan to ruin Ashland. Edgar doesn't care about the greater good. He's selling to make a buck—the highest buck possible—and that will jeopardize the entire future of OSF. We cannot allow money-hungry vultures like him to inflate the price. Have you seen the shack he's living in?"

Malcom didn't wait for us to respond. I wasn't even sure that he was aware that Lance and I were still there. "It's a complete teardown. It's not worth a penny, and he's trying to say the structure alone is valued at over $300,000. Do you know that he bought the entire property, land included, for $25,000 and hasn't done a single thing with it since 1970? It's ludicrous, and if the city doesn't do something to stop this market gouging then they are going to be in for a rude awakening, as are all of us. Am I right, Lance?"

Lance sighed and adjusted his tie. "Enough, enough." His long fingers brushed the air. "Do you smell that? Sourdough bread and vanilla cakes? That, my friend, is the stuff of dreams. Let's drop the high-pressure pitch and go get a better whiff." He kissed my cheeks and dragged Malcolm downstairs. Maybe the smell of wood-fired breads and hot-from-the-oven pies would ease Malcolm's stress. I've always thought that the scents from a commercial kitchen should be bottled and sold as anxiety reducers. Like a modern version of smelling salts. For me, there's nothing more calming than the smell of a working kitchen—whether it's a simmering pot of soup or sweet golden pastry.

Pam motioned for me to join her friends. "Jules, look what we wore for the occasion." She tucked her hair behind her ear to reveal cupcake earrings. "Aren't they cute? My friend Wendy makes them." All the women showed off their pastry-inspired jewelry—necklaces, bracelets, earrings, and bangles designed like miniature cakes and ice-cream sundaes. "We had these made for you." Pam handed me a package wrapped in red tissue paper.

Inside were a pair of earrings that were a perfect replica of our Torte aprons.

"Thank you. These are great." I immediately put them on.

Pam pointed to the coffee bar. "Hang on a minute, ladies, Jules and I will get some of those cold-brew samples for everyone." She pulled me toward the espresso counter. "I saw you speaking with Malcolm. What did he want? What did he say? Was he talking about me? I could tell from his body language that you weren't talking about pastries. Were you talking about me? Did he tell you about the letter?"

"No. What letter?" I was taken aback by her barrage of questions.

"Never mind." Pam waved me off. "He's trying to get you on his side, isn't he? Don't go there, Jules. The lot is going to sell to me or one of my neighbors. I met with Henry. He lives on the hill across from me. You'd probably recognize it because it's in a constant state of missing paint. The man cannot pick a paint color to save his life. He's an artist and regular fixture in Ashland. I think his family was one of the first to settle this area. Do you know him?"

I nodded, remembering my initial meeting with Henry, who had been splattered in paint. "Yeah, I met him the other day with Gretchen—the director of the homeless council."

"Don't put me in a bad mood, Juliet, by mentioning her name either." Pam's face scrunched in a scowl. "There is no way we're having a homeless camp in the neighborhood. That I can guarantee."

"Okay." I didn't ask for clarification. "You were saying something about Henry?"

Her face relaxed. "Yes, Henry has been an absolute doll. It's funny. We've lived near each other for years, but it took this debate to get us talking. Henry is on my side and so are the other neighbors who will be impacted the most by the sale of Edgar's lot, and everyone agrees that I should get the lot. My plans will preserve the neighborhood. He has such great perspective that can only come from someone who has witnessed the changes in Ashland over decades."

"What are your plans?" I intentionally didn't expand on my conversation with Malcolm.

"I'll demo Edgar's property. There's no value in it and it's an eyesore, and then I'll expand my driveway and add additional parking for my guests. Henry and I discussed drafting an agreement in which any neighbors directly surrounding the lot would have access to park there as well. It's the fairest option and will ensure that Ashland's most historic district will be preserved for future generations. Please don't align yourself with Malcolm. He's making enemies fast, and as a theater donor I believe that should have the board rethinking their policies. My friends and I are talking about pulling our support if OSF decides to forge ahead with this ridiculous plan."

"Wow, I had no idea," I said, arranging taster cups of cold brew on a tray for Pam.

She patted my arm. "I know you didn't, dear. That's why I wanted to make sure you were in the loop. By the way, I invited Henry. He said that he and Edgar might drop by. If you see him you should try to get him talking. You won't believe how much he knows about Ashland and the history of the Rogue Valley. He's like a walking encyclopedia."

We delivered the coffees and Pam dropped the subject. She and her friends left shortly after, and I returned to chatting with well-wishers. One thing was certain, if Mom and the Professor decided to build a dream house I was going to caution them to look for another lot. I didn't want them caught up in the growing battle for Edgar's property.

Chapter Ten

As the day wore on, I pushed all thoughts of the vacant lot from my mind. It wasn't hard to do, given the constant stream of customers flowing through the front door and Andy and Sequoia's constant bickering. They pulled shots with lightning speed but were barely civil to one another. On more than one occasion, I had to reprimand them for bickering in front of customers.

The other new staff appeared to be finding perfect rhythms. Rosa and Bethany tag-teamed between running the register and bringing trays of pastries and premade sandwiches up and down the stairs. Marty was right at home in the kitchen. His boisterous laugh carried up between the floors. Customers raved about his sourdough bread and sea salt and honey butter. Each time I checked in with Sterling he reported that Marty was a breeze to work with.

Late in the afternoon, I had gone upstairs to refill my coffee. The pro and con of owning a bakeshop was the constant access to a variety of caffeinated beverages. When I'm baking, I tend to drink—or as Mom claims, "guzzle"—copious amounts of coffee. It's hard to resist the lure of Torte's Mexican blend with notes of chocolate, allspice, and smoked cedar. I knew I should cut back, but when the scent of the roast wafted downstairs I couldn't resist.

"Hey, boss, you have to check this out," Andy said, as I poured myself a cup.

"What's that?" I glanced around, expecting him to launch into another round of complaints about Sequoia.

Sequoia was occupied with refilling coffee in the dining room.

He motioned to Rosa who was taking orders at the register. "You have to watch Rosa in action. She has mad skills."

"Mad skills?" I took a sip of my coffee, not wanting to tally how many cups I'd had thus far today. At least my hands weren't shaking. That was a good sign that I was still within my caffeine limit.

"Yeah. This is awesome. Perfect timing." He waved a greeting to a large group of tourists and two teenage boys who had just entered the bakeshop. Then he pulled me over to the register. "Rosa, do your trick for Jules," he whispered so that the tourists ogling the pastries on display couldn't hear him.

She smiled. "It is not a trick."

"What are you talking about?" I asked, cradling the warm coffee mug in my hands.

"Rosa can peg any customer's drink just by looking at them," Andy said with a touch of pride. "Mad skills, I'm telling you."

"It is nothing." She scoffed off his compliment. "It is simply that I have learned to observe people."

"Do it for Jules, before they order," Andy insisted,

giving the group a wide smile. They were still contemplating their pastry options. "Those two," Andy said, nodding to two preteen boys. "What will they order?"

Rosa studied the boys for a minute. "Chocolate-dipped meringue cupcakes and hot chocolates with extra whipping cream and marshmallows."

Sure enough, when the boys stepped forward to place their order, Rosa had nailed it.

"No, no, wait," Andy said. "That's too easy. Of course, teenagers are going to order hot chocolate and the sweetest cupcakes in the case. Do it again with the tourists." He clapped softly as the large group continued to vacillate over which decadent pastry to order.

Rosa laughed. I appreciated that she went along with Andy's request.

"Okay, I will try."

We huddled together. "This woman near the front with the expensive purse, she will order a nonfat latte with almond milk and no pastries. Her friend who is wearing the jean jacket will order an iced mocha and three strawberry macarons. The man near the back will order a black coffee and a slice of the chocolate-mousse pie, and the other man—hmmm—" She paused for a moment. "Oh yes, *sí,* I think he will order a cappuccino and a blue cheese, spinach, and chive scone."

Andy snapped his fingers. "Wait and get ready to be amazed."

He returned to the espresso machine to make the hot chocolates. I pretended to take inventory of the pastry case while Rosa rang up the group. Once again, she had predicted their order almost to the letter. Her only mistake was that the woman in the jean jacket ordered two strawberry and one salted-caramel macarons.

"Told you!" Andy called from the opposite side of the counter.

"Impressive," I said to Rosa.

She plated the pastries. "It is nothing. After twelve years of working in the food business you learn to watch and observe people, *sí*?"

I nodded.

She handed the customers their plates. When they were out of earshot she continued. "That and if you watch you can see where their eyes linger on the pastries. But do not tell Andy, he thinks I am a genius." She grinned.

We shared a chuckle before I returned to the kitchen. I liked Rosa's energy and having someone closer to my age. I had a feeling we were going to become fast friends. She and Marty brought experience to Torte. That would be a good thing when it came to mentoring some of the younger staff.

When I went downstairs I spotted Henry and Edgar seated near the fireplace. The two older gentlemen were deep in conversation, and from the furrow in Edgar's brow it didn't appear like they wanted company. I tried to scoot past them, but Henry saw me and raised his coffee cup. "Come join us."

Edgar was visibly irritated that his longtime friend had invited me over.

"Glad you two could make it." I kept my tone light. "I won't keep you, but have you tried the pastry samples upstairs?"

Henry clapped Edgar on the back. "I was just saying

that they didn't make coffee like this back in our day, did they, Edgar?"

"Nope." Edgar bristled at Henry's touch.

"Sit." Henry patted the empty chair next to him.

"I don't want to interrupt your conversation."

"No. Don't pay any attention to Edgar's scowl. He always looks like that." Henry patted the chair again.

I sat down. They both had black coffees in front of them. I wasn't surprised. Their generation hadn't grown up with lattes or espresso. "Pam tells me that you're an expert on Ashland's history," I said to Henry.

Henry chuckled. "I don't know about that, but when you've been around as long as Edgar and me you have some tales to tell."

Edgar, who hadn't bothered to change out of his tattered clothing, gave Henry a strange look.

"You were both here in the sixties, right? What was the plaza like back then?" I pointed behind us.

"Nothing like this." Henry broke off a piece of cookie. He had changed out of his painter's overalls, but his fingernails were caked with dried paint. "It was your typical small town. A drugstore, service station, market, cleaners. I remember I used to get to drive my dad's Ford Mustang into town to get supplies at the Coast to Coast auto store. It was right across the street, remember, Edgar?"

Edgar frowned. "No, the hotel was across the street. That I remember because I took Anna Mill to prom there."

"Anna Mill?" I interrupted. "Was she related to George Mill?"

One of them kicked me under the table. I wasn't sure

who had kicked, but I let out a little yelp and rubbed my calf. Neither of them responded.

"Yeah, Anna is George's younger sister," Edgar finally replied.

"You knew George?"

"Everyone knew George," Henry said, cutting off Edgar before Edgar could speak. "The Mill family owned almost all of the Rogue Valley. Unless you were living under a rock, you knew the Mills."

"Owned everything? Not everything," Edgar said.

I got the impression that his memories of the Mill family weren't happy ones.

"Do you guys know anything about what happened to George?" I couldn't resist at least asking. "The story I always heard was that he decided to stay when they flooded the lake."

"Nah. That's not what happened." Edgar knocked back his coffee like it was a shot of whiskey.

Henry was silent.

"What do you think happened?" I asked him.

He shrugged. "That's the million-dollar question, isn't it?"

Edgar scoffed. "I'd say more than a million."

There was visible tension between them.

"If anyone would know about George's investments, that would be you, Edgar, wouldn't it?"

"I'm not talking about this." Edgar threw back his chair with unexpected force. He stomped to the stairs.

Henry watched him for a minute and then returned his attention to me.

"Did I say something to upset him?"

"Don't worry about it. Anna Mill is a touchy subject.

You see, George and Edgar were best friends until Edgar fell in love with George's little sister."

"Anna?"

"Anna Mill. She was a beauty and a firecracker. George was protective of her. He was protective of everyone. She and Edgar snuck around in secret because George told Edgar he would shoot him if he so much as laid a finger on Anna. I don't know why. Edgar was a good guy. He treated Anna well, but George wouldn't listen to reason. Edgar was eight years older than Anna and George thought it was wrong."

"What happened?" I gathered Edgar's dishes and napkin.

"They dated in secret for a while and then it all came to a head after Edgar showed up at the prom with Anna. George flew off the handle when he heard the news. They got in a huge fight. Never spoke again. I always wondered if George's plan to disappear involved taking Anna with him." Henry wiped the edge of his weathered cheek with a napkin.

"Did Anna and Edgar continue to date?"

Henry crumpled up his napkin. "No. She was never the same after George disappeared. It broke Edgar's heart. He never dated. Never married. Anna was the one, but it wasn't meant to be. The man hasn't smiled since Anna took off for the Applegate." He stood. "I've bent your ear for far too long. I should let you get back to work. As I've always said, the past should stay in the past. No point in dragging up old, painful memories."

"Thanks for stopping by." I walked Henry upstairs and to the front door. Pam had been right. Henry was knowledgeable about the past. I thought about Edgar's heartbreak and George's bashed skull. Had Edgar's past just resurfaced thanks to Hannah and Ellen's discovery? Could Edgar have killed George over love?

Chapter Eleven

Customers continued to stream in for the next few hours. The party was a success. Everyone in town was amazed at Torte's transformation and excited to meet our new staff. After we closed for the evening, I was in the kitchen mapping out the plan for the remainder of the week with Marty and Sterling when the sound of angry voices came from upstairs.

"That's disgusting. We're never doing that. Never." Andy's voice ricocheted upstairs.

"What is your deal? You can't just say no," I heard Sequoia retort.

"Give me a minute," I said to Marty and Sterling, who both obviously had heard the disagreement too.

"You should quit. You're not cut out for this." Andy's tone was laced with bitterness.

The fight was escalating. I took the stairs two at a time to find Andy with his arms wrapped around his chest. "Thank God, the voice of reason is here. Boss, please tell her this is a terrible idea."

Sequoia twisted one of her dreadlocks. "What's your

deal, man? It's just an idea. You don't have to be such a downer about everything."

"ME? A downer? I'm the nicest person on the planet. Well, one of them at least. Tell her, Jules." Andy looked like he was about to jump over the counter.

"Let's calm down. Yes, Andy, you are one of the kindest people I know."

He shot Sequoia a look to say, I told you so.

"But you've also had a really rough time allowing Sequoia to help. We hired her for her skill and also for her ideas and suggestions on how to make Torte stronger. That's always been the tone here in the bakeshop. You know that. Mom and I greatly value everyone's opinions. It's our collective input that makes us the best coffee shop and bakery in town."

"Yeah." He looked at his feet. "Fine. But listen to her idea and then tell me that I'm not crazy."

I waited for Sequoia. She continued to twist her dreadlocks. "It might sound kind of weird, but it's like super delicious and really chill, you know? I think it will sell well."

"What are we talking about?" I stared at both of them.

"Cheese tea." Andy made a gagging sound.

"*Cheese* tea?" I couldn't hide my disgust at the thought. I'm sure my face must have contorted, because Andy snapped and pointed at me.

"See. Look! Look at her face."

Sequoia shook her head.

"It's gross, isn't it, boss? Cheese in tea. Ugh!" Andy stuck out his tongue.

I could tell that Sequoia was close to losing it. Her

fingers trembled. Up until now she'd been extremely calm even with Andy's bristly attitude, but how much more could she take? I was worried she was going to quit.

"Tell me more." I held up my hand to stop Andy.

"It sounds weird, but it's really popular. We used to serve cheese teas at the bakery cart I worked at in Portland. It's not like tossing a block of cheddar into a glass or anything. It's like a very beautiful drink with a subtle cheese flavor. It originated in Asia and has taken off here in the States."

"Okay, interesting." Now I was intrigued. In my travels I had never heard of cheese tea, and I considered myself a student of the global palate.

"You know, like, a combination of cheeses are used. Melted cream cheese that is whipped with cream, maybe a touch of melted cheddar, and then a dash of salt and sugar for a nice balance of savory with the sweet. One of my favorites is a floral tea with cheese. It's like a transcendent experience."

"That sounds amazing. We have to try it, don't we, Andy?"

Andy shrugged. "I guess." He looked at Sequoia. "You could have explained it like that from the start, instead of just saying cheese tea."

"You didn't give me a chance."

She had a fair point.

"Let's do it for our special tomorrow. Why don't you head down to the kitchen and make sure we have everything you need? If not, let me know and I'll be sure to grab the supplies."

"Cool. If you don't like it, I won't be offended. It just

seems like it could be a funky, unique offering here and the tea crowd is always looking for new tastes."

"Very true." I waited until she was out of earshot and stepped closer to Andy. "Is something else going on with you?"

He swallowed hard. "Why?"

"You're not acting like yourself. We already had a conversation a few days ago about your role here, your taking charge of the coffee bar, but you still seem uptight and antagonistic with Sequoia. That's not like you."

"I know. Sorry." He scuffed the floor with his tennis shoes.

"I'm worried about you, Andy. Is there something you're not telling me?"

He kept his gaze at his feet. I got the sense he wanted to say more.

"If there's something going on, you can talk to me in complete confidence, okay? I care about you, Andy." Maybe I was overstepping my role as his boss, but everything that I said was the truth. His behavior was so out of character that it didn't make sense.

"You promise you won't tell your mom?"

What did Mom have to do with Andy's shift in personality? "I promise," I agreed.

He picked up a stir stick and fiddled with it. "I love your mom. She's like a second mom to me, but I know what she'll say if I tell her this."

I couldn't imagine what Mom would say that I wouldn't.

"The thing is, I don't know what I want to do, Jules." He sighed.

"What do you mean?"

"I don't know what I want to do with my life. I mean I'm only twenty and I have no idea what I want to do next."

"That's normal, Andy," I assured him. "You don't need to know what you want to do. You're young. You have plenty of time to figure it out, and I can tell you that speaking from experience, it might change with time. In fact, it probably will change."

"Exactly." He tossed the stir stick in the sink. "That's exactly what I'm thinking. How in the world am I supposed to know what I'm going to do next?"

"Okay, then what's the problem?"

"The problem is I want to drop out of school."

"Oh." I was quiet for a second.

"Yeah, see, it's that response that I'm dreading. I've been trying to work up the nerve to tell my mom for weeks, but I know what she's going to say."

"Why do you have to drop out of school if you don't know what you want to do?"

"Because I'm wasting money right now. Sure, I love playing football, and I like school fine. But I want to work here. I could coach youth football on the side or something, but it's stupid to pay for a degree when I don't know what I want to do long-term. I tried to talk to my mom a little and she says it's just because I'm a Millennial. But the thing is, this is my generation. I don't want to spend money on getting a degree I'm not going to use. Maybe I go back later, or maybe I stay here and open my own shop one day."

I understood Andy's perspective. I had seen a shift in thinking in the workforce in recent years. It wasn't just Ashland either. It had been the same on the *Amour of the Seas*. Young people were content to work to support their lifestyle. They weren't as focused on traditional careers as my generation had been. Andy's struggle spoke of the greater cultural landscape. The American dream for Andy's generation didn't necessarily include working a nine-to-five job and buying a house with a lush green lawn and white picket fence.

I wasn't sure how to advise him. Dropping out of college was a huge decision and one not to be taken lightly, and yet if he opted to go that route, I would support him completely.

"You're not saying much," Andy said. "Are you preparing a lecture?"

"Not at all. I was thinking through the pros and cons." I went on to share my hesitations. I knew that if he dropped out and focused entirely on a career in the restaurant industry, the odds of him going back to school were slim. I also explained that having a degree (even if it was a general business degree) would set him apart from his competition long-term and give him a valuable skill set should he decide to own a business one day.

"Okay, okay, and what about on the other side?" Andy asked. "What about if I drop out?"

"If you drop out, I'll support that decision and I know my mom will as well."

"Would there be an opportunity to learn more about the business end of things?"

"Of course. We could create a training program for you internally." I thought of the many young chefs that Carlos had mentored over the years, many of whom had gone on to open their own restaurants. I would be thrilled to do the same for Andy, and in some ways, it would be a great help for me. Not that I would share that with him for the moment. I didn't want to influence his decision.

"Thanks for listening. It's helpful."

"Anytime." I could tell he needed some time to think over our conversation, so I made a joke. "I'm just glad that you told me. I was worried that we were going to have to stage an Andy intervention."

He smirked. "Yeah, I owe Sequoia an apology. I'll go talk to her. I guess I've been kind of taking out my stress on her."

"I get it, and I appreciate that you're able to see that and make some changes."

"Maybe some big changes, if my mom and grandma don't kill me." Andy winked.

I gave him a hug, before he went downstairs to talk to Sequoia. "I'm here for you, anytime. Understood? I might not have answers, but I'm always willing to listen."

"Thanks, boss." He gave my arm a light punch. "You're the best."

"That's right. Don't forget it." I tried to wink but ended up giving him a lopsided smile.

I felt better after our conversation. I had a feeling that Andy had already made up his mind, but as promised I would keep his secret until he had made a final decision and was ready to share it with everyone. At least now I understood why he'd been so on edge. Hopefully our talk had eased some of his burden. I knew that holding my struggles inside had never served me well. I wanted the best for Andy, and for his happy, easygoing personality to come back.

Chapter Twelve

I was about to call it a night. The team had cleaned the bakeshop from top to bottom after the party and had left for drinks at Puck's Pub. They invited me to join them, but I decided that it might be good to let them bond, especially after Andy's revelation earlier. I was flipping off the lights when a knock sounded on the front door.

Thomas and Detective Kerry stood in the door frame.

I let them in. "What's going on? Are you two in need of an evening pastry pick-me-up?"

"Is the Professor here?" Thomas glanced around the dark, empty dining room.

"No. Why?"

His face was serious. Detective Kerry looked equally concerned.

"Is it something with the Professor?" My stomach dropped. I couldn't imagine what losing the Professor would do to Mom. She had already lost one husband.

"No, no, sorry, Jules. He's fine. We're in go mode at the moment. There's been a murder and we're trying to find him. That's all. I thought since you had the big grand reopening today he might be around."

"Thank goodness he's okay," I said with relief. "That's horrible that there's been a murder. Here in Ashland?"

Thomas nodded. "Right around the corner. Edgar Hannagan. Did you know him?"

Detective Kerry cleared her throat. I knew that was her cue to Thomas to stop talking.

"Edgar Hannagan?" My jaw went slack.

"Yep," Thomas replied.

"I was just talking to him earlier. He and his friend Henry came to the opening. In fact, I was planning to talk to you or the Professor because I learned something that might have bearing on your investigation into George Mill's death."

"What's that?" Thomas asked.

I repeated what Henry had told me about George and Edgar's friendship and how they had come to blows over Anna. "I've been wondering if he could have killed George."

Thomas looked at Detective Kerry, who gave him a noncommittal look.

"But if he's dead that changes my theory, doesn't it?" I thought aloud. "Or maybe it has nothing to do with George and everything to do with his property that everyone in town seems to want to get their hands on."

Detective Kerry perked up at this news. She motioned for Thomas to get out his mini iPad. "Can you please expand?"

I told them about my conversation with Malcom, and how he had basically demanded that I lend my support to his plan to develop housing for the OSF company on the lot.

"And the other parties interested in the property?" Detective Kerry asked for clarification when I was done.

"Gretchen. I don't know her last name. She's the new director of the homeless council. The council is interested in putting up a permanent homeless village."

I waited for Thomas to take notes. "The owner of Nightingales, Pam, is hoping to buy the lot to keep it as is, and then there's a developer—Stella—who wants it for an expensive tiny-house development."

"How do you know so much about this?" Detective Kerry looked genuinely shocked.

Thomas chuckled. "Torte knows everyone's secrets. I think they sneak an elixir into their pastries."

"You never know." I laughed. "But, seriously, most of this I found out because Mom and the Professor were considering the lot."

Thomas and Kerry shared a strange look.

"Thanks for the intel, Jules." Thomas tucked the iPad back into his pocket. "If you see the Professor will you have him call one of us right away?"

"Will do."

They started for the door.

"Before you go, can I talk you into taking some hand pies or cupcakes with you?" I pointed to a couple of boxes resting on the counter. "We have a ton of leftovers from the party that I'm going to drop off at the homeless council."

"You're trying to butter us up, huh?" Thomas reached for his handcuffs. "We should arrest her for bribing cops."

Detective Kerry rolled her eyes, but I caught a glimpse of humor pass over her face as she took the box of sweets. "Let's go."

I watched them cross the plaza toward the Lithia fountains. Edgar was dead. He owned what might be the most coveted piece of property in Ashland and had been murdered. I wasn't a trained detective like Kerry or Thomas, but it didn't take a genius to figure out that the two might be connected. But then again, I couldn't discount Edgar's past. Could there also be a connection with George Mill? After what I had learned from Henry I had been fairly sure there was a solid possibility that Edgar had killed George. It made sense. Henry had said that Edgar was never the same again. What if he had lived with guilt for all these years and the discovery of George's remains had pushed him over the edge? Was there a chance that Thomas and Detective Kerry had it wrong? Maybe it wasn't murder. Could Edgar have taken his own life?

Two murders complicated everything.

I thought of my conversation with Malcom. He was an upstanding member of the community and a high-ranking figure at OSF. His contempt for Edgar had been apparent from the moment I met him. Could he have decided that he didn't want to try and become the highest bidder for the property? Maybe he decided to ensure that OSF could provide housing for its actors with drastic measures.

What's wrong with you, Jules? I shook myself free from my thoughts.

Perhaps before I started coming up with random theories in my head it would make sense to learn more about each of the people interested in the property. I was in a unique position to make that happen, as Thomas had pointed out. Not that he had exactly asked me to get involved in the investigation, but I already had an "in" so to speak.

I knew just who to start with: Gretchen at the homeless council. And I had the perfect excuse—pastry. I picked up the boxes of untouched baked goods and headed down the block. The homeless council offices were located directly across the street from Lithia Park. The council had taken over an authentic log cabin, known as Homesteader Hall, that had once served as Ashland's community center. When a new facility was built about ten years ago, the homeless council moved in. It was an ideal location for their staff and volunteers to do outreach in the park and the surrounding hiking trails. However, the hall had been built in the late 1800s and was in need of serious upgrades to bring it up to code.

As a stopgap measure, the city council had voted in favor of allowing the homeless council to use it as a temporary shelter last winter during a major snow and ice storm. It was never intended to be a permanent solution. The hall needed extensive repairs including a major overhaul of the plumbing and electric systems, a new roof, and flooring. Additionally, city engineers were concerned that the hall's brick chimney would fail and crumble in an earthquake. There had been an ongoing debate in the local newspaper about the future of the building and where to house the homeless council moving forward.

I had heard that the homeless council had negotiated using the space through the end of the summer, on the condition that it would only operate as a space for homeless families to access support services, without any overnight stays. The homeless council had been granted permission to open the hall daily to offer people in need wellness kits and prepackaged bags of snacks, nonperishable food, water, and drinks with electrolytes. Dehydration was a huge issue in the warm summer months for the street population. Additionally, homeless council staff were on hand to provide assistance with job searches and connections to medical and mental health services. The shelter served a free community dinner to anyone in need every night of the week. The dinner was staffed by volunteers. We tried to donate breads and pastries at least a few times a week.

I wasn't sure whether Gretchen would be there now, but I knew the building would be open for me to deliver the pastries and I could leave a message for her. Fortunately, we had made ample treats for the reopening party. I packaged tubs of basil-and-sundried-tomato butter, lavender scones, banana cakes, and savory ham and swiss hand pies. Then I locked the bakeshop for the evening and headed outside to the plaza. Warm evening air greeted me, along with the sound of happy diners eating at al fresco tables on the creekside Calle Guanajuato pathway. I strolled along the cobblestone sidewalks lit by antique street lamps and the glow of candlelight from the outdoor tables. The path ended across the street from Lithia Park.

A group of travelers had gathered in the open grassy area near the entrance to the park. They were lit up with glow sticks and performing an interpretive dance to the beat of a drum and the whistle of a flute. I smiled to myself as I passed by. A typical summer evening in Ashland.

Above the park I could make out the top of the Elizabethan theater and hear the sound of audience laughter. The outdoor show ran every night, except for Mondays, during the summer. I could time my evenings by the sound of the thunderous applause at the end of every show.

I stopped to smell a climbing rose that snaked along a wooden arbor. The homeless council building was farther down Winburn Way. I took the long route through Lithia Park, past the duck pond and across a bridge that ran over Ashland Creek. Even though the sun had begun to sink behind the mountains, dozens of families and children scampered through the park. Ashland summers were idyllic, with hot sun-soaked afternoons that transitioned into warm star-filled evenings. It was no wonder that so many people had opted to take advantage of the lingering twilight hours.

I crossed the bridge and headed across Winburn where the door to the homeless council building sat propped open. I had a feeling it was due to the heat. The cabin had been constructed in the 1880s long before the invention of central air-conditioning.

"Good evening," a woman seated behind a welcome desk called as I entered. "It looks like you have a delivery for us."

"Yes, I'm here with sweets." I held up the boxes.

"How wonderful. That will be such a treat." She turned her desk fan to low and stood.

"Is Gretchen around by any chance?" The converted cabin was humid.

"I think she's in her office doing paperwork. Do you want me to check?"

"That would be great." I handed her the boxes. "I think we've met before. I'm Jules from Torte."

"Yes, of course. Nice to see you again. I'll drop these off in our kitchen and let her know that you're here. Thanks again for the donation."

Gretchen appeared a few minutes later. Her thick dark curls bounced with each step. She dabbed her forehead with a hand towel. "Jules, what a nice surprise. I guess I always thought bakers kept early hours."

"Unfortunately, I rarely sleep."

"Ah, a no-sleeper? Welcome to my world." Gretchen motioned toward the back. "Do you want to come to my office?"

"Sure." I followed her.

Gretchen greeted a young family who had come into the community room seeking medical care for their daughter, who had cut her leg playing in the park. A staff member bandaged up the wound. Gretchen paused, reached into her shorts pocket and handed the girl a sticker.

"Would you like a sticker? I think you need a sticker. I have butterflies, flowers, and stars. Take two. Or maybe three. What do you think?"

The little girl gave Gretchen a shy smile and took a flower sticker.

We continued into her office. There were stacks and stacks of donations—clothes, food, bedding, pet supplies, and toiletries piled on the floor. Her desk was strewn with paperwork and used tea mugs. She cleared a comforter and sheet set from a folding chair for me to sit.

"Sorry. As you can see we are in dire need of space."

She wiped her brow with the towel and tossed it on her desk. "Sorry it's so hot in here. We've tried to add as many fans as we can, but they just seem to move the hot air around." She nodded to a large, freestanding fan in the corner that was turned off.

"No problem." I sat across from her.

She pushed a bunch of papers to the side of her desk. "I'm not usually this disorganized but we've been swimming in donations. Don't get me wrong, it's a fantastic problem to have, but there's nowhere to put anything. When we build the homeless village on Edgar's lot we're going to construct a shopping market and wellness center on-site. That way when our unhoused or transient families—as we like to refer to them—are there temporarily they can easily access medical care, community support services, and 'shop' at the market for donated clothes."

"That's a great concept." It sounded as if Gretchen thought it was a foregone conclusion that they had the lot.

"One of my first initiatives since coming onboard has been to change the language and culture of how we treat the unhoused. These are simply people—often families—who've hit a run of bad luck. A job loss, an illness, increasing rents, a lack of a support system, and suddenly they find themselves without a place to go. Our center is going to be warm, inviting, and a space that enables them to reenter the workforce or find permanent housing. Did you know that many homeless families are working, but can't afford the exorbitant costs of moving into a rental property?"

I shook my head.

"It's true. Many of our families have jobs, but for whatever reason they were displaced from a previous house or apartment, and even though they can afford the rent they don't have the funds to put down huge deposits and first and last months' rent."

"Right."

She reached for the towel and mopped sweat from her brow. "What really tugs at my heartstrings is the kids. You and I might joke about not sleeping but the stats on sleep deprivation in homeless children are staggering. Did you know that children in transition only get four hours of sleep on average?"

"No. That's terrible."

Her curls stuck to her forehead. "It is. It impacts everything—their ability to learn and thrive at school. And that's just sleep. We haven't even touched on nutrition and lack of medical care."

She took off her glasses and cleaned them on the edge of her T-shirt. "One of the things that I'm most excited about is the village. It's going to change so many lives. We're creating grant programs dedicated to helping our families with move-in costs. The market at the new village will have clothes, shoes, bedding—all the essentials. The shop will be run by our volunteers, but it will be set up like a boutique. Part of the stigma of being unhoused is taking charity. Our families are proud—they don't want handouts. They want a hand up. Instead of giving our families one of these bags with predetermined clothing and stuff, we'll give them a shopping pass. They can try on clothes and choose things that flatter and make them feel good. It's life-changing. Helps build confidence to go out on a job interview or tour a rental property."

"That's wonderful. Ashland is lucky to have someone as dedicated as you at the helm of this program. Especially for the children." Gretchen's passion was evident. Her hands moved as rapidly as her lips as she spoke about her vision.

"Don't even get me started on the kids. Aw, the kids." She paused and put her hand to her heart. "They are so resilient and thankful. I'm constantly amazed and humbled by how grateful they are and how their energy perks up with the slightest little thing—like those stickers."

"Yes, I noticed that."

"Well, I have even bigger plans. The market for kids will include clothes and shoes, but also backpacks, books, stuffed animals, and toys. We want them to feel like they have tangible items that are solely theirs."

"It sounds like you have a very clear direction."

She brushed me off. "I don't deserve any credit. I'm borrowing ideas from other places I've worked. I just want to know that we have the lot once and for all so that we can break ground and start building. I've been trying to get the city to realize it's their responsibility to care for the unhoused. We can build the village, but they have to relax the building codes for us. It's been an absolute nightmare trying to get any traction with them on the issue."

Sweat began to pool on my back. How could Gretchen and her staff work in conditions like this? I couldn't even imagine how hot the building must get during the peak heat of the day.

"I was at Edgar's a little while ago and I'm about ready to kill that man. He's making me pull my hair out—literally." To demonstrate she yanked a strand of long dark hair from her head.

It sounded as if Gretchen didn't know that Edgar was dead. "You haven't heard, have you?"

"Heard what?"

I hated to be the person to break the news. "Edgar is dead."

Her jaw fell open. "What? How? I was over there less than an hour ago and he was fine."

"I don't know the details. My friend who is a police officer just broke the news before I came to drop off our donations. They're investigating as we speak."

Gretchen stood up. She walked over to a stack of pre-packaged food and began sorting canned beans and boxes of macaroni and cheese. "Edgar's dead. He's dead?"

"I know. It's terrible news." I hated having to be the person to share it with her. This must be how Thomas and the Professor felt every time they had to inform family and friends of loss.

"This can't be happening. Who killed him?"

Had I said anything about murder? I replayed my words. I was sure I had said that Edgar was dead—not killed. "I don't think they know that at this point," I lied.

"He was killed. I know it." She thrust canned goods into a plastic tub with such force I thought she might dent them. "Look, I need to go. Sorry to cut this short. Can we talk tomorrow?"

"Yes . . ." I started to say, but she was already half-way out the door.

I left feeling completely perplexed. Gretchen obviously had a tender heart and was doing tremendous things for Ashland's transient families, but could her passion have led her to a crime? She had admitted to being at Edgar's and knew that he had been murdered. I didn't want to think the worst. But Gretchen left me no choice.

Chapter Thirteen

The next morning, I went through the motions at Torte. I couldn't stop thinking about Edgar. Who'd killed him? And why?

"Jules, you cool?" Sterling asked midway through the breakfast rush. He and I were alone in the kitchen, which was a rare occurrence. Bethany had taken Marty to show him the bread delivery route, and Stephanie was hand-piping a lace pattern on a custom cake. She had her headphones in to drown out any distractions. Piping work was tedious and required concentrated focus.

"Is it that obvious?" I massaged my temples. Sterling had a rare gift. He was completely in tune with emotions. Since we had first met I knew instantly that he was a kindred spirit and an old soul. It was likely one of the reasons that he had struggled with addiction in the past. He had used alcohol and drugs as an escape from the grief over losing his mom, but thankfully he had tapped into his inner strength to overcome his addictive behaviors. I hadn't known him during those darker years, but he was open and honest about his commitment to sobriety as well as his intention to live a fully realized life. He had become one of my most valued friends and was like a brother.

"You seem distracted." He motioned to a half-decorated four-layer dark chocolate cake. "Your layers are uneven. Something must be up."

"Uneven layers." I gasped. "Unacceptable. I should fire myself."

He set a wooden spoon on a trivet. "What's going on? Are you worried about Andy?"

"Did he tell you?"

"Tell me what?"

"Nothing." I didn't want to break Andy's confidence.

Sterling must have sensed this. He didn't press me. "I've told him he has to chill with Sequoia. I'm sure he's going to figure it out. It's just an ego hit, you know?"

"Exactly." I brushed chocolate cake crumbs from my apron. "It's not Andy. Although you're right, I have been worried about him and intend to keep an eye on him. It's another murder."

"What?"

"Edgar Hannagan, the owner of a vacant lot that Mom and I went to look at, was killed last night."

"Geez." Sterling ran his fingers through his dark hair. It was no wonder that the twenty-somethings swooned over him. He had a distinctive look—dark hair, piercing blue eyes, and enough tattoos to give him a bad-boy appearance, even though he was one of the kindest people on the planet. "Did you find the body?"

"No. Thank goodness. Thomas and Detective Kerry stopped by last night. They were looking for the Professor. I feel totally wrapped up in the case, though, because I've come across a number of people who are all vying for the property. What if one of them is the killer?"

"You should probably share what you know with Thomas or the Professor," Sterling replied in a matter-of-fact tone.

"I will. Trust me." I rested a flat spatula coated in dark chocolate ganache on the counter. "I just can't believe that someone in this community could be a killer. I hate the fact that I'm staring suspiciously at everyone who comes into Torte and adding people I've known for years, like Pam, to the list of potential suspects." I thought back to Pam's reference to a letter yesterday. Had she written an official complaint to the city? Was she working with Malcolm or were they adversaries in their quest for the lot? When I saw her next I would have to see if she would tell me more.

"Jules, come on." Sterling gave me a look as if to say I was acting insane. "It's normal. I'd be worried if you weren't thinking about it. If it was just business as normal at Torte in light of a murder in town, I would be reevaluating my employment options."

My hands were dotted with spots of ganache. I had to resist the urge to lick it off. "Thanks." I smiled at him. "It's hard though. Ashland has been a sanctuary for me. I hate seeing crime touch this community. I guess I live in a bubble sometimes. I want to believe that the world is a kind place, like Torte, where people genuinely care about each other."

"The world is what we make it." Sterling ladled vats of soup into plastic containers.

Like always his words resonated. "You're right. I have to shake out of this slump and help right this wrong."

"That's the Jules I know." Sterling twisted a lid on a soup container. "Seriously, don't let it get to you."

"I'll try not to." I paused and stared at the lopsided cake. "Now the question is, what am I going to do with this mess?"

Bethany appeared with empty bread delivery boxes. She studied the lopsided cake for a minute. "Ooooh, I have the best idea." She set the boxes down and pulled out her cell phone. "I'm totally hashtagging this #bakingfail."

"Great." I put my hand to my forehead.

"No. No. It's awesome, Jules. It will get tons of shares and comments. People love to see flubs and mistakes just as much as they love to see our beautifully styled products. You're the one who always talks about kitchen mistakes making us better bakers."

"She has you there," Sterling agreed.

"It makes Torte more real." Bethany clicked another shot. "Can we cut it up into tasting bites? We might as well use it, right? I was thinking it would be fun to take a tray out to the plaza and shoot some quick little videos for our social media. Something clever like tasting bites. Give our followers a glimpse outside Torte's walls, you know?"

"Sure. Go for it. But aren't all of our followers here in Ashland?"

She scrunched her face. "Are you for real?"

I looked to Sterling for help.

Bethany proceeded to scroll through dozens upon dozens of bakeries from all over the country that were following our social media profiles. "Jules, we have a huge following on Instagram. Torte has become one of its most popular baking feeds."

"That's amazing. I had no idea."

"It's nothing." Bethany's cheeks blotched with color. "But it is super fun to connect with bakers in Miami and Chicago from here in Ashland."

"We should do something with this. You and Steph have completely exceeded my expectations." I started slicing the cake fail into small slices.

"What do you mean? What would we do with it?" Bethany tugged at her gray T-shirt. It had an outline of a whisk and the words: WHIP IT GOOD.

"I don't know." I thought for a minute. "What if we did a big giveaway?"

Bethany perked up. "Like what?"

"Like a trip to Ashland? Spend a day here at Torte? I'm sure I could talk to some other business owners in the plaza. Maybe we could partner to give away a stay at Ashland Springs, wine tasting at Uva, tickets to a show at OSF. There are so many possibilities."

"Fork yeah!" Bethany shouted.

"What?" I cracked up.

She threw her hand over her mouth. "Sorry. Did that sound bad? I said '*fork* yeah.' It's just a funny saying that one of my favorite celebrity chefs says on his show."

"I heard you correctly."

"Okay, whew. But, OMG, Jules. OMG! I love it! I absolutely love it!" Bethany clapped so fast that her fuchsia-pink-nail polish flashed in a blaze of color. "Steph is going to flip out. I mean like totally flip out. Should I interrupt her?" She paused and shook her head. "No, I'll wait. She looks pretty intent on that piping. I'll go tell Andy instead. He'll be totally into the idea."

I couldn't picture Stephanie flipping out, but I was glad to see that Bethany was excited about the idea. I watched her rush upstairs. At least my staff was happy and oblivious to Edgar's murder.

I knew that the only thing that would help clear my head was baking. First, I needed to bake another round of cakes for the one I was ditching and then I wanted to bake something sweet and summery to take my mind off murder. I decided on Neapolitan cupcakes. We had received four flats of fresh strawberries. I would start with a strawberry cake, filled with vanilla buttercream and frosted with chocolate buttercream. Then I would drizzle each cupcake with white and semisweet chocolate sauce and finish it with a whole strawberry. It should make for a delicious afternoon snack or postshow treat.

I got to work whipping butter and sugar in one of the industrial mixers. Then I incorporated fresh vanilla bean seeds, buttermilk, eggs, and sifted in flour, salt, and baking soda. As I rinsed and destemmed mounds of juicy, ripe strawberries my thoughts drifted away from Edgar's murder. Soon I was lost in thoughts of a grand Ashland tour. There couldn't be a better way to show off the wonderful, creative things happening in the Rogue Valley than with a custom tour of the places that had helped shape me. The more I thought about it, the more I loved the idea.

I pressed the strawberries through a strainer. I wanted the cupcakes to have chunks of strawberries and their juice. Soon I had a fragrant pulpy mash to add to the batter.

Once the batter had turned a dainty pink I used an ice-cream scoop to pour equal amounts of batter into cupcake tins. They would bake for ten to twelve minutes and then I would allow them to cool before frosting them.

With that task complete and the kitchen humming, I decided to take a quick walk over to Ashland Springs and pitch the idea. Two Eurasian doves swept above my head as I crossed the street and headed south to Ashland's iconic hotel. The summer tourists were out in force. They walked four-across on the sidewalk, their arms loaded with shopping bags. Not a day went by when I didn't feel grateful that with the plethora of vacation options in this world, people still chose to come to our little corner of Oregon. Without the revenue that the tourist crowds brought in, Ashland might become a ghost town, like Malcolm had warned.

I was about to head into the historic hotel when I spotted two young travelers panhandling by the Lithia fountains. They had two cats on makeshift leashes. I did a double take. Were those really leashes? On cats?

Yep. My eyes weren't playing tricks on me. The well-groomed cats were tethered together with leashes made of braided rope.

The travelers were easy to spot with their tattered clothes and cardboard signs. One read: THIS CEREAL KILLER NEEDS SOME DOUGH.

Ha! I chuckled internally. I had to give them credit for thinking outside of the standard "I need cash" box. The difference between Ashland's vagabond population and the homeless families that Gretchen had been tasked to serve was that travelers had opted for a wanderlust lifestyle. They hopped from city to city along the West Coast. Sometimes following the weather. Sometimes a hiking trail. Or even a band. Many of them drove Priuses and had nicer cell phones than any of my staff. These weren't desperate people in need of food and shelter. They simply embraced a different path.

I walked up Main Street where many shops were hosting summer sidewalk sales. I stopped briefly to say hello to a few of my fellow shop owners. One of them pointed up the street in the direction of Ashland Springs. "Have you heard about the protests?"

"No. What protest?"

"Malcolm from OSF has staged a walkout for minimum-wage workers. They've shut down the street in front of the hotel. They're protesting the lack of affordable housing."

I thanked the shop owner for the tip and hurried to the hotel. Sure enough a few hundred people had gathered on Main Street in front of the iconic historic hotel. They waved cardboard signs and chanted, "Affordable housing now! Affordable housing now!"

Malcolm was in the middle of the action. He held a sign that read: ACTORS NEED BEDS AND ROOFS OVER THEIR HEADS!

Thomas and a handful of other police officers were trying to gain control over the swelling crowd. He stood on one of the hotel's outdoor bistro tables and raised his voice, trying to get their attention.

Everyone chanted louder. "Inclusion not exclusion zones!"

"Listen up," Thomas yelled from the table. "Your cause deserves a hearing, but you can't protest here without an official permit."

This made the group roar. Malcolm led the protestors in a freedom song. "I want to know what freedom is. I want to know where freedom lives!" They repeated this over and over.

It seemed strange that as a mid-level employee of OSF, he would personally be involved in an unsanctioned protest.

Thomas tried to quell the boisterous cheers. He looked to his reinforcements. They were outnumbered. Five police officers and cadets in blue uniforms flanked both sides of the hotel. Detective Kerry stood blocking the hotel's entrance.

As I stared at the crowd, I realized it was a mix of actors and retail, hotel, and restaurant workers who were protesting the ever-growing housing costs, but there were also several homeless people and travelers. Their mission was different. They were protesting in response to the city's exclusion zone downtown and along Main Street that banned camping and panhandling.

"Let's start moving along, folks." Thomas remained calm. "If you want to hold a formal protest you need to go through the permitting process."

Malcolm raised his fist in the air. "Let's take this to the green stage! Let's show our patrons the real Ashland!"

A huge portion of the crowd followed him. Traffic swerved to avoid them as they marched toward OSF in the middle of the street. About twenty or thirty protestors remained. These were the travelers and homeless advocates who were unhappy with the city's panhandling ordinance.

"No exclusion zones! No exclusion zones!" they shouted.

Thomas might have been able to get the crowd to disperse, but Detective Kerry stormed toward them with a megaphone in her hand. "I command you to clear the sidewalk immediately." She didn't waste any time trying to break up the gathering. "Move. Now."

This infuriated the homeless protestors.

"I'm going to start arresting people if I don't see movement—now!" Detective Kerry whipped out a pair of handcuffs.

A few of the protestors took off.

Thomas stayed on his perch on the table. "Listen, folks, there's a right way and a wrong way to do this. Let's all remain calm."

Kerry continued to direct the protestors with the help of her bullhorn. Tourists began to gather at the ice-cream shop to see what the commotion was all about.

"We are human beings! You can't exclude us!" a woman near the front of the group shouted and then spit near Detective Kerry's feet.

Kerry took this as a personal assault. In a lightning-fast move, she had the woman's hands secured behind her back. "Let's go. I'm taking you in."

Thomas looked pained. I knew that he had built personal relationships with the vast majority of Ashland's travelers and homeless. Kerry's style was in complete opposition to Thomas's. While she dragged the woman down toward the police station, Thomas used a different tactic. "Can I buy everyone a slice?"

The leader of the group nodded. "Okay."

"Meet you at Tony's Flying Pies in ten minutes. Take a minute to think about what you want to accomplish, and I'll see what I can do to help."

With that the crowd dwindled apart.

"That was impressive," I said, as Thomas climbed off the table.

"Nah. None of these guys are a threat. They want to cause a scene more than anything. I've learned that a slice of pizza or a hot cup of coffee can do wonders for negotiating and for keeping the peace."

"Well played."

He took out his mini iPad. "You know that police app that I've been working on?"

"Yeah."

"Well, this is the first alert that came through on it."

"Alert?"

He clicked on the iPad and showed me the Ashland City Police app that he had created. The goal of the app was to keep citizens informed, share alerts, and further community support. "We've had a few people running the beta version of the app, and the owner of the ice-cream shop sent in this picture and notification that there was a group gathering. Isn't that cool?"

Sure enough there was a picture of the crowd and a note from the ice-cream shop owner in Thomas's app. "That's great, but there's one problem."

"A problem?" Thomas stared at his phone. "What? You don't like the design? I went with yellow and blue because they're Ashland's signature colors and we want the app to be user friendly and positive. See the cute little police dog in the corner? That's Rover—for our roving reporters."

"I like the app, but I can't believe I didn't make the cut for the beta. I thought we were friends."

He grinned. "We're friends, Jules, always." There was a subtle shift in his posture. If I hadn't known him for so many years, I probably wouldn't have even noticed it. "You can make the cut. I'll send you an invite. The only reason I didn't ask you was because I knew how busy you've been with the expansion."

"I'm never too busy to help a friend."

"Thanks. You have to be brutally honest. Anything that feels clunky, or you don't like the flow, design, whatever, you have to promise to tell me, okay?"

"Deal."

He turned in the direction of the pizza place. "Hey, what are you doing here anyway? Were you looking for me?"

"No. I was going to Ashland Springs." I told him about our social media giveaway idea.

"That's awesome. Count me in. I'll give the winner a guided police escort through town, and I'm sure my parents will donate flowers."

"I'll stop by the shop later," I said, crossing the street with him. "Is there any more news on Edgar's murder? Are you sure that he was murdered?"

"We're never sure until we see the coroner's report, but it's definitely looking that way. Why?"

I told him about my theory that Edgar had killed himself because he couldn't live with the guilt of killing George any longer.

We waited at the next intersection for a family of deer to cross the street. Tourists snapped photos and clapped in delight as they watched the deer trot across the street. "It's an idea," Thomas said. "I'll share it with the Professor, but why now? Sure, there's the skull, but that alone isn't enough for a conviction."

"Did you find anything else in the lake? The Professor mentioned something the other day about a potential murder weapon, but he didn't elaborate."

"Actually we did. We found an old rusty hammer that matches the blunt-force trauma on the skull, but there's no chance of getting prints off it. It's been submerged underwater for fifty years."

We continued on. "I know you're due for a pizza roundtable soon, but I wanted to tell you about my conversation with Gretchen last night if you have a minute."

Thomas squared his shoulders. "I'm all ears."

I explained how I had dropped off pastries at the homeless council and about Gretchen's odd reaction to Edgar's murder.

"Really. That is interesting." Thomas made a couple notes on his iPad.

"Why?"

He glanced around us to make sure that no one was listening. "This is between us, understood?"

I gave him a solemn nod.

"We have a reliable witness who spotted someone fleeing the scene last night. Guess who they saw sneaking down the alley right around the time of death?"

"Gretchen?"

Thomas pursed his lips. "Yep. The Professor is on his way to question her again, but this case might be closed before the end of the day." He tucked his iPad back into his pocket. "Can I tempt you with a slice of mile-high meat?"

"No, thanks." I declined. He left to go appease the protestors with pizza. I wondered if he was right. All signs pointed to Gretchen as a killer.

Chapter Fourteen

As expected Ashland Springs and every other business I approached with the giveaway idea agreed. I couldn't wait to tell Steph and Bethany that we had a package that was sure to give one lucky winner a weekend to remember. There was one more person I wanted to ask before I headed back to Torte—Lance.

I retraced my steps along Main Street and turned left on Pioneer Street. The OSF welcome center on the corner had a display of Belle's costume from last year's production of *Beauty and the Beast* in the window. The dress was a work of art with miles of yellow silk and a hand-darted bodice.

I headed up Pioneer toward the bricks, as locals refer to the outdoor brick courtyard where the green show takes place before every evening performance. The protestors had dispersed but many of their abandoned signs littered the steps above the Green Stage and had been propped up along the outside of the Elizabethan theater.

Lance, flanked by his entourage, stood with his back propped up against the Bowmer Theater. He did not look happy. The object of his anger was none other than Malcolm.

I moved closer past the stage where a couple of OSF workers were gathering the protest signs. A band, which I assumed was the evening's headliner, was trying to unload their equipment but had to wait for the crew to clear the discarded cardboard.

"Pull a trick like that again and you're fired," Lance said to Malcolm, scolding him with his index finger.

Given Lance's status with the company most staff members would have acquiesced and left with their tails tucked between their legs. Not Malcolm. He squared his shoulders. "If we want to solve the housing crisis we're going to have to break some rules. We're going to have to play dirty. The city isn't going to listen unless we demand that they listen."

Lance fumed. "Enough, Malcolm. Enough. This is not how we operate. There's a time and a place for protests. You crossed a line and you've trashed the bricks."

Malcolm started to respond.

Lance held his finger in the air. "Not another word. Go help the crew clean this mess up."

I knew from experience that it took a lot to rattle Lance. He didn't get angry often, but when he did, it was like a scene from *Henry V*. I thought about ducking back to Torte. Lance didn't appear to be in the mood to chat about Ashland giveaways. But he spotted me.

"Well, well, to what do I owe the pleasure?" he asked with a catlike grin, strolling over to the stage.

"Do you have a minute? I want to run an idea by you, but . . ." I trailed off and pointed at Malcolm who had begun picking up the signs.

"For you, my darling, I have all the time in the world." He rolled his eyes. "Malcolm is low on my list for the moment. Very low."

He walked with me to a shaded area in front of the Tudor Guild gift shop. "Please tell me you're here because of our latest case. I could use a happy distraction."

"What are you talking about?"

"Our case, of course, darling. Why else would you be here?"

"I came to talk to you about donating some tickets for a giveaway we're planning."

"Pish-posh." Lance flicked his hand in disgust. "Take as many tickets as you want. Name your show. You don't need to ask. Tell the box office I approved the request."

"That's very generous of you, but don't you want to know more about the giveaway?"

Lance placed his long, slender hands on each of my shoulders and pretended to shake me. "Juliet, the game is afoot, and you want to talk about giveaways? Have you lost your mind?"

"The game is afoot?" Sometimes Lance was too much for me.

"Murder, darling. Murder."

"Are you talking about Edgar?"

He let out an exasperated sigh. "Finally, the lights go on." He flashed his fingers open and shut, mimicking a spotlight turning on and off. "Yes, I'm talking about Edgar."

"How did you know?"

Lance folded his arms across his chest. He narrowed his eyes and stared at me. "Please. This again?"

"Okay, okay." I threw my hands up in surrender. "I forgot you are always in the know when it comes to anything in Ashland."

"Exactly. And don't you forget it." He brushed his hands together. "Now, let's get on to the details. What do you know so far?"

"Not much." I shared a condensed version of what I had told Thomas.

Lance stopped me. "No. No. That's impossible."

"What?"

"The mousy homeless advocate. I'm all for a jaw-dropping plot twist, but I don't see it. Not Gretchen."

"But she was seen in the alley and when I spoke with her last night she knew that Edgar had been murdered. Why would she jump to that conclusion? He was old. I have to think that most people would have assumed that he died of natural causes."

"Not necessarily. And, let's not discount what we've learned in our past sleuthing adventures."

I wasn't sure that was how I would describe it. "What's that?" I said to Lance.

"You know as well as I do that simply being seen at a murder scene does not make one the killer."

"Yes, but it's more than that. She wanted Edgar's property. She's desperate for a place for her new homeless village." I fanned my hand in front of my face. The temperature was climbing.

"And." Lance looked bored. He stared at the band who had started warming up on the green stage. They had no reprieve from the sun. It glinted off their instruments.

"And, if we've learned anything from the past, it's

that you can't judge a book by its cover. I agree that Gretchen doesn't look like a typical murderer, but there's a lot of evidence stacking up against her."

"Evidence? Ha!" Lance threw his head back in a mock laugh. "Hearsay. I'll tell you what we really know about this case."

I waited for him to continue.

"It needs us. The case is calling. Can't you feel it drawing you in?"

I must have looked skeptical because Lance tapped my chin. "Angles, darling. I do believe that Gretchen is being falsely accused. Perhaps even set up. She needs our help."

"How are we going to help?"

"For starters why don't you scoot over to the shelter again with another stack of sweets. Get her talking."

"Okay, and what are you going to do?"

"I have some sources that should be quite helpful in our quest."

"Lance, this isn't a quest. Someone is dead."

He stabbed his chest. "Ouch. As your best friend and dearest confidant, I would have thought that you would understand me better by now. I jest as a coping mechanism. Nothing more." He dropped his affected manner of speech. "I assure you, Juliet, after all that I've been through—that we've been through—I want nothing more than to help the police figure out whodunit and see them brought to justice. Are you with me?"

I couldn't refuse his sincerity. "I'm with you."

"Excellent." He blew air kisses at each of my cheeks. "Now, run along, and let's reconvene over cocktails later. Ta-ta."

Once Lance was on the trail of an investigation there was no chance of deterring him. I returned to Torte feeling more confused. My talk with Thomas had made me think that Gretchen was the most likely suspect, but after chatting with Lance I wasn't sure. I distracted myself by sharing the good news on the giveaways with Bethany and Steph. They were jubilant and decided to head out after their shifts to shoot some videos at each of the businesses. I was happy to see them enthused about the project.

By late afternoon the dining room had cleared out and most of the staff had gone home. Sterling and I sat down to look through catalogs for an ice-cream case and ice-cream-making equipment. As part of his new role at Torte he would be taking on concrete production and helping me set a rotating weekly lunch menu.

"I've come up with a few recipe ideas," Sterling said, handing me a sketchbook with pencil drawings of his vision of the ice-cream counter with colorful swirls of smooth and creamy custards.

"These are fantastic sketches. I knew you had a talent when it came to words, but I didn't know you were such an artist."

"Steph drew those," Sterling said, flipping to the next page. It was covered with notes and measurements. "The recipes are mine. Like we talked about, I came up with five standard flavors and then we can offer seasonal specials."

"Excellent." Sterling's flavor combinations had my mouth watering. His summer concrete line included a strawberry lime and basil; lemon with chunks of crunchy gingersnaps; milk chocolate with a touch of chipotle, honey and sea salt; and vanilla double cream. Our concretes would be made fresh daily.

A concrete (or frozen custard) is a smooth, silkier version of ice cream. It's made with butterfat and egg yolks. The key difference between a concrete and ice cream has to do with the amount of air beaten into it. A custard achieves its delicious creaminess through a low overrun. The more air that an ice cream contains, the coarser the texture. Ice cream gets its name because of the ice crystals that form in the churning process. We wanted our concretes to be silky smooth without any ice chunks.

"These sound so good that I want to rip out the page and eat it."

"Don't do that, Jules," Sterling teased. "Hopefully there's something in the menu for everyone. If not, I'm sure we'll get feedback and requests."

"I'm actually formulating a request list in my head right now."

"Hey, are we going to revive Sunday Suppers?" Sterling asked. "I know they've been on hold during construction, but your requests reminded me that we've had a bunch of people asking if we're going to do another one soon."

"Thanks for the reminder. Yes. I definitely want to bring them back, and we should put one on the calendar, as long as you're still willing to help."

"Yeah. I've been craving chicken cacciatore. My mom used to make a version of it for my birthday every year. It's a great summer dish. We could serve that over noodles, with field greens and some rustic Italian bread."

"And don't forget about the concretes. Let's debut them at the next Sunday Supper. It will be great marketing—word of mouth."

"Literally." Sterling chuckled.

"You're quick." We finalized a date for the supper, ordered an ice-cream case, and I gave Sterling the green light to proceed with testing the concrete flavors. Sunday Suppers had been one of my first initiatives when I took over Torte. The concept was simple. Guests paid a flat fee for a three-course dinner, including dessert. We served everything family style, encouraging strangers to mingle. They'd been such a hit that we had had to create a waiting list for the last one. Planning a new Sunday Supper was yet another thing to look forward to.

After everyone left for the evening, I turned on some salsa music, poured myself a glass of earthy malbec from Uva, and jotted some thoughts about Edgar's murder in my cake sketchbook. My list of suspects included Gretchen, Stella, Pam, and Malcolm. At the moment Gretchen sat at the top of the list. She had a motive and had been seen at the crime scene, but like Lance I couldn't reconcile Gretchen's do-gooder personality with murder. I wanted to talk to Stella. My initial, albeit brief, interaction with her had left a bad taste in my mouth. Her cold, biting personality matched that of a murderess, but that wasn't exactly fair. I knew nothing about her, other than that she was a successful real estate developer. Pam was an even less likely suspect in my mind. She was a friend and Nightingales was one of Ashland's most beloved bed-and-breakfasts. However, I had to put aside my personal biases. Pam had motive for killing Edgar. Both the proposed homeless village and tiny-house development would directly impact her business. The last suspect on my short list was Malcolm. I wondered how well Lance knew him. Could there be an outside chance that Malcolm had killed Edgar to ensure his position at OSF? It seemed unlikely, but not outside the realm of possibility.

I savored my wine. What if I was approaching this wrong? Maybe there was another motive for killing Edgar. What if his death had nothing to do with his property? I thought of the recovered skull of George Mill. I couldn't discount the fact that the two murders might be connected. My imagination ran wild. I needed another theory besides Edgar being the killer and one began to emerge.

What if Edgar knew something about George's murder? Maybe the killer struck to keep him quiet after all these years. Edgar would have been in his early thirties when George was killed. Could he have seen something? Witnessed the actual murder?

But why would he have stayed quiet for decades? I rationalized with myself.

Yet it did seem like a remarkable coincidence that two murders had occurred in our small corner of Southern Oregon within days of each other. Yes, technically one of the murders was linked to the past, but what were the odds that Ashland would be the site of killings? Tomorrow I would ask the Professor if they were looking for any potential connections between the two.

I made a note in my sketchbook and finished the last

sip of my wine. The sun hung low on the horizon, casting a warm peachy tone on the plaza. I made up my mind on the spot to take a short walk past Edgar's property before calling it a night. What harm could come of that?

Chapter Fifteen

Apparently, I wasn't the only one with that idea. When I arrived at the vacant lot I spotted Stella and Gretchen arguing in front of the FOR SALE sign. I didn't mean to eavesdrop, but they were debating so loudly it was impossible not to overhear their conversation.

"This property is officially off the market," Stella said as she yanked the sign from the ground. She lost her footing in the process. Her strappy high-heeled sandal stuck in the grass, causing her to flail her arms to regain her balance.

"No," Gretchen wailed. "You don't understand. The property is supposed to be ours. Edgar promised."

"Edgar 'promised' everyone who walked by a piece of this land. He probably offered it up to that herd of deer." She pointed to a family of deer nibbling on the lawn across the street. "I have orders to take the lot off the market, and that's what I'm doing. You'll have to take it up with Edgar's trust." With that she propped the sign in one hand and marched toward her SUV.

Gretchen dropped to her knees. She ran her fingers through her mop of wild curls. If it weren't for the look of utter despair on her face she reminded me of a reporter on a nature TV show the way she sat in the grass in her khaki shorts and white T-shirt, staring at the herd of deer.

I waited until Stella had zoomed up the alleyway and out of sight before approaching Gretchen.

"Is everything okay?" I asked.

She looked up at me with tear-filled eyes. "What am I going to do? I can't believe Stella would do something so shady and try to rip this property right out from under me." She took off her bulky frames to wipe away tears. "I mean it's not even me. It's people in our community who are in desperate, desperate situations. That woman is so callous. She doesn't even care. It's all about the money."

I offered her a hand.

Once she was on her feet, she blinked a few times. In a matter of seconds her tears turned into fury. "She's not going to get away with this. I won't let her. I poured blood, sweat, and more blood into this. I'm not going to stand by idly and let her walk all over our unhoused community. She will not get away with this. I can't let her for the sake of the children. Think of the children. I've got to talk some sense into her," Gretchen wailed.

Gretchen's reaction gave me pause. Had I misread her? Maybe Thomas was right.

"Why are you staring at me like that?" she snapped.

For a minute I thought about taking off. I didn't want to have a confrontation with a potential killer, but then again Gretchen was so distraught that this might be my best chance to learn something.

"It's Edgar's murder," I started.

Gretchen cut me off. "Wait, wait, wait . . . hold up. Are you saying you think that I killed Edgar?"

How had she jumped to that conclusion so quickly?

"I didn't kill Edgar. Why would I kill him, when he had offered me the biggest financial donation that the homeless council has ever received?"

"What do you mean?"

She ran her fingers through her wild curls. "After many discussions and days and days of negotiations Edgar finally agreed to gift us the lot. That wasn't even my end goal. I was hoping to negotiate on price, but I never imagined that he would donate the entire property. He was a hard man to read, but he had a kind heart. You know what finally pushed him over the edge?"

I shook my head.

"That family you met last night. Edgar met them too and came to the conclusion that he wanted to leave Ashland a lasting gift. A legacy. He didn't have family. This was his opportunity to do something generous—we are going to name the community after him. It will have a plaque and a small water feature dedicated to him."

She was speaking so fast that her words blurred together. Edgar had intended to donate the property? I couldn't believe it.

"Stella was furious. She's not used to losing out on any deal—big or small—and especially to a measly little nonprofit like us. I saw them fighting. She probably did it. He broke the news that he was going to bequeath the land to us and she flipped out and killed him. I know it. I know she did. We can't let her get away with this."

"Slow down." I placed my hand on her forearm.

"Take a nice long breath. Let's go find Thomas or the Professor and fill them in on this. It's going to be really important for their investigation."

Gretchen's shoulders heaved as she attempted to take a deep breath.

"Do you have anything about the deal in writing? Did you and Edgar finalize the deal or was it only a verbal agreement?" I guided her toward the sidewalk.

"The deal is final. At least it's final in my mind. He signed an initial letter of intent, but we hadn't had a chance for our lawyers to go over the paperwork. Why?"

I didn't know if I should tell her that Thomas and the Professor considered her a suspect.

"Do the police think I did it?" she wailed. Was she some kind of secret mind reader? It was as if any thought that passed through my mind landed straight in Gretchen's head.

"You'll have to talk to them, but like I said, this is vital information, and could be instrumental to their investigation."

"So they do think I killed him. My God. I have to go to my office and get that paperwork."

"I can walk with you, if you'd like?"

"No. I'm fine." She brushed me off. "Just keep your eye on Stella. She killed him—I swear."

She ran off without another word. I stood in the empty lot feeling dumbfounded. Was Gretchen to be believed? If Edgar had had a change of heart and decided to give the land to the homeless council then her motive to kill him disappeared. While I tried to make sense of what I had just learned a voice interrupted my thoughts.

"You back for another look?" It was Henry, Edgar's neighbor.

"No. I'm just passing by," I replied.

Henry was dressed in painting clothes again.

"You look like you're in the middle of a project." I noted the paint splatter on his hands.

He stared at his overalls. "Nah. This is my everyday wear. Doing some touch-ups on an old canvas that refuses to become what I want it to. That's how it goes most days."

"I didn't realize you were an actual painter. I guess I assumed that you were painting your house when we met earlier."

"Yep. I'm doing that too. I can't stay away from the paint. My late wife used to say it was because of the fumes." He gave me a toothy grin. "You want to come see? It's not a gallery or anything fancy, but I've got a few canvases lying around."

"Sure." I was interested in seeing Henry's work, but more importantly maybe I could get some more information about Edgar from him.

When we passed Edgar's house, Henry stopped and gave a solemn nod of respect.

"You were good friends, weren't you?" I asked.

"I don't know about friends. Edgar liked to argue about anything and everything, but he was a good neighbor. Stuck by me when my wife died last year. Told me the cure for heartache was a hefty shot of gin. We've had one every night for the past year. It's not going to be the same without him." He cleared his throat twice.

"I'm sorry for your loss."

Henry picked at a piece of dried paint on the top

of his palm. "When you get to be my age death is inevitable. I'm thankful for every day that I wake up breathing."

"You look pretty energetic to me."

"Don't say that to an old man like me." He put his hand over his heart and pounded his chest. "You'll make the old ticker go crazy."

I laughed.

Nightingales sat to our right. I pointed at Pam's English garden in the backyard. The rear of the Victorian was as ornate as the front of the house. "Pam mentioned that she's been talking to the neighbors about trying to preserve these older homes and make sure that Edgar's property isn't turned into a new development."

Henry reached into his pocket and pulled out a handful of hard candies. "Peppermint?"

"No, thanks."

"Peppermints are my vice. And gin." His laugh was throaty. "Pam is one woman I wouldn't want to dance with," Henry continued with the peppermint on one side of his teeth. "She's gonna get her way if you ask me. She's talked to everyone on both sides of the block. Told me I can have extra parking, whatever I want. Sounds good to me. I don't exactly want a big eyesore to go up there."

He stopped and turned around. "I like having a view of the hills and Mount Ashland." He pointed to the far mountain range.

"I never realized you could see Mount Ashland from here," I said.

"Yep. She's a real beauty in the winter. It would be a shame to lose that view."

He showed me into his workshop in his garage. There were canvases on every wall. To my surprise, Henry's style was very modern. Each piece used bold colors with stark, often angry brushstrokes. I wasn't sure what I had been expecting, but I had imagined bucolic Impressionist-style paintings of Ashland's surrounding hillsides and mountains. Henry's artwork looked as if it could be displayed in the lobby of a swanky futuristic hotel. I chided myself for judging Henry based on his age.

I wandered through the garage. Some of the paintings had to be over twelve feet long and six feet tall. There were a variety of canvases in various stages. Henry had paintbrushes and jars of paint in nearly every corner of the workshop. Splattered paint coated the floor. I got the sense that Henry became completely immersed in the process when working on a new painting.

"These are really impressive. Some of them are huge. How did you manage to lift them?"

Henry shrugged. "Easy. They are light. It's only canvas and a thin strip of framing."

"Still, I'm impressed. I like how you can see the brushstrokes in some of them."

He looked pleased with the compliment. "Glad you noticed. Most people don't. That's on purpose. I wanted to represent the angst of our culture. Those thick, ugly strokes pull out the darkness that simmers just below the surface. Ever since I was a kid I've been interested in our shadow side. The piece of ourselves we try to mask. You can't mask the darkness when painting. It finds a way out."

I understood his point but embracing darkness didn't

resonate with me. I had made it my life's work to spread light in the form of warm, comforting pastries and handmade pies.

Henry showed me a collection of new works. These were smaller. Unlike the broad, sweeping strokes on his bigger pieces, the new art was on small canvases and resembled human form, only each body was contorted so that prominent features like a nose or arms were missing or placed in the wrong spot. Like an ear sticking out of a toe.

"These are . . ." I struggled to find the right word. "Interesting."

If Henry noticed me pause he gave no indication. "Yes. I've been morphing my stroke work lately and am enjoying where these are taking me."

"Do you have a background in art?"

He stared at me for a minute. "I thought you grew up in Ashland."

"I did." I got the feeling that I had offended him.

"I taught at SOU."

"Oh, I had no idea. Sorry."

"Yeah, you're too young to remember that far back." He laughed. "Not many of us old fogies around these days."

"Were you an art professor?"

"Yep." He nodded. "It used to drive Edgar crazy. We were like oil and water when it came to art. He didn't understand the process, the result. My work made him squeamish. I was good with that. Art is supposed to move you. I would tell my students not to fear negative reactions. Good art—great art—evokes a response. Any response. If you walk by a painting and don't even turn your head, that's an insult, but if you tell me that my work is too dark or revolting, I've done my job." He reached for a tiny paintbrush and dabbed the corner of a canvas. "I suppose that doesn't work in your line of business, does it? People don't want revolting pastries."

"We try to avoid serving revolting pastries." I laughed. "This is amazing. You should do a showing in town. People would love knowing that a retired SOU professor is still here and painting prolifically."

"Nah." Henry used the softest touch with the edge of the paintbrush. "I'm a hermit. My days of showing my work are over. This is for me. Keeps me out of trouble as my wife used to say."

I didn't press him, but when I got back to Torte I was going to do a little research into Henry. Even if he didn't want to do a formal gallery showing, I was sure that the local paper would want to do a feature story on him and his connection to the university.

"Did you see anything out of the ordinary at Edgar's place the other night?" I asked, steering the conversation to Edgar. "The police are saying that someone killed him. I keep wondering if maybe he had something to do with George's murder and couldn't live with the guilt."

Henry dropped the paintbrush. "What?" He reached down to pick it up and then wiped paint on his overalls. "Why?"

"Well, in part because of what you told me about him and Anna Mill. If George broke them up, do you think Edgar could have killed him?" I hoped that I sounded causal.

"Edgar? No."

I could tell that I had made him uncomfortable. I felt bad for suggesting that his longtime friend could be a killer.

"I happened to bump into Gretchen, the director of the homeless council, right after Edgar was killed; do you know her?" I changed the subject again.

"Gretchen, yeah, I know her." He didn't elaborate. Nor did he look enthused when I mentioned her name.

"It seems like a lot of people are vying for the empty lot," I continued. "Gretchen, Stella the developer, even OSF."

"Good luck to all of them."

"Why do you say that?"

"Edgar wasn't going to sell to any of them."

"Really? Did he tell you that?"

"Not in so many words. But I knew the man for far too many years, and I can tell you this. He was motivated by one thing and one thing alone."

"What was that?"

"Money," Henry huffed.

"But he lived in such a rundown space."

"Right. Because he refused to put a dime into it. I told him a thousand times he couldn't take his cash with him to the grave, but the man was cheap and because of that he was also a millionaire."

"What?" I couldn't picture it. Edgar's house was falling down—literally. When I had met him, he looked as if he could use Gretchen's service. Now Henry was telling me that he was rich?

Henry nodded. "Yep. The man saved every single

cent. He was the cheapest person I've ever met. You know who bought every bottle of expensive gin we drank together? Me. We argued all the time about the fact that his cabin was slowly sinking, a potential death-trap, but he didn't care. He kept piling up the nickels and dimes. I guarantee you that his net worth account is triple that of any of the people who live in the huge mansions up on Scenic Drive. He owned more land in the Rogue Valley than God."

"I believe you, but it's so strange to think about someone who lived like Edgar being a millionaire."

"Believe it. Remember, we're from a different era. These days students spend twenty minutes making a video and end up bringing home millions. In my day we had to work and save and then work and save some more. That's what Edgar did. He bought the cheapest property on the cheapest lot in Ashland back in the day and then saved every red cent that he made. He was a hoarder. Have you ever seen inside his shack? It's like something straight out of the depression era. He saved every coffee can, every newspaper."

"You're right. You definitely wouldn't know from the outside that he was rich."

"That's the way he liked it. For all I know he kept his stash of cash under his mattress. He didn't trust anyone with his money. Not banks. Not a single living soul." An alarm beeped on Henry's wrist. "Time to take my meds."

"I'll let you go. Thanks for the tour and letting me see your art. It's incredible."

"Stop by anytime. I'm usually here."

He shuffled into the house. I left armed with new information. Edgar was a millionaire. I wasn't sure what that meant in terms of the case, but I knew that he had money—and plenty of it. Could that have given someone yet another motive for murder?

Chapter Sixteen

The next morning Mom called to ask if I would take a second look at the Emigrant Lake house with her. I didn't hesitate. The house was meant for her and the Professor. Plus it would give me a chance to wander around the lake for a few minutes. I couldn't shake the feeling that there might be a connection between Edgar's murder and the discovery of George Mill's body. I kicked myself for not asking Henry more about it last night.

When we hit a lull between the morning and lunch rushes, I scooted out to meet Mom at the lake. Glorious summer weather greeted me. The hills glowed in golden tones. A vast blue sky stretched before me. There was no sign of police activity at the lake. Kids jumped from the docks and floated on inflatable rafts. It was surreal to think about the fact that an abandoned town lay under the lake's calm waters.

Mom and I toured the house again, without Stella breathing down our necks. She ran her fingers along the cool countertops. "I love this kitchen, honey, don't you?"

"It's perfect. I can see you here. Can't you imagine Thanksgiving and Christmas? You can put the dining room table there." I pointed to the wall of windows opposite the open kitchen. They boasted a spectacular view of the lake below. "We can watch the winter birds migrating while we feast on your homemade Parker House rolls and the Professor's chestnut stuffing."

"You're making me hungry. That's not fair. I'm supposed to be of sound mind and body when making a decision about purchasing a new house." Mom winked.

The Professor appeared in the door frame. "Did someone mention chestnut stuffing?"

"Guilty as charged." I threw my hands up.

"It's the middle of summer and Juliet Montague Capshaw is trying to sway me by painting a perfect picture of the holidays here in this house."

The Professor walked toward the gleaming windows. "Watch out, Juliet, she's pulling the middle and last name. That spells trouble." He gave me a knowing look, then addressed Mom. "Helen, I must agree with your only daughter's astute assessment. These ceilings must be at least twenty feet tall. A blue spruce would work quite nicely in that corner near the fireplace, don't you agree?" He nodded to the adjoining living room. "As the Bard would say, 'If all the year were playing holidays; To sport would be as tedious as to work.'"

"Doug, that's not fair." Mom shook her index finger at him. "We're making a lifelong decision here."

"Indeed, my dear. Indeed." He caught her eye. They shared a tender look that made me lose my breath for a moment. "All the more reason to do as Juliet has so wisely suggested. Imagine gatherings, merriment, a welcoming space for friends and neighbors. I do believe that this house more than any that we've seen feels right. Does it for you?"

Mom's eyes welled. I took that as my cue to make my exit.

I let them have a moment together in the house. It was obvious that they had already made their decision. Watching them go through the process of finding their dream home had made me nostalgic for Carlos. When he and Ramiro had come to Ashland for Mom and the Professor's wedding he had asked about the possibility of coming to stay for an extended time. He would take leave from the ship and Ramiro would have a chance to study abroad. On paper it sounded ideal. Carlos could manage Uva. Ramiro could help at Torte after school or on weekends. But was it a pipe dream? Would Carlos really be happy here? As much as I longed for him, I didn't want to tie him down if he was meant for the sea.

We had spoken weekly ever since. Carlos was intent on making a long-term stay in Ashland a reality. He'd been in touch with Ramiro's mother, the schools, and had already started the paperwork for obtaining temporary residency. Technically we were still married, even though we'd spent the last two years apart. In the eyes of the court we were a happy couple, which would make it easier for him to get a green card and a student visa for Ramiro. It was happening so fast that I worried Carlos wasn't putting enough thought into the reality of life in Ashland.

What if he hated it? What if he ended up bored?

What are you really worried about, Jules? I asked myself as I navigated slippery loose rocks on the hillside trail that led down to the lake.

If I was being honest with myself, I was worried that this was our last chance. I wasn't going back to the ship. If Carlos and I couldn't make it here in Ashland, we couldn't make it anywhere. The thought terrified me, and yet was also freeing. I loved Carlos—deeply. Maybe this was the final push we needed to make a decision about our future together once and for all.

Or maybe it will be a complete disaster, I mumbled as I reached the shoreline.

I stared out in the direction of the spot where the girls had recovered George's skull. My thoughts shifted to Edgar. There were many similarities between him and George. They were both recluses, who opted to live alone and not participate in Ashland's active and vibrant community. That was a rarity around here. They had both attempted to hold on to their land and perhaps their way of life. They had both been unmarried and died alone. The thought made me shiver.

What could the connection between them be? Or was I just grasping at air?

I felt like the lake waters. On the outside, calm and composed, but down below swirling with questions and a secret life. Carlos was my not-so-secret life. I could hear his thick Spanish accent ringing through my head from our last conversation. "*Mi querida,* do not worry. You think too much. You must follow your heart. What does your heart say about us coming to stay with you?"

My heart said run. It was wounded. Not permanently broken, but the layers of scar tissue had finally begun to heal. Yes, I missed Carlos, but Ashland had taught me that I could live without him. If he came and left again I wasn't sure how I was going to mend.

"A penny for your thoughts." The Professor's baritone voice interrupted my downward spiral into worry.

"Nothing. Just thinking about how sometimes things appear perfect on the surface." I motioned to the lake.

"Ah yes. Quite true. That makes me think of words by the Duke of Suffolk in *King Henry VI, Part Two*."

"What's that?"

"'Smooth runs the water where the brook is deep.'"

"It's a lovely quote, but I'm not sure I understand the context. I'm a bit rusty on *Henry VI*." I smiled. No one was as well versed in Shakespeare's works as the Professor. And that wasn't exclusive to Ashland either. The Professor could hold his own against an Oxford scholar.

"The Duke of Suffolk is referring to deception in that passage. He's suspicious of Gloucester's calm exterior. Too calm for his taste, as he is quite sure of Gloucester's treachery."

"Ah, I see."

"It's one of Shakespeare's most popular quotes, and I might add, a metaphor for life. Steer clear of calm waters. They say to avoid rocky waters, but in my line of work I've learned not to trust eerily still water. Sometimes we need a hint of a swift current or an errant wave." He gave me a knowing look.

"Right." I wasn't sure if he was alluding to my love life but opted to change the topic. "Any news on the investigation?" The smell of baking pine needles hit my nose as we walked along the path toward the picnic area.

"Which one?" He strummed his fingers on his auburn beard.

"Good point. I was thinking of George, but I've learned a bunch about Edgar too."

"Would you care to elaborate? I'm most interested." He reached into the breast pocket of his short-sleeved buttoned-up shirt. It was dotted with silhouettes of Shakespeare's profile.

"What about Mom?" I looked back toward the house.

"Not to fear. I wouldn't abandon her. She and our real estate agent are having a chat about positioning furniture and paint color while they wait to hear about the status of our offer."

"You put in an offer?" I clapped.

His eyes twinkled. "We did. Hopefully it's a formality. Our agent thinks we'll know within the hour."

"That's great." I stopped and gave him a hug.

"Thank you for supporting your mother and me through this. I know how much it's meant to her to have you by her side."

"I'm her biggest fan."

"The feeling is obviously mutual. It's one of the many reasons I fell for her. Your relationship is one for the ages. It's a rarity to see a mother/daughter team like you two. I'm grateful you both allow me to bear witness to your extraordinary love."

"Thanks. You know, she's pretty into you too," I joked.

"That makes me one lucky man." He gave me a half bow. "Now to your previous question; there have been a few developments. We've learned that Edgar ingested medication typically given to patients with heart arrhythmias."

"Did he have a heart condition?" We continued on to

the park. I could hear kids on the waterslide and the sound of a motorboat cutting through the water.

"None that the medical examiner has been able to determine, but this medication taken in high dosage can lead to a heart attack. We are working on the theory that someone delivered a deadly dosage to Edgar, although we can't rule out the possibility that he intentionally overdosed."

"But why?"

"My thoughts exactly. I was explaining to Thomas and Detective Kerry the other day that over time a good detective learns to hone his or her senses. You'll get a sense of knowing, for lack of a better term. There might not be anything obvious at first glance, but I was encouraging them to trust their intuition. Those hunches tend to lead us down the path of discovery." He opened his Moleskine notebook. "As I'm sure you can imagine, Thomas finds this concept easier to digest than Detective Kerry."

"She's definitely a rule follower."

"A wonderful asset for a detective. I wouldn't discourage her from her pristine practices when it comes to police protocol, but I would like her to also lean on her feelings. That will come with time."

"You think?"

"Juliet, would you believe that when I was first learning the ropes, I too was uptight?"

"Never."

"'Tis true. I had a fabulous mentor, whom I hope you'll get to meet one day. He retired to the desert in Arizona, but I have invited him for a stay this fall. If it weren't for him, I wouldn't be the detective I am today. He taught me everything I know and then some."

"Does Mom know him?"

"She does. He was a frequent customer when your parents first opened Torte. As was I. You might say that I've loved your mother from afar for many, many years."

"That's so sweet."

The Professor's cheeks reddened ever so slightly. He fumbled momentarily. "I don't mean to imply that I ever would have acted on my feelings when your parents were together. Please forgive me for how I worded that. I have always adored your mother, but I respected her first and foremost. I never would have done anything to jeopardize their relationship."

I put my hand on his arm. "I know. It's okay. I understand, and it makes the fact that you and Mom have found each other that much sweeter."

He looked relieved. "Good. I wouldn't want you to think poorly of me."

"As if that could ever happen."

"Since the topic has arisen naturally, would you allow me to ask a favor?" He plucked a broken twig from an overhanging branch.

"Of course."

He extended his arm. "Might we go sit on that bench down by the water and have a brief chat?"

"Sure." I didn't know what the Professor wanted to tell me, but for the first time in memory I could tell that he was nervous.

He tripped on loose lava rocks twice as we descended the sloped hillside and found a shady bench under a giant white oak tree.

We watched as an osprey circled the lake in search of food. For a minute I wondered if the Professor had lost his nerve to ask me whatever favor he was hoping for, but after the osprey flew away he crossed one leg over the other and leaned back against the bench.

"Please forgive me if I'm potentially stepping into uncharted waters." He acknowledged the lake with the slightest of nods. "Juliet, as you know, I never had children of my own. I'd never known love—the kind of love that set the Bard's quill on fire—until your mother and I found one another. I suspect that you and I are alike in that way. I was content to live alone, knowing that one day love would find me. Or it wouldn't. Either way I would be fine. I never wanted to settle for something unworthy of a sonnet. I would have been happy living out my days alone if it weren't for your mother."

"I know she feels the same," I said.

"Indeed. But, this conversation is not about your mother. It's about you." His gentle eyes held my gaze. The tender look made my throat tighten. "As I've said before I would never dare to attempt to fill the very large shoes that your father left behind, but I want you to know, my dear, that I've come to think of you as my family."

"Me too." I squeezed his hand. The lump in my throat grew.

"My favor is this: I would be so very, very pleased if you would consider your mother's house as our gift to you."

I started to interrupt, but he patted my hand.

"Grant me this brief plea."

"Okay, sorry."

"You see, Juliet, I lived a relatively simple existence until your mother came into my life. I never felt the need for extravagant vacations or a luxurious home without someone to share them. I've saved a rather large amount over the years and neither your mother nor I feel right about you buying the house. You're investing in Torte right now. You're growing your parents' legacy. That is such a gift for your mother and the entire community."

I couldn't contain my tears. They spilled from my eyes and trickled down my cheeks.

The Professor reached into his pocket and handed me a monogrammed handkerchief. "I've watched you with such pride," he said after I'd had a chance to regain my composure. "I take no ownership of the young woman that you've become, but I'm filled with the deepest gratitude every day that I get to be a small piece of your life."

"That's one of the nicest things that anyone has ever said to me."

"I mean it with the utmost sincerity. You are the daughter I never had, and while I will do my best never to overstep my role, as one of your father's dearest friends I'm positive that he would be so proud of you. And I also want you to know that I am always here for anything you need."

His words spurred another round of tears. After I wiped my face again he gave me a hug. "We can't be blubbering messes like this for much longer. Your mother will scold me to no end."

I laughed. "That's true."

"Will you consider the offer?"

"Yes." I folded the handkerchief.

He sat up on the bench. "Shall we go see what furniture arrangements your mother has come up with?"

While we walked back to the house, I relayed everything, from Gretchen's insistence that Edgar was going to bequeath the lot to the homeless council to Henry's assertion that Edgar was rich. When I finished the Professor returned the notebook to his pocket. "Aha, so it continues to unfold."

I wished I had a clue what he meant by that.

Chapter Seventeen

I returned to Torte in time for the lunch rush. Andy and Sequoia were actually laughing as they pulled shots and steamed milk at the espresso machine. Thank goodness for small miracles.

"Hey, boss," Andy called. "Check out the specials board."

I looked up at the chalkboard that hung next to the counter. Stephanie had outlined our daily specials in chalk along with a new quote that read: "You raze the old to raise the new. —Justina Chen."

"Oh, I like that quote. It's very fitting for our new space," I commented. "Who's Justina Chen?"

Sequoia deftly poured foam on top of a latte in the shape of a leaf. "I think she's a YA author."

"Yeah, Steph loves her," Andy offered. "But that's not what I'm talking about. Did you check out the special?"

I looked up again. Below the quote Stephanie had drawn a teacup and hunk of cheese along with a clever saying: "Feeling cheesy? Try our cheese tea latte. Mmmm. Creamy, cheese, tea latte. That's right. The big cheese."

"Has anyone ordered one?" I asked.

Andy held up two fingers to make a peace sign. "Two. That's right. Two brave souls have ventured into cheese territory so far this morning."

"And, what's the verdict?"

He looked to Sequoia. "Props to my cheese girl here, they've loved it."

"Yeah, but two is pretty lame. I thought people might be more adventurous." Sequoia sounded disappointed.

Andy reassured her. "Don't sweat it. Once word starts to spread, it's gonna be a hit. I can feel it."

I mouthed "thank you" to him and went to check on how things were going downstairs. I had to admit that it was going to take a while to get used to overseeing staff in two separate areas. I was happy to have more space, but it felt strange to have the team spread apart.

When I went downstairs there was music playing in the kitchen. I could hear Sterling and Marty laughing. The smell of baking rosemary-garlic focaccia bread enveloped me. I paused at the bottom of the stairs to breathe it in.

At a table near the fireplace, Stella and Malcolm were sitting together, deep in conversation. It couldn't be a coincidence that they were both vying for Edgar's lot and meeting together here at Torte. I ducked into the kitchen. Sterling and Marty were working the stove together. Bethany and Steph were frosting two-tiered cakes for a bridal show. Rows and rows of dark chocolate cupcakes and lemon sugar cookies cut out in the shape of flowers and hand-piped with marionberry buttercream sat in lovely splendor.

"Do you mind if I steal a couple of these?" I asked

Steph. Who as usual shrugged and didn't brother to look up from her work.

"Aren't they so cute?" Bethany gushed. "The yellow cookies with the light purple frosting look beautiful together. Steph and I have a couple dozen more to finish, and then I'm going to shoot some pictures for Instagram. This is our special cookie for the day, so we're going to give one away to the first person who comes in and mentions the post."

"You two are amazing."

"We're just getting started, Jules. The Ashland weekend giveaway has already had more likes and comments than anything we've ever posted. I think it's going to be huge. Not only for us, but for all of the downtown businesses."

"That's exactly what I'm hoping for." I placed two lemon cookies on a plate. "Keep me posted." With that I went out into the small seating area to offer cookies to Stella and Malcolm. Stella jumped when I held out the plate. "Can I interest either of you in a lemon marionberry cookie? They are today's special and I'd love some feedback on what you think."

Malcolm cleared his throat. "I'll try one."

Stella leaned back against her chair and crossed her narrow ankles. "No, thank you. Waistline." She pinched her small waist. Her steel-gray outfit matched her steely, untrusting eyes.

I tried to think of a subtle way to bring up the lot.

Malcolm took both cookies. "If you're not going to eat these, I'll gladly try two."

"Please do," I said to him.

Stella unzipped her purse. Then she proceeded to

open a compact and dab her cheeks with powder. "Rumor has it that your mother put in an offer on the Emigrant Lake house."

Wow. News did travel fast in Ashland.

"How did you hear already?"

Placing her compact in her purse, she reached in again and removed an expensive tube of lipstick. "Thirty years in real cstate. I make it my business to know everything. Plus, I had already opted out of that property. It wasn't worth the excavation costs. Flat parcels like Edgar's are so much easier to work with."

She had given me the perfect in. "Have you heard anything about Edgar's lot?"

Malcolm choked on his cookie.

Stella glared at him. "That deal was done weeks ago."

I pretended like I had no idea what she was referring to. "Really? I thought the lot was still for sale."

Malcolm coughed twice. He stood, leaving an uneaten cookie on the table. "I realized I'm late for a meeting," he said, trying to clear his airway.

"Are you okay?" I asked.

He cleared his throat. "I'm fine. Must run."

Stella shot him a look I couldn't decipher.

"I'll be in touch," he said to her and took off.

She rolled her eyes.

"Do you mind if I sit?" I asked.

"Go ahead." She waved at the empty chair that Malcolm had vacated.

I decided to be straight with her. She was clearly an astute businesswoman, and I had a feeling that she would see through any feeble attempt at skirting the issue. "I heard that you were at Edgar's the day that he was killed."

With a simple flick of her fingers she dropped her lipstick tube into her purse. "Yes. I've been at the property nearly every day finalizing details. Why does it matter?"

"Finalizing details? I was under the impression that the lot had already been accounted for."

Her jaw tightened. "What?"

"I heard that Edgar had decided to donate the lot."

"Who have you been talking to? Gretchen?"

I didn't reply.

"That's wishful thinking on her part. Believe me, Edgar had no intention of giving away the land. He might have looked like a tattered, old hermit but the man knew money. He wasn't about to let the lot go without a huge payout."

Her words mirrored what I had learned from Henry.

"Edgar was motivated by money. He had been holding on to the lot for years, waiting for the land to appreciate. Gretchen is dreaming if she really thinks that he would give it away."

"I think he led her to believe that."

"That may be true, but he was toying with her. Or maybe he had an ulterior motive. Maybe he was trying to drive the value even higher by ensuring there were multiple interested parties. Perceived value can't be discounted when it comes to real estate. I've seen it time and time again. A cash buyer is interested, and they learn that there is more than one offer on the table. The price gets bid higher and higher. I had a lot listed a few months ago that sold for fifty thousand dollars over asking price because of a bidding war. The parcel wasn't even that desirable, but once the bidding war started everyone wanted in. That's real estate."

"I don't understand how Gretchen's interest would help. The homeless council couldn't outbid anyone."

"No," Stella agreed. "They didn't have to. That's what I'm saying, *perceived* value. Not actual value."

"You mentioned that the property was already sold. Do you know to whom?"

"To me." She said it as if it was a known fact.

"Edgar sold *you* the property?" I'm sure my face must have reflected my confusion.

"Yes." She brushed an imaginary crumb from her shirt. "I cut him a check for one hundred thousand dollars in earnest money last week."

"That's a lot of cash."

She didn't flinch. "Not in my line of work. It was intentional, to secure our interests."

Like a bribe, I thought to myself.

"Edgar and I have been finalizing the contract and paperwork. It's a shame that he died when he did. I had drawn up the documents and had gone over to have him sign them. When I arrived, he was already dead."

She didn't sound shaken up over that fact. More upset that she hadn't had a chance to ink the deal before Edgar's untimely death.

"I was under the impression that the city wasn't going to approve a development for tiny houses," I said, waiting to gauge her reaction.

"Codes can always be worked around. Sometimes it takes some extra nudging, but it can be done."

"What about Malcolm? Isn't he interested in the lot too?"

Stella pursed her lips. "I'm not at liberty to divulge any details about my clients." She picked up her purse. "I'm off to another signing."

With that she left.

I sat for a moment, trying to absorb what she had just said. She, like Gretchen, believed that the lot was hers. Edgar hadn't had a chance to sign the deal before his death. That didn't give her much of a motive for murder. However, there was one detail that lingered in the air. She had just divulged something new. Malcolm was her client. Is that why they had been meeting? Her client for what?

I picked up the cookie plate and their empty coffee mugs. I had been under the impression that Stella and Malcolm wanted Edgar's property for their own separate purposes. What if I was mistaken? If Malcolm and Stella were working together that changed everything. The question was, how did this news connect to Edgar's murder?

Chapter Eighteen

"Hey, Jules, do you have a minute?" Sterling called from the kitchen. I brought the dishes with me and placed them in the sink.

Marty and Sterling had assembled an eye-popping assortment of concretes. Half of the island had been taken over by colorful tasting dishes. "We sort of got out of control." Sterling looked sheepish.

"Don't let the kid take the blame," Marty said, patting his plump belly. "I can't resist a good frozen custard. Sorry—concrete. It's a nice upscale term, isn't it?"

Sterling cracked his knuckles. "They're the same. You can call it whatever you want."

"Custard, concrete, ice cream—you name it. I used to tell my late wife that ice cream is always cheaper than therapy." His warm brown eyes lit up at the mention of his wife.

I chuckled. "That's a sentiment that we take to heart here at Torte. My mom's mantra is: 'Never underestimate the power of pastry.'"

"I knew there was a reason I was supposed to work

here." Marty smiled. Then he slid a dish filled with a creamy scoop of pale pink custard my way. "Try this first."

I picked up the dish to study the custard's appearance. One of the first things I taught chefs-in-training is the importance of presentation. We eat with our senses. The custard was smooth without any icy chunks. The texture was like butter. It had a lovely color that reminded me of spring and an intoxicating smell. "This looks divine."

Marty and Sterling shared a look of pride.

Next, I took a taste. The juicy flavor of vine-ripe strawberries instantly melted in my mouth, followed by an earthy finish with a touch of basil.

"You guys, this is amazing." I took another bite.

"It's good, isn't it?" Sterling reached for another dish. "Try this one. It's super chill—vanilla bean with sea salt, but I think we nailed the sweet-versus-salty balance."

"You don't have to ask me twice." The snowy white custard was flecked with tiny black vanilla bean seeds and sprinkled with coarse sea salt. My taste buds rejoiced at the first bite. Sterling hadn't oversold the custard. Often, in baking, simplicity provides the best results. This was certainly the case in the simple yet full-flavored vanilla-and-salt combination. "I'm at a loss for words."

Marty clapped Sterling on the back. "Our work here is done."

I couldn't resist spooning another heaping bite of the custard into my mouth. "There's only one problem with flavors this decadent—we are going to go through this fast. Are we sure that we're going to have the capacity to make enough with everything else we have going on?"

"We've already worked it out," Sterling replied, looking to Marty for confirmation.

Marty adjusted his apron. "Right. We'll add custard production to the top of the list each morning. The magic is in the machine. We dump in the ingredients and set it and forget as they like to say on TV."

Sterling picked up a lavender-colored cup of custard. "Yep. We'll shoot for three flavors to start and work our way up to five or six for daily rotations. Once we run out, we run out."

"I have a feeling we might run out quickly."

"Supply and demand." Marty opted for a serving of dark chocolate custard dusted with chopped hazelnuts and drizzled with homemade caramel. "We supply, and they will demand."

I liked his sense of humor and could tell that Sterling did as well.

"Speaking of supply and demand, I'm going to make some flyers to put out for the next Sunday Supper. We're confirmed on the menu, right?"

Sterling polished off his custard. "Yep. And Marty's agreed to help too."

"That's great."

A brief look of sadness passed over Marty. "I have more time than I know what to do with. Being here has been a good distraction from . . ." He trailed off.

Sterling patted his arm. "Distractions are good, man."

Truer words couldn't have been spoken. I was happy to have them paired together in the kitchen. They were good for one another. Sterling knew about loss, and I could already tell that Marty was going to be a parental figure for Sterling.

I said a silent prayer of thanks to the Universe for bringing Marty our way and then went to check on lunch service upstairs.

Rosa was circulating through the busy dining room, refilling coffee and clearing tables. She paused at a table with four older women to speak in Spanish. Andy was pushing cheese teas at the espresso bar while Sequoia was working the register and sending happy customers out the door with our boxed lunches and lemon marionberry cookies.

This was exactly what I had pictured when we began the expansion process. Torte was humming with life, with fantastic smells wafting from downstairs and the easy chatter of customers enjoying a leisurely lunch. Contented that all was well, I went to the office to work on the Sunday Supper flyers.

Our office hadn't changed in the renovation. We didn't need much space for paperwork and both Mom and I agreed that any square footage we would be gaining should go to the pastry counter and espresso bar. The office was cozy with a small desk, filing cabinet, and a whiteboard with ordering information and staff schedules.

I logged onto my laptop and pulled up the flyer from the last Sunday Supper to use as a template. It didn't take long to update it with the new menu. Once I had made the changes I hit print. To kill time while I was waiting for the flyers to print, I decided to see what information I could find online about George Mill.

A quick search returned dozens of articles about his disappearance. Police reports from the sixties surmised that George had opted to "go down with the ship" so to speak. Or in this case, submerge himself under lake waters. I read up on the Mill family. Interestingly none of George's three sisters had ever married. Two of his older sisters moved to Eastern Oregon after Emigrant Lake flooded their homestead. They lived out their later years on a cattle farm. Each of them died of natural causes within a few years of one another. The Mill family trust had amassed acreage throughout the Rogue Valley. I read up on the family's preservation efforts. After losing their homestead to the lake waters, they had carved out a policy of purchasing fertile farmland and wild acreage on the edge of the national forest to leave it untouched. I was impressed with their legacy.

I hit a dead end when it came to finding out more information about George's youngest sister, Anna. She had stayed in the Rogue Valley after George's disappearance. She worked as a teacher at an elementary school. I discovered a small article about her starting a farm school in the Applegate Valley in the 1970s but there was nothing after that. She could still be living. I did the math—she would be in her late seventies or early eighties today.

A new sense of urgency pulsed through me. What if I could find Anna Mill? She might hold the key to George's unsolved death. What if she knew who killed him? She was probably the only living person who knew if Edgar had been involved.

Did the Professor and Thomas know about Anna?

I didn't wait. I found my phone and called Thomas.

He answered on the second ring. "Hey, Jules. This time you had better be calling to tell me that you have a pastry emergency and need a taste tester stat! You know, I should add that to our app."

I heard someone in the background. I assumed it was Detective Kerry.

"She's not feeling me on this one, Jules. Back me up," Thomas continued. "Pastry 911, this is Torte speaking, what's your emergency?"

"Classic, Thomas."

"I'm outnumbered, aren't I?"

"This time, I'm with Detective Kerry."

"Women," he muttered. "Fine. If you're not calling about pastry, what can I do for you?"

I told him about Anna Mill.

"Thanks for the intel, Jules, but we've already followed up on that lead."

"Did you find her?"

"Anna? Yeah. She has a small farm out in the Applegate."

"Does she remember anything about George's death?"

"She remembers everything. Sharp as a tack. Detective Kerry and I said that we hope our memory is that strong when we're her age. But she's feisty. I wouldn't want to be on her bad side, that's for sure."

"Did she tell you anything that would help with the case?"

I heard Detective Kerry in the background again.

"You know I can't share details of an open investigation with you, Jules. Sorry." I could hear the regret in Thomas's voice and wondered if he would have been more forthcoming if Detective Kerry weren't standing right next to him.

After we hung up, I placed another call. This time to Lance. If Thomas wouldn't tell me more about Anna Mill, I knew that Lance would be game to take an afternoon drive out to the Applegate Valley with me. Lance agreed before I could finish my sentence.

"Be there in thirty minutes, darling. Must have a brief tête-à-tête with my lighting director. For some reason he keeps insisting on floodlights when I want a soft, easy touch. After that I'm yours. All yours. Ta-ta."

I knew that Lance and I should leave the investigation to Thomas and the Professor, but I also knew I couldn't let it go.

Chapter Nineteen

Lance and I drove through the lush Applegate Valley past vineyards and lavender farms. Horses and llamas ran free on acre upon acre of grassy organic land. The sun backlit the forested mountains that stretched to our left, casting filtered golden light through their sturdy branches.

"There's nothing as ambrosial as a slow drive through the countryside," Lance commented as we breezed past a father and son fishing in a stream. "It's as if we've stepped into a postcard."

"It's true," I agreed. "This area still feels untouched by time."

"Well said." Lance gazed out the window.

The Applegate loop took us through a scattering of tiny towns. Most consisted of nothing more than a gas station, small grocery store, and the occasional bar. Anna Mill's town resembled the dozens we had passed, with one exception. In the center of Main Street sat a statue of a wooden covered wagon. A sign hanging next to it read: "In Honor of the Mill Family Who Brought Their Pioneering Spirit to the Applegate."

"Did you see that?" I asked Lance.

He gazed out the window. "Yes. Very intriguing. Does this mean that Ms. Mill established this town?"

"I don't know. I guess we'll have to add that to our list of questions for her."

Lance steered the car off the main road and followed the directions on my GPS. They took us to a bumpy gravel road with huge potholes.

"Buckle up, it's going to be a rough ride." Lance tugged at his seat belt.

The road hadn't been maintained. I held on to the side of the passenger door. We nearly bottomed out twice. Somehow Lance managed to navigate over the rocky terrain and deliver us safely to Anna's front door. The house needed some serious TLC. It was a one-story bungalow with a wraparound front porch. In its heyday it was probably a lovely family home, but from the looks of the boarded-up windows, moss-caked roof, and weeds growing up between the porch slats, it hadn't been loved in years. The white paint was chipped and cracked. The porch looked as if it was sinking.

"Do you think anyone's living here?" I asked Lance. "It's in bad shape."

"Only one way to find out." He opened the car door, reached into the backseat, and tossed me a camera.

"What's this?"

"A prop." He made a beeline for the porch.

"Be careful," I called, hurrying after him. "That porch looks like it's about to collapse."

Lance held on to a wobbly railing and placed a toe

on the first rotted step. He shifted his weight. "Seems okay."

I watched him move with purpose. He reminded me of one his actors prancing on stage.

"She'll hold. Move slow," he said when he made it to the top.

I mimicked his footsteps, waiting for one of my feet to break through slippery, moss-coated steps at any minute.

"If Anna is living here, it's no wonder that she's a recluse. She has to be," Lance said, stepping over a broken board to knock on the front door.

We waited in silence. There was no sound of shuffling footsteps.

"I'll knock again," Lance said after a few minutes. This time he pounded on the door.

"Are you trying to terrify her?"

He wiggled his earlobe. "Aging ears. Maybe she can't hear."

We waited again. I was ready to give up and head to the car when Lance pressed his fingers to his lips. "Shhh. Do you hear that?"

"Hear what?" I cupped my hand over my ear.

"A creaky floorboard. I'm sure that someone is in there." He raised his arm to knock again when the door swung open.

I wasn't sure what I had been expecting Anna to look like, but the woman on the other side of the door didn't match the image I had conjured up in my mind. She was stout and stocky with wiry gray curls. I suppose I had envisioned a frail older woman, but Anna was the opposite. She wore a pair of steel-toed work boots, a pair of jeans, and a bulky sweatshirt that had a map of the state of Oregon in the center with a silhouette of a gun and the word ORY-GUN.

"I see you understand the correct pronunciation of our great state," Lance commented.

Anna bent her head toward her sweatshirt. "I understand how to use a gun and I'm about to go get my rifle if you don't move on off my property."

Lance swept his hand across the dilapidated deck with a flourish. "Oh dear, no, no. There's no need to get your gun. Although I must say I could cast you in *Annie Get Your Gun* in a heartbeat. You were made for the role."

Anna looked at Lance as if he was speaking a foreign language.

Lance took no notice. "Now, as I was saying, my colleague the lovely Juliet Montague Capshaw and I are here on important business."

Anna folded her arms across her chest.

"You might recognize me from the newspapers," Lance continued.

"I don't read the newspapers anymore." Anna's voice had a twangy quality to it. "Nothing good in them."

"Ah, well, that explains the confusion." Lance gave me a nod. "You see, I am the artistic director at the Oregon Shakespeare Festival and Juliet is my literary consultant."

Literary consultant? Where was Lance going with this?

He stood as rigid as one of the queen's guards. I might have believed he was royalty in his formfitting black suit, crisp white shirt, and skinny black tie. "The festival is working on a living history of the Applegate Valley and its founding members for an upcoming production in partnership with Southern Oregon University. I've been told again and again that I absolutely must speak with Ms. Mill. Apparently you're a legend around these parts."

If Anna had had any qualms about our intentions before, now her armor was definitely up. She stared from Lance and then to me out of the corner of her dark eyes. My estimates had placed her in her early eighties, but she could have easily passed for seventy.

"You want to know about this dump?"

Lance smiled broadly in an attempt to pacify her. "A dump? However could you say such a thing? Rustic, yes, but a dump, hardly."

Anna humphed.

"As I was saying, we're trying something entirely new next season—we're calling this revolutionary experience 'live history.' We'll have displays, historical relics, and hopefully people—not actors—regular people like yourself and your parents and grandparents, who've lived through the incredible changes in the valley. The railroad development, the flooding of Emigrant Lake. We need living legends like yourself to share your valuable knowledge and history."

Anna flinched.

Lance shifted tactics. "There will be compensation involved of course."

"What kind of compensation?"

Lance whispered a number in her ear. "That will be for our time today. Juliet and I will take photographs of everything inside your house, with your permission, of course. If you have a few minutes to spare we'll ask you a few questions today and then I'll have you come to the theater and we'll shoot an in-depth live interview that will be aired later. If you're so inclined you can be one of the living members at the event next spring, or we can simply roll the video that we shoot of your family's personal journey to the west."

I could tell that Anna was swayed by Lance's offer. She uncrossed her arms. The tight muscles in her neck relaxed. I had to credit Lance for his quick thinking. Compensation in exchange for snooping around her house.

"What's this live theater you're talkin' about? I don't need a bunch of people sniffin' around here."

"I assure you we will conduct ourselves with the utmost professionalism. If there's anything you don't want us to take photos of, please do let us know."

"How long is this gonna take?"

"Not more than an hour or two."

"Okay, but be quick about it. I've got beans cannin' and need to get back to the stove."

"Of course. You do whatever you need. We'll snap photos of the house and property and stay out of your way. Just holler when you're ready for us and we'll go over a few preliminary interview questions." Lance's typically polished voice had a hint of a twang as he spoke to Anna.

She returned inside with a skeptical glance at me.

"Were you planning that the entire time?" I whispered.

Lance shook his head. "No. I let the moment guide

me, and it worked." His smile was like that of a cougar about to pounce on its prey.

"How are we going to ask her about George though?"

"Follow my lead, darling. We'll dig around as much as we can first, and buy ourselves some time to craft Plan B. Why didn't we bring pastries?" He shook his head in disgust. "A terrible oversight on both our parts, but wallowing will get us nowhere. Let's get on with it, shall we?"

I wasn't sure what I had gotten myself into, but there was no turning back now. I tagged along with Lance as he tiptoed over broken sections of the porch. Hopefully Anna wouldn't catch on to our real motive. I had a bad feeling that she wouldn't hesitate to turn her gun on us if she figured out the truth.

Chapter Twenty

"Lance, what are you doing?" I whispered as he pulled up a loose floorboard on the deck and peered underneath it.

"Looking for bodies, of course."

"You think Anna has a body buried under her front porch?"

He stood, brushed dust from his hands, and straightened his tie. "Isn't that always where the bodies are hidden?"

"What?"

He rolled his eyes. "Really, darling. You have much to learn when it comes to the world of murder."

"Wait. How did we go from trying to learn what we could about George from Anna to considering her to be a murderess? Not to mention who do you think she murdered? We already have two bodies. You think there's another?"

He scoffed. "You're no fun sometimes."

"How? I'm asking a pretty basic question, and if there's even the slightest chance that Anna is harboring a body under her front porch, then isn't it the worst idea in the world to be drawing attention to that fact?"

"Like I said, way to kill the fun." Lance whipped his head toward the front door. "Am I allowed to venture inside, or is that off-limits too?" His tone was icy, but his eyes glinted with a devilish playfulness. "Shall we?"

The door creaked like a scene from a horror movie. The rotting floorboards sagged with each step. This was a bad idea. Every cell in my body screamed to turn around. What were we doing?

Anna had been less than welcoming. Lance's excuse for our visit was flimsy at best, and most importantly, she had a gun. No one knew that we were here. What would stop her from shooting us and hiding our bodies under the porch?

"It's us!" Lance called in his singsong voice. "Juliet is going to shoot some pictures of your kitchen as long as we aren't disturbing you." He turned to me and whispered, "Get the camera ready."

Anna didn't answer.

An uneasy feeling made the tiny hairs on my arms stand at attention.

The house smelled of beans and decades of neglect.

Lance spoke in an exaggerated theatrical tone as he dragged me into the kitchen. "Don't you absolutely love how quaint this kitchen is? Would it make for a wonderful tight shot?" While he spoke loudly for Anna's benefit he motioned for me to open the drawers and cupboards.

I shot him a look of confusion. What was I searching

for in Anna's kitchen? And where did she go? The pot of beans bubbled on the stove.

"Oh, wonderful shot, Juliet. I adore that angle. It's a slice of Americana, isn't it?" He glared at me, making a sign to hurry up. I opened a couple of cupboards and drawers to find rusty old canned food, dusty silverware, and what appeared to be the remnants of a loaf of bread, although it was impossible to tell whether it was French or whole wheat from the layer of green mold consuming the crust.

I fought back the urge to gag from the smell. How could Anna (or anyone) live like this?

Lance continued talking at a volume that the neighbors a half mile away could probably hear. I wondered if Anna was buying his act.

We moved into the dining room. It was in worse shape than the kitchen. Stacks and stacks of old newspapers, ripe with mildew, filled every square inch of the farm-style table and had been piled in the corners. Anna might not read newspapers anymore, but clearly at some point she had. Some of the stacks looked precarious, as if they might topple at any minute. That would make a good headline, I thought. Death by newspaper.

"Give those a look-through," Lance commanded in a hushed whisper.

Where would I even start? There had to be decades' worth of old newspapers in the room. Even if I could manage to take one from the stack without it falling on top of me, reading through them would take years.

"We don't even know what we're looking for," I shot back.

"Clues. Remember? Clues."

I pointed to one stack that had to contain a month's worth of daily papers. "A clue to what?"

"George Mill's disappearance." Lance stared at me with expectant eyes. "Why someone decided to bash his head in."

"There are probably thousands of newspapers here. That would take forever." I pointed to the adjoining office. "Let's try in there."

He threw his hands up in exasperation. I ignored him and moved toward the office. It was more of the same from the dining room. Stacks of newspapers, yellowing magazines, books, and old letters. I'd never been inside a hoarder's house, but I was sure that Anna's would qualify. This was a lost cause. I doubted that Anna could locate anything in here. Lance and I could be at it for weeks and have nothing to show other than newsprint stains and the need to take a long, hot cleansing shower.

"What are we doing here?" I said to him. Anna was nowhere in sight. I didn't know if that meant she had decided to trust us or that she was waiting for us in the next room with her gun at the ready.

"I don't know." Lance hung his head. "This is a disaster. And shockingly sad."

"I know." I was glad to hear that he was finally seeing the flawed logic in our sleuthing plans.

"How has she survived like this?" He pressed the palm of his hand under his nose. "The stench is starting to get to me."

"I think she needs help."

"Obviously." He cleared his throat and tried to wave away the odor with his free hand. "Who would we call?

Didn't you say that Thomas and the authorities have already been here?"

"Yes, but that doesn't mean she let them inside. The exterior is in poor shape, but I'm sure that if Thomas saw these living conditions he would have done something."

Lance stifled a gag. "Let's go. I can't fake it for a minute longer. We'll have to find another way to learn what we can about George. If I don't get some fresh air stat I'm going to lose my lunch."

I didn't argue. Once we were back outside, Lance drew in a long breath. He was about to say something when Anna appeared in the door frame. She had a shotgun slung over her shoulder.

My heartrate spiked.

"Juliet, get that shot." Lance tittered. "Oh, I do crack myself up sometimes. Shot? Get it?"

He moved toward Anna. Panic pulsed through my body. What was he doing? "Do you mind if we get a picture of you with the gun? It's so very Wild West."

Anna shrugged.

Lance whipped his head in my direction. "The picture, Juliet."

I pretended like I knew what I was doing. Fortunately, I'd watched Bethany frame dozens of photos at Torte. I stood on my tiptoes to shoot at an angle from above.

"Excellent. Do you have a few minutes to spare? We'd like to do a quick interview."

Deep crevasses lined her forehead. "You didn't even see the whole place. There's a lot of good stuff in the back and out in the barn. You want me to show you?"

My senses were on high alert. Why did she want to show us the barn? So she could shoot us?

Knock it off, Jules.

What was wrong with me? Lance's crazy suspicions were getting the best of me. I needed to stay calm and focus.

"We've seen what we need to for the moment." Lance's words were as smooth as butter.

"Fine. You want to sit?" Anna pointed to rotting rocking chairs on the far end of the porch.

"That would be lovely." Lance led the way.

The decaying wood sagged as I sat down.

Anna's chair creaked as she rocked back and forth. "What do you want to know?"

Lance began by asking her some basic history of her family and how they came to be one of the biggest land preservers in the valley.

As Thomas had mentioned, Anna remembered things about her early life in pristine detail—from strawberry picking in some of the region's first farms to her first teacher's name. The sun began to sink, casting a honeylike glow on the front grass as she recalled stories of digging a swimming hole behind her family's homestead and big outings to Sears for school shoes in the fall.

Finally, Lance shifted the conversation to George. "Please stop me if this is too painful to talk about, but one of the things we might want to touch on in the interview is your brother George. He went missing when the lake was expanded. Is that right?"

Anna's eyes narrowed. "He didn't go missing. He was murdered."

Lance threw his hand over his forehead. "What? Do tell."

Anna rocked her chair faster. "I already told the police. George was murdered."

"Do you know who killed him?" I asked.

"I can't say for sure, but I know he was murdered."

"Did it have anything to do with Edgar?" Lance caught my eye and made a slicing motion across his neck.

Tears welled in Anna's eyes. "How did you know about Edgar?"

"Research, dearest." Lance stood. "We must be off. Will you be available tomorrow to discuss specifics? I'd like to spend at least a few hours with you. Plus we'll need to get you in hair and makeup, and have our costume designer find something from the period to put you in. I'm thinking covered-wagon era. We'll re-enact your grandparents' westward migration. I can have a car pick you up. Shall we say three o'clock?"

Anna scratched her head. "What are you talkin' about, a car?"

Lance rested his hand on her shoulder which made her flinch. "Yes, you'll be treated with the height of luxury. I'll send a car, complete with some snacks and warm drinks for your travels."

"What kind of warm drink?" Anna arched her eyebrow.

"Whatever your heart desires. Tea? Coffee?"

"How about gin?"

Lance chuckled. "Why, of course. Gin it is."

Anna still didn't look convinced, but she gave him a nod.

"Excellent. A car with a bottle of my best gin will be here at three o'clock on the dot. My driver will bring you to Ashland where we can have a lovely chat. Sound good?"

Anna scowled. "I guess."

"Wonderful. Wonderful. See you tomorrow." He practically dragged me off the porch. Once we had backed out of the driveway and turned onto the gravel road that led to the main highway, he exhaled. "The first order of business when I get back to the office is a scalding shower."

"Lance, what was all that about your car and driver? You don't have a driver."

"Details, darling. Details. I'll send an Uber to pick up Anna or send my personal assistant. Actually, yes, I'll send my assistant since Anna would like a bottle of gin." He shuddered.

"Come to think of it," he continued. "I quite like the idea of a living history production. Can't you see it? The halls of OSF draped in the pictures of our past. A look at how we've come full circle. Sometimes the best ideas strike spontaneously, don't they?"

"I guess." My skin was sticky with sweat. I couldn't wait to take a long, cool shower.

Lance sounded put out. "You of all people should agree with that assessment. I have it on good authority that the pastry muse strikes you at the most random and often inconvenient times."

"You're not really going to write up a contract for her, are you?" I changed the subject.

He frowned. "Hardly. No. You and I have work to do before tomorrow afternoon. I will spend the evening digging up anything I can in the theater's archives about the Mill family. I need you to call that boyishly handsome detective friend of yours and his siren of a partner. We need to stage an intervention for that poor woman immediately."

"I'm not sure that's how it works."

"Exactly. The minute we arrive in town, track down Thomas or Detective Kerry and fill them in."

"Okay."

"After we get her cleaned up and sort through the filth in her house I'm quite convinced that Anna Mill has some serious secrets to spill."

"Nice rhythm."

"It happens without even trying, my dear." Lance winked. "But seriously, we have a deal, yes?"

"Yeah, but why did you cut me off? We were just getting to the good stuff."

"I know. Many apologies, but we need this on film. Anna is a broken woman. She's warming to us. Trust me. If we ever want Thomas and Detective Kerry to take us seriously we need proof. What better proof would there be than getting Anna on film? She knows who killed her brother and we are going to be the ones who uncover that."

We drove in silence for a while. I hoped Lance was right. I felt terrible leaving Anna in the state she was in.

Chapter Twenty-one

True to my word, I called Thomas after Lance dropped me off at Torte. He promised he would stop by when he finished his shift. While I waited, I decided to experiment with dessert options for our Sunday Supper. I knew that Sterling and Marty were planning to prepare a few of their new frozen custards to share with the guests, but since part of our motivation would be getting feedback on our soon-to-debut custards, I wanted to offer something to pair with them. An ice-cream treat called for something crunchy. I knew just the thing—cookies.

I headed for the basement. I would bake three cookie varieties, one to accompany each of the custards. For the strawberry, lime, and basil, I would make a vanilla crunch cookie, for the lemon, a gingersnap, and for the chocolate, a lacy oatmeal cookie.

I started with the oatmeal lace cookies because they were a favorite of mine. Their name originates from their baking process. The dough spreads as the cookies bake, causing it to bubble, which in turn creates tiny holes in the cookies—much like a lacy doily. I creamed butter and brown sugar together in the mixer. Next, I added eggs, vanilla, and a touch of salt. These cookies didn't require a leavening agent. The goal in baking them was to keep them as flat and crispy as possible. Once the batter was smooth I incorporated flour and rolled oats. They would bake for six minutes until they turned a lovely golden brown.

My recipe made dozens upon dozens of cookies. Some cookies are meant to be warm, right from the oven, but not these. They are best when they've had a chance to cool and become crisp. As I removed trays from the oven, I placed them on cooling racks. With a nice rest overnight, they should be perfect come morning.

Before I could start on the next batch, I heard a knock upstairs and went to answer it, holding a tray of cookies in one hand. Thomas and Detective Kerry had both come. I was shocked to see Detective Kerry in a pair of jeans and a red V-neck T-shirt. She had rolled the cuffs of her jeans over her ankles and wore a pair of red checkered Chuck Taylors. Her auburn curls hung loose. She looked like a completely different person.

"Wow, you look . . ." I paused for a minute trying to find the right word. Detective Kerry was beautiful, but she was typically so buttoned up that she gave off an almost unapproachable vibe. "Relaxed," I finally said, resting the cookies on the coffee bar.

She tossed her hair. "Oh this? I'm working undercover."

"In Ashland?"

"Don't you think she can pass for a grad student at SOU?" Thomas asked.

Detective Kerry shot him a look.

"I won't blow your cover," I promised. What was Detective Kerry doing undercover at SOU?

She didn't offer more.

Thomas headed straight for the cooling cookies. "Is this what smells so good? I swear I think you guys pipe the scent of your delicious baking onto the plaza to lure us in." He pointed to a lace cookie. "Can I?"

"Please. Help yourself. You too, Detective Kerry."

I figured she would refuse, but she took two. "Are these lace cookies? My mom used to bake these every Christmas. My brother and I would eat an entire plate. They're caramel, right?"

I couldn't believe it. Detective Kerry and I finally had a point of connection? It had only taken a few months. Well, that wasn't entirely true; I had initially greeted her with a box of jelly doughnuts which she had also taken a liking to. "You're right, they have a very caramellike taste and texture. That comes from the butter and brown sugar, which are the basic building blocks for caramel. I love the combination of the crispiness of the oats and the taffylike texture of the caramel."

She bit into a chewy cookie and closed her eyes. "This is exactly how I remember them."

"I can give you the recipe. They're super easy to make."

"Trust me, you don't want me anywhere near a kitchen. I can't bake."

Thomas nudged her waist. "That's one strike against you."

She chewed the cookie. "Just one? Wait until you really get to know me."

Their playful banter was fun to watch. Detective Kerry was definitely loosening up under Thomas's and the Professor's influence. And I could tell by Thomas's eager gaze that he was smitten with Kerry.

"Anytime you have a childhood craving, come by and I'll whip up a batch for you. I'm serious that they are one of the easiest cookies to bake."

She twisted her hair into a high ponytail. To my surprise she had on a pair of doughnut-shaped earrings. "I might have to take you up on that, especially if I have to hang out on campus with the coeds much longer."

"Hey, where did you get those?" I asked.

"My earrings?" She massaged her earlobe. "Thomas gave them to me."

Thomas's cheeks swelled pink. "A friend of my mom's makes them. I know Kerry's a big doughnut fan, so I thought she might like them."

Ashland was such a small world sometimes. "I have a pair like them myself. They look good on you."

"Thanks." Detective Kerry smiled.

I knew it was futile to ask what her assignment on campus was, but I hoped her presence at SOU didn't mean that the students were in any danger. Steph and Andy (at least for the time being) both took classes at the university and Stephanie lived in the dorms.

Thomas chomped on a cookie. "So what's the scoop? You mentioned something about Anna Mill on the phone."

We went and sat in the dining area. I told them about how Lance and I had taken a day trip to Anna's house and described the living conditions inside.

"Wait one minute." Thomas clicked off his iPad. "Are

you telling us that you and Lance entered Ms. Mill's home under false pretenses?"

"I wouldn't exactly say that." I could hear how feeble my reply sounded.

"This is a murder investigation," Detective Kerry replied.

"I know. You're right. We should have left it alone, but you know how Lance gets. And quite honestly, I'm just as bad. I promise I'll encourage him to tell Anna the truth, but isn't there something you can do about her house?"

Thomas scrolled through a file on his screen. "The fact that you two busted into her house isn't going to help us."

Detective Kerry shook her head. "Nope."

I felt terrible. I shouldn't have let my curiosity get the better of me. "Not busted. We simply said we were doing research for a living history performance, which I think is true, by the way."

"We're going to have to pass this over to social services. Adult protective services will allow you to place an anonymous tip. They can then send an investigator to assess the situation and interview Anna Mill."

"Why anonymous?" I asked.

"You can use your name if you want. Ask them, but I think they prefer to keep reporters anonymous for personal safety issues. Of course since you and Lance were the last people to visit Anna, unless she's not with it mentally, she'll probably figure out that you reported her."

"That's okay. I'm willing to risk that. I'm willing to have a conversation with her. This isn't coming from a place of judgment. I'm genuinely worried about her. That house is not safe. One spark and the entire place would go up in flames."

Detective Kerry's phone rang. She stepped outside to answer it.

"Look, Jules." Thomas's voice was filled with empathy. "I get it. I know how involved you get and I know that the Professor doesn't exactly discourage your input and information when it comes to investigations. I don't either. I appreciate your candor and the fact that everyone in town opens up to you. You get more information out of suspects by offering them a cup of Joe and a scone than I do sometimes, but this is sketchy territory we're in. People get kind of nuts about their personal property and their independence. I only spoke with Anna for a few minutes, but my read on her is that she won't be happy to have social services show up at her door."

"No. I don't think she will, but Thomas, it's the right thing to do. Even if it's the hard thing, I know that it's the right thing."

"Okay. I appreciate that. It's one of your best qualities, but I want to warn you that if you go down this path you're involving yourself in Anna's world and there's no turning back."

"I understand."

He sighed. "In that case, let me call a friend at adult protective services and put her in touch with you."

"Thanks, Thomas."

"You bet, Jules. Just be careful, okay?" His eyes narrowed. "I'm not sure what's going on with these two cases right now, but I can tell you that I don't like either of them. They're dredging up the worst in Ashland and it's not making me sleep easy at night."

"Is there anything else I can do?"

He shook his head and headed for the door. "Be careful. Watch your back. And don't let Lance talk you into any more crazy schemes."

"Deal."

I watched him leave. Thomas wasn't usually so glum. Did he know more about the case or cases that he couldn't tell me? Probably. I would definitely heed his warning and have a chat with Lance about doing the same. Regardless of what transpired with Anna Mill I was confident that I was making the right choice. The woman clearly needed help. If I didn't step in, who would?

Chapter Twenty-two

Andy was the first staff member to arrive at Torte the next morning. I had already brought all the trays of my cooled oatmeal lace cookies upstairs. They looked tempting in the pastry case.

"You've already baked cookies?" Andy stretched as he reached for an apron. "It's barely possible to call this ungodly hour the morning. You are not human, boss."

"I made these last night." I reached into the case and handed him a cookie. "Try one. It'll put a spring in your step, guaranteed."

"That's what coffee is for." Andy ripped off a piece of the cookie. "Although this will do in the meantime."

I waited for him to finish his cookie. Then he went through his precoffee ritual, washing his hands, warming up the espresso machine, and doing a quick inventory of the large bags of coffee beans.

"I could make a latte to go with that cookie. Maybe something with a touch of caramel and Irish cream and a hit of cinnamon. That could be good."

"It sounds amazing. Go for it."

"You always say that." Andy grinned. He began steaming milk.

"So have you given any more thought to school?" I asked, keeping my eyes focused on the pastry case.

He ground fresh beans. The smell was instantaneous. Rich, earthy coffee scents enveloped the enclosed area. "I think so."

"And?" I walked around to the other side of the counter, so I could see his face.

"I'm going to quit, Jules. I've made up my mind. I know that you and my mom and my grandma and your mom are all going to tell me that I'm making a mistake, but I'm not feeling it right now. Maybe it's a mistake to drop out, but I don't think so. I can always go back."

"What about football though? I thought you loved being on the team."

He twisted the tamper into the machine. "I do. I love the team, but it hasn't been the same lately. Something's going on with the coach. Rumor has it he's leaving. He hasn't been at practice. Hasn't checked in with me or any of the other guys. I'm sure he's out."

"You mean fired?"

"No. I think some bigger school came calling and probably offered him a lot more dough." He winked. "Hey, I set myself up for that one."

"But you'd be giving up football too."

"That's what my mom is going to say. But, come on, what am I going to do with football? That's not a career. I'm not good enough to play professionally. I could play for the Raiders for another year or two and then what? A few guys have gotten really hammered lately.

One of my friends had to sit out for four weeks with a concussion. I don't know that it's worth it. I don't want to mess up my head just because I like to play a stupid game."

"Good point. I worry about you all the time when it comes to taking hits, but you could stop football and still get your degree."

"Yeah. Except I want to do this. If I were working here full-time I could learn just as much if not more about the coffee and restaurant business. You know my generation doesn't care as much about a piece of paper. We want to get out into the world and create our own futures." Thick espresso dripped into a stainless-steel shot glass.

"I get that, but I don't want you to do something rash and regret it."

"I won't regret it. You'll be my mentor. Remember, you talked about sending me to barista competitions. I'd love to learn more about the coffee trade and even get into roasting. There are so many things I can do if I have the time. Right now, between school, and football, and work, I'm totally scattered."

"Andy, you're far from scattered. You are one of the most reliable staff members we've ever had. Have you even missed a single day of work?"

"See, that's it right there. Doesn't that tell you something? This is my passion. This is what I want to do. When I'm in class I'm daydreaming about coffee."

I couldn't argue with him. When I wasn't at Torte, my mind was never far from thoughts of future menus or new cake designs. I knew it borderlined on an obsession. That was often the way it went with things we were passionate about—a blessing and a curse as Mom would say.

"See, I can tell you get it," Andy continued. "If I didn't love this place and what I'm doing, why else would I show up before the sun? My friends sleep until noon. I'm already halfway through my day by then. You don't pick this life. It picks you. This is what I want to do, Jules."

"You have my support." I breathed in the aroma of the coffee. "When are you going to break the news to your family?"

Andy poured a shot into a coffee mug and then began steaming milk. "I'm not sure who I'm scared of more. Your mom or my mom."

"If you explain your decision to them the way you have to me, I'm sure they'll understand."

"Right." Andy laughed. "Have you met either of our moms?"

"Okay, maybe they'll freak out at first, but they'll come to terms with it. They know you're an amazing guy."

A foamy froth spilled over the side of the metal steaming pitcher. "Thanks, boss. At least I know that you've got my back."

"Always." I wiped a smudge off the countertop. "Once things settle down, let's talk about next steps for you. I would love to plan to send you to some competitions and have you take a bigger role with procuring coffee and working with our local roasters. I'm sure that we can arrange an internship of sorts with one of the roasters to have you learn the steps."

"That would be awesome." Andy's cheeks flamed

with excitement. "You're seriously like the best boss in the world. You know that, right?"

"The feeling's mutual," I replied with a smile. "But the bread calls. I can smell the batch I have in the ovens. I better go check on it."

"I'll have a java ready for you in five. I want to play around with the ratios of caramel, Irish cream, and cinnamon." He swirled milk over the espresso. "Thanks again. All kidding aside, you are such a good listener and I appreciate you taking the time to help me through this."

"Anytime. You know that you're not staff—you're family."

He held up the coffee mug in a toast.

I left to check on my bread, wondering how everyone else would react to Andy's news. It wasn't my story to tell. I would let him take the lead on when and how he decided to share his decision.

Our morning bread orders had doubled over the summer months. In the height of the theater season every restaurant and pub in town was bursting at the seams with hungry visitors. We supplied breads, rolls, a selection of our pastries, and even a few custom cakes to businesses throughout the plaza and town. I enjoyed doing the delivery rotation. It allowed me a chance to stop in and say hello to my fellow business owners. I packed up boxes of crusty sourdough and marble rye.

Andy came downstairs with a sample oatmeal cookie latte. Sterling and Stephanie accompanied him.

"Have you heard that you have a dropout on your hands?" Stephanie asked, shooting Andy a sideways glance.

I was taken aback. I hadn't expected that he would tell everyone right away.

I looked to Andy.

He handed me the latte. "Yep. I'm the new Torte delinquent, I guess."

"Someone finally usurped my title." Sterling punched him in the shoulder. "Thanks, man."

"Happy to help." Andy saluted him.

Stephanie scowled. "This is great. Now I'm going to be the only one around here who's stuck doing homework on my lunch break."

"All part of my master plan." Andy shot two thumbs up in the air. "No more homework, suckers."

Stephanie rolled her eyes. "You're sure about this?"

I appreciated that she was concerned too.

Andy launched into the same argument he had used on me. Sterling and Steph listened attentively. When he finished Steph pursed her lips and twisted a stud earring. "I guess that makes sense. It's going to be weird not to walk over to campus with you or see you in the library."

"But you'll see me here every day."

"I guess. It's just going to be weird." Stephanie dropped the conversation and walked over to the sink.

Sterling clapped him on the shoulder. "It's you and me against Jules now, watch out."

"Nice." I chuckled.

"Seriously, man, that's cool. I can see you owning your own roasting company one day."

Andy gave him a look of thanks. "That's the goal." He returned to the coffee bar.

"What do you really think, Jules?" Stephanie questioned. Her startling, almost violet eyes were heavily lined with black and dusted with purple eye shadow. "You can't let him drop out of school."

"I don't think she has any control over Andy's decisions," Sterling said.

"Whatever. You know what I mean. This is a terrible idea."

"Honestly, I'm not sure if it is," I said. The oven buzzed. I walked over to check on the next round of bread.

Sterling gathered a pile of applewood to start the fire in the pizza oven.

Stephanie reviewed order sheets for custom cakes and cupcakes. "Have you lost it? You think that dropping out of college is a good idea?"

"No, but I understand Andy's perspective and if I've learned anything over the course of my life so far it's that sometimes you have to trust your gut instinct. Sometimes we have to make choices based on where we're at in a particular moment of time. Andy's decision to leave school reminds me of when I left the ship. It was rash in hindsight. I left without giving it as much thought as Andy's giving to his decision right now. Would I make the same choice today? Who knows. But I don't regret it. All of my collective choices have led me to where I am now."

"Yeah, but Andy's giving up his future. Do you know how many people go back to school once they've dropped out?" Stephanie was more animated than I'd ever seen her. "Zero." She made an *O* with her hand.

"I know. I told him the same thing."

"And that's it? You're not going to try to stop him?"

"Steph, Andy is an adult. I can't stop him."

She muttered something under her breath and then walked over to the fridge for butter, eggs, and heavy cream. "It just sucks that he's throwing away his future."

"Yeah. Although, again, you could argue that I did the same when I left the ship. I gave up great pay, and I had basically no expenses. Not to mention leaving my husband."

Stephanie set her baking supplies next to one of the industrial mixers. "That's totally different. You were an adult. And you've said a million times that you were ready to leave long before you realized it. You just needed a catalyst."

"True, but that's my point about Andy. It sounds like he's been simmering on this for a long time."

Sterling had stoked a fire. The kitchen filled with the scent of sweet, woodsy smoke. "Speaking of simmering. I should probably get today's soup special going. Any requests?"

I was happy for the change of topic. I didn't think I could win this argument with Stephanie. Nor did I need to.

"We got a huge delivery of new veggies yesterday. What about summer vegetable minestrone? We can offer a vegetarian option and a meat option. Maybe with shredded chicken?"

"Sure." Sterling and Steph shared a look. I knew that he had stepped in as much for her sake as for mine. I didn't blame her for her resentment. Attending college and working was a huge commitment. Seeing one of her coworkers opt out must be hard to stomach. I just hoped that it wouldn't cause a permanent wedge between them.

Marty's boisterous voice cut through the tension.

"Morning, everyone. Who's ready to bake the bread as they say?" He clapped Sterling on the back.

Sterling laughed. "For sure, man."

Stephanie went to her workstation to start rolling out fondant for a custom cake order.

Marty set down his things and washed his hands. "What's on the docket this morning?"

We reviewed bread orders. Within minutes Marty had yeast proofing on the counter and milk and butter simmering on the stove.

"Let's start with a hearty chicken stock for the base," I said to Sterling, who had gathered veggies and canned jars of tomatoes for the garden minestrone soup. "We have some in the freezer, but I can use my quick-stock recipe for today. If you want to chop everything for the soup, I'll get a batch of chicken stock going."

"Works for me." Sterling arranged the vegetables on a cutting board and began dicing onions, garlic, carrots, celery, Yukon gold potatoes, and fresh herbs.

"It's starting to smell like my grandma's kitchen in here," Marty said over the sound of the dough hook whirling in the mixer.

I rough-chopped onions, carrots, leeks, and celery and added them to a pot along with large handfuls of rosemary, parsley, peppercorns, whole cloves of garlic, bay leaves, and a healthy glug of olive oil. It didn't matter how the vegetables were cut because I would allow the stock to slowly boil for a few hours and then strain it. While the vegetables were sautéing on low heat, I hacked whole, organic chickens with a meat cleaver into two- to four-inch pieces.

"Watch out!" Marty called, placing his hands behind

his head. "Don't mess with a woman and her meat cleaver. I learned that lesson a long time ago."

"What?" Sterling looked up from chopping veggies.

"I'll tell you about it later, kid." Marty made a goofy face.

"That's right. Don't mess with me." I lifted the cleaver above my shoulder. "Otherwise, you might get the ax."

"Yeah, right. Jules wouldn't hurt a fly," Sterling bantered with Marty. "I mean literally. There was a fly in the dining room during construction and she refused to kill it."

"Not true," I chimed in. "It was a ladybug. Not a fly."

"I rest my case," Sterling said to Marty.

Once the chicken had been cut in smaller pieces I added it to the stockpot and browned it on both sides. The key to any good stock is a low, slow boil. Often, we would use leftover chicken carcasses to make our stocks and keep them on the stove all day. I didn't have that kind of time today, so I sped up the process by sautéing the chicken and veggies just until the chicken released its juices.

Simmering the chicken (bones and all) would infuse it with dense flavor as well as iron, collagen, and rich vitamins from the marrow of the bones. By the time we were ready to add it to Sterling's soup, it should be rich and herbaceous, and the chicken should fall off the bone. We would shred that by hand and add it to the soup.

My stomach grumbled at the thought.

With the herbs, veggies, and chicken nicely browned, I added water by the gallon.

"What are you doing down there?" Marty asked as

he passed by me with a tray of beautifully shiny loaves of bread.

I had crouched to get at eye level while measuring water.

"Morning exercises?" Marty teased.

"No, this is an old trick I learned from the chef in culinary school. When measuring liquids get at eye level. You can't get an accurate reading looking from above." I did a couple of lunges. "But you're right. Maybe we can start a new trend. Kitchen weight training."

"I like it." Marty heaved the tray of bread. "Bread push-ups and measuring squats."

"Don't let Bethany hear you guys," Sterling said. "She'll want to film you for social media."

I winced. "Good point." I poured water over the chicken and vegetables until they were completely submerged. Then I brought it to a rolling boil, turned the heat down and covered the stock with a lid. It would simmer on low for two to three hours. Then I would scoop the bones and big pieces of chicken out with a slotted spoon and put the stock through a large sieve, lined with cheesecloth, to strain the remaining broth.

"I'm going to deliver more bread to the Green Goblin. The stove is all yours," I said to Sterling as I picked up one of the boxes that Marty had packaged as well as a box of cookies I had set aside to donate to Gretchen. "They're hosting a cocktail tasting this afternoon and asked for a few extra loaves. Be back soon."

The rest of the staff had arrived when I went upstairs. Andy was telling them his news. Bethany's reaction was the opposite of Steph's. She squealed and threw her arms around him. "That's so great! You're going to be here all the time now."

Andy returned her hug. "Yep. You're not getting rid of me."

I left them chatting about bigger and better plans for social media involving daily coffee art and documenting Andy's ventures into the world of coffee roasting. I hoped that my advice was right. Andy had to carve out his own future and captain his own ship.

Chapter Twenty-three

My delivery route took me through the plaza's busy sidewalks. It was later than usual for our morning delivery loop which meant there were already tourists getting an early start on the day. Thomas's mom waved from A Rose by Any Other Name as I passed in front of the colorful flower shop. She was bundling up a cheerful bouquet of bright yellow daisies for a customer. Galvanized tins bursting with vibrant blooms sat in front of the shop. Twinkle lights and strings of pink paper peonies hung from the windows. I made a mental note to stop by later and ask about some flower arrangements for our next Sunday Supper. Antique lampposts lined the plaza. Banners announcing the annual Daedalus project flapped in the warm morning wind. The event had been a favorite among locals and theatergoers since 1988. It was a fund-raiser for HIV/AIDS organizations. There would be a staged reading of a play, a remembrance ceremony, a bake sale, and actor talks throughout the day. The highlight of the evening was a variety show put on by the entire company. Actors showcased a plethora of hidden talents from magic to the electric guitar. Fans waited with bated breath for the pièce de résistance—the underwear catwalk where members of the company strutted through the aisles of the Elizabethan while sweet little old ladies shoved one-dollar bills into their skivvies.

I dropped off a box of baguettes at Puck's Pub and continued on toward the Green Goblin. My posture stiffened as I hurried past the Merry Windsor Hotel, which sat across the street from the Lithia bubblers. A run-in with Richard Lord was the last thing I needed today.

No luck.

Richard's booming voice echoed in the plaza. "Juliet! A word!"

Did he have spy cameras planted outside? It couldn't be a coincidence that anytime I passed his hotel he came out on the porch to flag me down.

"Can't stop, Richard." I shifted the boxes of bread. "I'm on my way to the Green Goblin."

"Stop on your way back," he countered. He was dressed in plaid golf shorts and a Merry Windsor T-shirt. The hotel had used Shakespeare's bust as their logo, and Richard had recently added the tagline WHERE EVERYONE COMES TO EAT, DRINK, AND STAY AT THE MERRY. My staff and I had gotten a good chuckle out of Richard's lame attempt at a pun.

"No can do. Busy day." I didn't wait for a response. Instead I made a beeline for the Green Goblin, which sat at the far end of the plaza. I could sense Richard's beady eyes burning into the back of my head. Sooner or later I was going to have to face him, but I was fine with avoiding a Richard Lord confrontation for the moment.

After I delivered the Green Goblin's order, I headed for the homeless council headquarters. Inspired by Gretchen's impassioned plea the other day, I had made a few dozen sugar cookie cutouts in fun summer shapes—a pineapple, bee, watermelon, flip-flop, pool float, sunglasses, and sea turtle. Each cookie had been flooded with royal icing and hand-piped with bright colorful frosting. We would sell them to our regulars, but I thought they would be a special treat for the children that Gretchen served.

I stopped in my tracks when I saw Stella and Gretchen talking in hushed tones in front of the rustic building. I was too far away to hear their conversation. Gretchen had her back turned to me, and as usual Stella's face was completely stoic. I considered interrupting them, but before I had a chance Stella motioned to her car, parked across the street near the entrance to Lithia Park. Gretchen hopped into the passenger seat and they sped off.

Gretchen had been furious with Stella when I had seen her at Edgar's lot. Where were they going? And what were they doing together? I was more than curious. Alas, there was no chance that I could chase after Stella's car, so I dropped off the cookies instead.

The same receptionist sat behind the desk when I entered the already warm building.

"Another Torte delivery?" She grinned.

"These need to stay pretty cool, otherwise the frosting will melt," I said, handing her the box of decorated sugar cookies.

"May I?" She lifted the lid. "These are the cutest. That pineapple. It's adorable. The kids are going to love these. Thank you so much."

"They were fun to make." I turned toward the door. "Did I see Gretchen taking off a minute ago?"

The receptionist closed the lid to the cookie box. She glanced around to make sure no one was listening. "Yes. It's all hush-hush. She told me she had a very important meeting that might change our fate. I'm dying for her to come back so I can get more details."

"Fingers crossed." I crossed my fingers in a show of support and left. Gretchen and Stella had scheduled a meeting about the homeless council's future. What did that mean? Had Gretchen convinced Stella that Edgar wanted to bequeath the property to the council? But why would Stella be involved? Nothing added up.

I let out a sigh and decided to take the long route back to Torte and turned toward the Shakespeare Stairs that led up to the OSF complex. I doubted that Lance would be in his office yet, but since I was already in the vicinity I might as well give it a shot. Maybe he could lend some insight to the puzzle. The bricks were awash with sunlight. A handful of company members rolled heavy carts between the theaters and a gardening crew filled a fresh layer of bark dust in the flower beds and trimmed the ivy snaking up the Elizabethan's retaining wall.

A couple of tourists posed in front of the historic open-air theater to take a selfie. "Would you mind?" the woman called. "I'm terrible at taking photos."

"I'm not much better," I admitted. Then I set the empty delivery boxes on a bench and clicked a few photos of them. "Hopefully one of these works," I said, handing her back her phone.

She pointed at the delivery box. "Are you from Torte?"

"I am."

"Our friends in San Francisco raved about your bakeshop. They said we *had* to do two things while in Ashland—see a show and eat at Torte."

"Have you been into the bakeshop yet?" I asked.

"No." She looked at her husband. "We were out for a morning walk and thought we'd come to Torte for breakfast after we burn off a few calories."

"It's a good plan. We don't skimp on the butter." I grinned.

"No one should ever skimp on butter," her husband chimed in.

"That's our mantra." I was about to pick up the delivery boxes when the woman gasped and grabbed my arm.

"Is that an actor? Is he famous?"

I turned and followed her eyes. Malcolm had just opened a side door on the Elizabethan theater. I could understand how she might have mistaken him for an actor. He had a black OSF baseball hat shielding his face and a cell phone glued to his ear. "No," I said, returning my attention to the woman. "He's not an actor, but keep your eyes open. You'll spot familiar faces all over town."

The woman looped her arm through her husband's. "How exciting. Maybe we'll rub elbows with someone famous at Torte."

"It's been known to happen." I excused myself and went to track down Malcolm. He was unlocking the main doors at the Bowmer Theater. "Malcolm," I called.

He paused, swiveled his head, and then acknowledged me with the slightest of nods. "Juliet, hello."

I jogged down the bricks to meet him at the theater entrance. "Wow, you're working early."

His key was inserted into the lock. "I needed to get some paperwork. This isn't my typical start to a day. What are you doing out this early?"

"Morning deliveries." I realized I had left the boxes up on the bench.

"We get morning pastry deliveries? How come no one ever told me that?" He turned the key. "I guess that's indicative of the fact that I'm still too low on the food chain around here."

"No, I'm sure it's not that. Sometimes we deliver morning treats to the cast and crew, but not today. I was delivering to a few businesses in the plaza and thought I'd see if Lance happened to be here."

Malcolm glanced at a fitness tracker that doubled as a watch on his wrist. "Now? I highly doubt it."

"Yeah, it was worth a shot, right?" I shrugged.

"Is there something I can help you with?" He turned the handle and opened the door to the main stage. "I'm heading to my desk, but you're welcome to join me."

Since he had offered I jumped at the chance to ask him about Edgar's murder. I wasn't breaking my promise to Thomas, not exactly. Malcolm had invited me in.

"Actually, I was hoping to talk to you about Edgar and his property," I said as we entered the lobby. The six-hundred-seat theater had been constructed in the late

1960s due to growing demand for tickets to the festival's sold-out productions. Its stadium-style seating had a surprisingly intimate feel, due to the fact that no seat was more than fifty-five feet away from the stage. The spacious lobby's huge arched wooden beams reminded me of the ship, the *Amour of the Seas,* where Carlos and I had sailed together.

Malcolm locked the doors behind us. "What do you want to know about Edgar's property?"

"I spoke with Stella yesterday after I saw you at the bakeshop. She hinted that you might be a client."

"What's your point?" He stuffed his keys into his jeans pocket. They were dark charcoal with intentional tears in the knee.

"I was under the impression that there was another party who had already acquired the lot."

"Who?" Malcolm's voice echoed in the open lobby. The faintest hint of popcorn lingered in the empty space. From February through October, the Bowmer hosted performances daily, except Mondays. Day after day theatergoers from around the globe entered these doors and queued up for refreshments while waiting with eager anticipation for the show.

"I'm not sure," I lied. Maybe I should have stayed out of it.

"That's too bad for whoever thinks that they're getting the lot, because it's ours. We haven't made an announcement to the press yet, but that's coming later today. The initial survey work is complete. I met with the survey crew the day Edgar died, and we have the preliminary site reviews done."

"Wait, OSF officially purchased Edgar's lot?"

Malcolm nodded. He motioned to the stairs. "That's why I'm here early. I need to bring a copy of the contract to our legal team."

"You have a signed contract?" I don't know why I couldn't do anything other than to repeat Malcolm's words.

"I do. Had to pay thirty percent over asking price. That stung, but the board agreed that housing for our actors is of paramount concern for the future of the festival."

"You paid thirty percent over asking?"

Malcolm raised one brow, making the left side of his lip curl. "Yes, that's what I just said."

"I know. Sorry. I'm trying to make sense of that." I didn't want to go into the fact that there were not one but multiple parties who claimed the same thing.

"Want to walk to my desk with me? I have to get the contracts anyway. You can see them for yourself."

"If you don't mind?"

"No, it's fine. It's going to be public record soon anyway. I don't have anything to hide."

The Bowmer Theater was deserted. I hesitated for a second. No one knew that I was here, but Malcolm sounded transparent. It was morning, and soon actors and crew would be arriving to prepare for the matinee and backstage tours. It was a calculated risk to go with Malcolm, but I liked my odds.

His office was close to Lance's, but unlike senior members of the management team, Malcolm shared an office. His corner of the cramped space was sparsely decorated with a desk, filing cabinet, and bookshelf. Lance's office was nicer than most hotel suites, with a built-in bathroom, wet bar, dozens of awards on display, and a comfortable couch and seating area. Malcom's space was utilitarian. A few of his coworkers had personalized their desks with photos, but his was void of anything unique.

He thumbed through a neat stack of files. "Here. Take a look." He thrust one of the files labeled "OSF Trust" at me.

Sure enough, the file contained a contract, signed by Edgar. I couldn't believe it. How many people in Ashland had contracts with Edgar? His unethical business practices must have gotten him killed.

I leafed through the contract, not sure what I was looking for. What was more than evident was that someone—Malcolm, Gretchen, or Stella—was lying. One of them must have learned about the other contracts and decided to seek revenge.

Malcolm knocked on the top of his desk. "It's all right there, like I said."

"Thanks for letting me see it." I handed him the file.

"You look upset." He tucked the file under his arm.

"No. I'm confused. I can't figure out what Edgar's end goal was. He promised the lot to a bunch of people."

"Maybe he promised, but he only inked a deal with us." Malcolm gloated. "Who else thinks they have a claim to the lot?"

I figured that Malcolm would hear about Pam and Gretchen soon enough. I had a feeling that the battle for the land would play out in the courts for many months. When I finished telling Malcolm what I knew his face blanched.

"That can't be true."

I shrugged. "It's what I've heard."

He scratched his head. Then he rifled through the stack of files again. This time he removed a letter. "You should read this."

"What is it?"

"A letter I received yesterday."

I opened the letter. It was written in a woman's hand in gorgeous cursive. The letter was scathing. Demanding that Malcolm stop pursuing the empty lot. The letter was obviously written by one of OSF's biggest donors. The threats escalated as I read on—claiming that the donor would pull all of her funds from the theater if Malcolm didn't withdraw his offer for Edgar's lot.

I paused halfway through. "She's not happy with you."

Malcolm shook his head. "Keep reading. See who wrote it?"

I read on. There was more of the same, but when I got to the last line, butterflies assaulted my stomach. It was signed Pam Denke, owner of Nightingales.

Chapter Twenty-four

"Pam wrote this?" I bent over to pick up the letter.

"Yes. I haven't done anything with it yet. Pam is one of our best donors, but we can't let our patrons' wishes dictate best business practices."

"Why is she this upset?"

"She's convinced that any additional housing units near her property will greatly devalue Nightingales. She's not entirely wrong about that, but that's business. She's gone off the deep end. I think she's unstable."

My throat tightened. Not Pam. Pam was a friend. She wouldn't do something so extreme. Would she?

I thought through every interaction I'd had with her. She had been on the property. She had access. She knew Edgar's routine. Pam couldn't have gone so far off the deep end, as Malcom had said, that she killed Edgar. Could she?

"Are you okay?" Malcolm reached across the desk to steady me.

"I'm fine. I need to go. Thank you for sharing this information with me. Did you show Pam's letter to the police?"

Malcolm shook his head. "No. I didn't see a need. She wasn't threatening me personally. Only to stop funding the theater. That happens all the time."

"You should call the police. I think they're going to be very interested in that letter."

"Okay," Malcolm agreed.

I left in a rush, taking the stairs two at a time. What did this mean? I hadn't wanted to believe that Pam was a murderess, but had I intentionally ignored the clues right in front of me?

On my way out the front door I ran right into Lance.

"Juliet, where's the fire?"

Without taking a breath, I explained what Malcolm had told me along with relaying my conversation with Thomas and Detective Kerry about Anna Mill from last night. "You've got to drop your plan to invite Anna to the theater under false pretenses. It's serious, Lance."

He scowled when I finished. "You're telling me that I have to cut the theatrics? Impossible. It's in my blood."

"No, I'm telling you no car. No bottle of gin. No more elaborate lies. Thomas and Detective Kerry are taking it from here. I'm waiting for the social worker's call."

"That certainly puts a damper on my morning."

"Same here. Lance, do you think there's a chance that Pam could have killed Edgar?"

He flipped his wrist. "I don't see it. Sweet Pam who hosts literary salons with wine and cheese and nibbles on her back patio a stone-cold killer? Doubtful."

"But everything tracks back to her."

"Perhaps."

"Did you have any luck with the archives?"

He smoothed his pocket square. "Not yet. That's why

I arrived early. I was swept up by my adoring fans after the show last night. They practically kidnapped me and forced me out on the town for evening cocktails."

Knowing Lance, I doubted that he put up much of a protest.

"Would you like to join me?"

"No. I need to get to Torte and give Thomas a call. He needs to know about Pam."

"Suit yourself. If I find anything of interest I might keep it to myself."

"You know that you'll call me right away if you find anything."

"Fine. But I'll gloat." He stretched his lanky neck to the sky in a show of superiority. "Ta-ta, darling."

I retrieved my delivery boxes. My cell phone rang. It was the social worker assigned to Anna's case. We had a lengthy discussion about the state of Anna's house. She asked me a few questions about Anna's cognition as well as my opinion as to whether she was able to live independently. I answered honestly, yet with a feeling of regret, as I imagined she was building her case to place Anna in the state's care. There wasn't anything more I could do in the short-term. At least Anna was connected to services. Hopefully she would be able to get the support she needed to clean out her house and stay there with visits from nursing staff or social workers.

Torte was packed when I returned. The couple I had taken a picture of in front of the Elizabethan theater sat at a booth in front of the windows. They waved when they spotted me. I returned their greeting and made a beeline for my office.

I called Thomas and left a message about Pam, then

I tried the Professor. He didn't answer either, so I left a message for him too. I didn't want to believe that Pam was a killer, but I couldn't ignore the possibility.

The morning passed in a blur. I circulated the dining room with pots of hot coffee and delivered pesto-and-egg croissants with thick-sliced bacon. Not even Bethany's enthusiasm over our skyrocketing social media numbers could shake me from my funk.

I went through the motions as the morning wore into the afternoon. Sterling's fragrant vegetable minestrone was a hit, as were the oatmeal lace cookies and Andy's accompanying latte. Sequoia continued to encourage customers to try her cheese tea, and even had a handful of takers. I kept my cell phone close by, anticipating that Thomas or the Professor would call, but it never rang.

Rosa swept into the kitchen in the late afternoon with a tray of empty soup bowls and sandwich plates. "This lunch was a winner. The customers very much enjoyed the soup."

"Did we sell more of the vegetarian or the meat?" I asked.

"We sold out of both." She pressed her fingers to her lips and blew a kiss to Sterling and Marty. "Our wonderful cooks have done very good work."

"That's what we like to hear."

"I did a count of the tickets for the Sunday Supper and it too is sold out," Rosa added.

"Great."

"Maybe you will consider expanding the suppers? You could host them at the winery in the summer when it is warm. We would often have outdoor dinners at the B and B. Our guests enjoyed getting to sit by the gas fireplace and eat under the stars." Rosa's soft brown curls framed her heart-shaped face. "I would be happy to help if you decide it's something you'd like to try."

"That would be great," I said with a smile. I was thrilled that the new staff were fitting in so well, and that Rosa felt comfortable suggesting new ideas. Uva would be the perfect space to host summer farm-to-table dinners. Our Sunday Suppers at Torte were cozy and intimate whereas at the winery we could set up large picnic tables and double or triple the number of guests. I would have to add it to my ever-growing to-do list.

With lunch service complete, I wandered over to A Rose by Any Other Name to place our order for flowers for tomorrow's event. It was such a relief to have Torte running smoothly. I was irritated with myself for not hiring more staff sooner, but in the same breath reminded myself that there would have been no way to cram Rosa, Marty, and Sequoia into our old space.

At the flower shop, Thomas's mom suggested red roses, artichoke hearts, eucalyptus leaves, and white hydrangeas to capture the rustic, Italian vibe of the dinner. I loved adding some extra touches to the dinners like flowers, candles, and plenty of wine.

At least preparing tomorrow night's feast would give my mind respite. My cell phone rang on the walk back to Torte. Finally, the Professor or Thomas was returning my call.

Alas, it was Lance.

"Where are you?" he asked without waiting for me to answer.

"A Rose by Any Other Name."

"Wait there. Don't move a muscle. I'll be there in five minutes."

"Why?" He hung up.

Less than five minutes later, Lance's car sped up to the curb. "Get in."

"Where are we going?"

He threw open the passenger door. "Get in, darling. Time is wasting."

I got into the car. "Where are you taking me?"

His face held a puckish delight. "Anna Mill's house."

"What?" I considered opening the car door, even though we were already moving. "We can't go back there."

"Relax, relax. I've taken care of it." Lance looked regal as always. He wore a pair of tailored teal shorts, a gray shirt, and matching loafers. Not many men could pull off teal shorts, but Lance wasn't like most men.

"Taken care of what?" I fumbled through my purse in search of my sunglasses.

"Of everything, darling."

"But the social worker. I already talked to her. They were going out to do their assessment earlier. Thomas made me promise that we wouldn't snoop again. I told you all of this."

Lance cranked the air-conditioning to high. "I know. Don't worry your pretty little head. I made my own phone call to the social worker. I explained my position and my connection to Anna."

"What connection?" I found my sunglasses and put them on. The glare from the afternoon sun made my eyes hurt.

"That her house is a treasure trove of invaluable Oregon Shakespeare Festival history."

"Lance, stop!" I shouted for him to brake for a family of deer crossing the street.

"Damn, deer." He pressed the brake just in time. The deer trotted across unscathed.

"No more schemes, remember?" I shot him my best scolding look.

"This isn't a scheme. We're simply going to take a look around the property. We'll scour every room and corner for any valuable items that might hold historical significance and then I'll report back to the social worker." He pointed to a massive magnolia tree. "It's like that gorgeously devastating tree. Did you know that it's officially on the historical registry? It's one of Ashland's oldest trees. Planted in 1880. The state deemed it a heritage tree a few years ago thanks to a wise homeowner who did some sleuthing into the tree's past. When she learned that the tree had been planted by one of Ashland's original political powerhouses, the tree's status shot up and it's now to be preserved forever. That's exactly what we're doing for Anna Mill. You should consider it your civic duty."

I stared at the magnolia's shiny leaves. "I don't understand. How are we going to get in? Anna will never let us in, especially after involving the authorities."

"Don't worry. It's all taken care of. Anna is safe and sound. I personally chipped in for a full spa day for her, followed by a shopping excursion, and the very best of housecleaning teams who will sort and scrub every inch of the farmhouse. The house is vacant. The social worker and my hired team did their initial intake assessment earlier. They'll begin going through the house later in the week, but they have deemed it unfit for living in, which means it's sitting there empty. Waiting with eager anticipation for us to come along and allow the house to spill its secrets."

"Lance, this is a terrible idea in a string of terrible ideas."

"No, it's a golden opportunity that we need to seize. You're missing the key point here. Don't get stuck in the details, darling. Think about the big picture. We are on a mission to preserve the past."

I sighed and stared out the window. Lance changed the topic. "Do tell, what's the news with your staff? I heard word of a Sunday Supper." He unclutched the wheel momentarily to clap.

It was futile to argue. I told him about Andy's decision to drop out of school and Sequoia's unique drink ideas while we drove past organic farmlands and wound through twisting mountainous curves.

A notice had been posted on Anna's fence and front door warning of NO TRESPASSING when we arrived.

"Lance." I pointed to the sign.

"That's for strangers. We're here on official business, remember?"

"We're going to end up in jail."

He shuddered. "Banish the thought. I've done my time. Never again. Never. As I said, Anna's social worker knows that I'm here."

"She thinks that you're here to recover OSF documents, not snoop through an old woman's personal items."

"Details, darling. Details." He carefully placed each

toe on the gravel to avoid getting dirt or dust on his leather loafers.

Lance opened the creaky door. "The question is where to start."

"We don't even know what we're looking for."

"Anything on George's disappearance." Lance held the door for me. "Why don't you start with the papers in the dining room and I'll tackle the office?"

"For the record, this is a bad idea."

"Noted. Now, on with you. The faster those pastry fingers search the faster we'll be out of here."

Getting out of Anna's house was motivation enough for me.

"Lance, finding anything about George in the ten-foot-high stacks of newspapers is going to be an impossible job." I pointed to the towering stack of papers. "Why don't we go to the library or the historical society?"

"What? Please, that would take all the fun out of sleuthing." He blew me a kiss. "Good luck. I'll be in the office."

I started by sorting the piles. It didn't appear that Anna had had a system for stacking the discarded papers. Dates ranged from the 1950s to the 1970s in the same stack. I didn't want to sit on the floor for fear of contracting a virus, so I removed all the stacks from the dining room table and worked my way around the room. I piled papers by decade.

It was hard to concentrate. The room was musty and thick with the smell of old newsprint and mold. Not to mention the fact that my pulse pounded in my chest as I leafed through Anna's discarded newspapers. Lance had been known to stretch the truth in the past. Had he even asked permission of the social worker? What if someone from the state or the police came by and caught us?

Sweat dripped down my neck as I scanned each paper. Anna's house, like the homeless council's headquarters, had been built long before the invention of air-conditioning. The afternoon heat was sweltering. I willed myself to work faster.

"Find anything yet?" Lance called from the office about a half hour later.

"No. What about you?"

He appeared in the door frame. The heat must have been affecting him too. His usually pale cheeks were red and dewy, and his shirt was splotched with sweat. "That depends on what you consider anything."

"You found something about George?" I perked up. "Thank goodness, because it's miserable in here."

"I know. How could the poor woman live like this?" He fanned his face. "Alas I've yet to find anything on our dear departed George, but I found an old playbill from a production at OSF that starred Ginger Rogers. As I suspected there's a treasure trove of history from the Rogue Valley in here."

"Don't take anything," I cautioned him.

"I won't. But I am going to begin cataloging a pile that OSF will likely be very interested in acquiring."

"Yes, and the instructions were NOT to take anything, right?"

Lance let out an exasperated sigh. "Always the stickler for rules, Juliet. Always."

My fingers were black from the newsprint residue.

My shoulders ached, and I was starving. I realized I hadn't eaten lunch. My eyes started to burn, as I had to squint to make out the year on some of the papers that had been badly damaged by water over the years.

The smell of mildew was giving me a headache. I wanted to quit. For a change of pace, I walked to the closet and opened it. I should have looked there much sooner. Stacked in the dusty closet were dozens of paintings. I recognized the artist immediately—Henry. Like some of his more modern paintings I had seen, these were of dismembered body parts. A yellowed letter was taped to one of the paintings. It read: "To Anna, my one and only love."

Chapter Twenty-five

"Lance! I found something," I yelled. The letter felt like it was burning my fingertips.

He dashed into the dining room. "What?"

Everything felt like it was moving in slow motion as I showed him the letter.

"Don't just stand there. Open it."

My mind swirled through every conversation I had had in the past two weeks. I flashed back to the fateful afternoon at Emigrant Lake when Hannah and Ellen had recovered George's skull. I thought about everyone whom I had suspected and wanted to kick myself for not trusting my first instincts.

"Juliet, read the letter."

I peeled open the envelope. The letter was written in gorgeous calligraphy—obviously by an artistic hand. In it, Henry professed his love for Anna, begging her to run away with him and leave her family and brother behind. Had he lied to me about Edgar being in love with Anna? He had been in love with her.

"My God." I handed Lance the letter.

"What does it mean?" Lance stared at me with eager anticipation.

"Give me a minute. It's right on the tip of my brain." I closed my eyes for a minute and tried to center my thoughts. I blocked out the stuffy room, the dank smell, and the fact that I felt like I was trapped in a sauna. The word "connection" repeated again and again in my mind.

"The two cases are connected," I said to Lance. "They had to have been from the start, but the issues over Edgar's property distracted us. Edgar's murder was never about the lot or property."

"Okay, go on."

"I think Henry killed George because of Anna. Edgar must have known. The question is, was he involved somehow and living with guilt, or did he suspect that Henry had killed his friend but could never prove it because there wasn't a body? When Hannah and Ellen found George's skull at the bottom of the lake, Edgar finally had proof. Henry must have gotten desperate. He had to kill Edgar to keep him silent. If there was a body, Edgar could go to the police and tell him what he knew and had been keeping quiet all of these years. Henry has a heart problem. He told me the other day that he had to go take his medication. They had a drink together every night. It would have been so easy to slip some of his heart medicine into Edgar's drink."

"My God, Juliet, I think you've cracked the case." He swept sweat from his forehead with the back of his hand.

"Why didn't I think of it sooner? I was just talking to my staff this morning about learning to trust their instincts. My instincts told me from the beginning that the cases must be connected, but this entire time I've been so focused on the lot. I was sure that Edgar's real estate was the killer's motive for murder, but I was wrong. It didn't have anything to do with the lot."

Lance whipped out his cell phone.

"What are you doing?" I asked.

"Calling the police."

My mouth must have hung open. Lance never called the police. He lived for a big reveal. I was always the one who had to convince him that we needed to loop Thomas or the Professor in.

He handed me the phone. "It's Thomas. Tell him everything you said to me. Spare no detail. You were brilliant, darling. Absolutely brilliant. A pastry maven and murder-solving mastermind."

"You can drop that phone." A loud voice echoed behind us. I was so startled that I did drop the phone.

I turned to see Henry standing in the doorway holding Anna's gun. He blocked the doorway

"Henry. What are you doing here?"

"Coming for you." He positioned the gun directly at me. My heart rate spiked. How did he know we were here?

Lance threw his arms up. "Let's all take a step back and calm down. There's no need for a gun. Juliet and I were just on our way out." He started to take a step toward Henry.

"You're not going anywhere." Henry shifted the gun toward Lance, then he held it at eye level and nodded at the letter in my hand. "Drop the letter on the floor and both of you move back against the wall."

Lance and I complied with his command. I pressed

my back up against the tattered dining room wallpaper. I kept one eye on Henry and scanned the room for any potential weapon.

"Stay calm," Lance whispered through clenched teeth. "Keep him occupied."

"I don't understand. How did you know we were here?" My voice quivered. If my theory was correct, Henry had killed two people. What would stop him from killing us?

"I've been watching you. For someone who makes pastry, you sure ask a lot of questions. You should have listened earlier when I told you the past needs to stay in the past." His eyes were hard, but they were strangely clear and focused, which sent my stomach swirling. "I followed you out here. Should have stayed out of it, but you kept snooping."

I placed one hand on my stomach in an attempt to quell my nerves. "So did you lie about Edgar being in love with Anna?"

Lance had scooted slightly toward the dining room table.

Henry moved closer to me and placed his foot over the letter. "No. Edgar loved her too. He didn't have a chance. I loved her more. He took her to prom, but she was in love with me. I was the one she would sneak off with every night. George found out. We got in a fight. I didn't mean to kill him. It was an accident, but a well-timed one. He had already been going on about protesting the loss of that dirtbag of a town, Klamath Junction. I dumped his body in the abandoned auto shop and let Mother Nature take care of the rest. I started the rumor that he left town. No one was ever the wiser, except Edgar."

Lance muttered something under his breath that I couldn't understand.

"Edgar knew?"

"He suspected, but he never had proof. I made sure of that, until those two girls went and ruined everything."

"But why now? And why come get the letter from Anna?" I realized that Lance was slowly working his way toward one of the dining room chairs. I had to keep Henry talking.

"Edgar told me he was going to see Anna and then to the police. I had to kill him."

"You were going to kill Anna too?" The overstuffed room was beginning to feel claustrophobic.

"No. I still love her. I would never hurt her."

"You told me that you were married and that your wife died."

Henry shifted the gun. He hadn't noticed that Lance was almost parallel with him. "That doesn't mean I didn't love Anna. I told her she should run away with me, but she wouldn't listen. She said she loved Edgar. I knew that wasn't true. She never looked at me the same after George disappeared."

Sweat poured from the palms of my hands. Anna's musty house felt like it was closing in on me.

Lance motioned for me to keep talking. He was inches away from the chair.

"Did she know that you killed her brother?"

"No. I was there to console her when George went

missing." He let out a half chuckle that sent a cold shiver down my spine. "She thought her family was cursed. Moved out here and lived alone all these years. We could have been together."

Lance picked up a chair. In a flash he slammed the chair on the side of Henry's head. I shielded my face and ducked in anticipation of a gunshot, but nothing happened. I looked up to see Henry facedown on the carpet.

I couldn't move. My feet felt like they were cemented to the stained green carpet. "Thank God, Lance. You move like a cat. I don't think Henry ever noticed."

"Teamwork, darling." Lance held out his hands. His fingers were shaking like crazy. "I think it's time to call the police."

Chapter Twenty-six

I reached for Lance's phone, while he picked up the gun and placed it on the dining room table. I'm not even sure what I said to Thomas, but whatever it was it must have worked because within minutes the sound of sirens wailed nearby. Lance clutched the chair that he had used to knock Henry out. When the first police officers arrived on the scene, Lance was still hovering over Henry with the chair ready to strike. "We'll take it from here, sir," one of the officers said, prying the chair from Lance's hands.

They had us sit and drink some water. Shortly after, Thomas appeared. He was wearing his typical summer uniform of navy blue shorts. "Guys, seriously?" He surveyed the scene, making sure that the first responders had Henry contained before coming over to take our statements.

"You better start from the beginning," he said, pulling out a rickety dining room chair and straddling it backward.

"Juliet figured it out," Lance said. I noticed his hands were still shaky. "It was quite masterful if you ask me."

Thomas took notes on his iPad while Lance and I relayed what had happened. When we finished he let out a sigh. "I don't approve that you took matters into your own hands, but I will say it was synchronistic timing. We were on our way to meet the Professor at Henry's place. He obtained a warrant for his arrest."

"You guys knew?" I felt a twinge of disappointment.

Two police officers restrained Henry, who had begun to come to.

"Go ahead and take him out to the car," Thomas said to his colleagues.

Lance placed his hand on my knee. I squeezed it.

Thomas returned his attention to us as the two uniformed police officers lifted Henry and escorted him out of the dining room. "Not until today. The Professor has been looking into potential connections with the two cases, but I thought it was someone who wanted the lot too." Thomas clicked off his iPad. "Look, I need to go. I'm supposed to be on my way. I'll fill you in after we process Henry."

Lance tapped my chin after Thomas left. "Cheekbones, darling. Hold your head high."

"Can you imagine what that must have been like for Edgar? Knowing that your friend was probably a killer for all these years and keeping that inside?"

"The question is why? Body or no body, why didn't he share his suspicions sooner?"

"Maybe Henry paid him off? Blackmail."

"It's possible." Lance brushed dust from his damp shirt. "I think we've seen enough for today, shall we make our exit? I think an ice-cold martini or two is in order."

"Yeah, Ashland is calling." I followed him to the car.

I felt a sense of closure knowing that Henry would see justice, but I still had so many questions. Hopefully Thomas and the Professor would be able to fill in some of the gaps.

Back in Ashland, Lance steered us straight to Puck's Pub. He swept inside with his usual flourish. "One martini, ice-cold, and a glass of your coldest brew for the lady."

"How did you know I was going to order a beer?"

"Please." He rolled his eyes and dragged me to a table in the back of the cozy pub that was designed to resemble an Elizabethan forest. Stepping into Puck's made me feel like I was entering scene from *Midsummer Night's Dream* with its twinkly lights, old-world-style wooden keg barrels and tap handles, and fake greenery that decorated the ceiling.

Our drinks arrived as we sat down. Sometimes it paid to be pals with one of Ashland's celebrities.

"To us, darling. Yet another case closed." Lance lifted his martini glass and clinked it to my frothy pint glass.

"Why don't I feel like celebrating?" I held the cool pint glass. The beer had a bright hoppy scent with notes of citrus.

"This particular case had a certain melancholy. A palpable sadness about it." He popped an olive from his drink into his mouth. "There's no need to look so glum. Justice will be served. The dead will get their due."

His words brought me little comfort.

I nodded. A waiter came by to take our order.

"Dinner?" Lance asked, catching my eye.

"Yes. I'm famished."

"In that case bring us an order of your world-famous turkey legs," Lance said to the waiter.

"I'm not that hungry." Puck's was known for their turkey-leg dinner, served on a platter fit for a king. It came with heaping mounds of smashed potatoes, vegetables, cheeses, breads, and a turkey leg the size of both my arms put together.

"We'll share." Lance shooed the waiter away.

"I can't stop wondering—assuming our theory is right—why Edgar never told anyone."

Lance closed his eyes. Then he took a lengthy sip of his martini. "We won't be able to discuss anything else until your unrelenting questions are put to rest. True?"

I shrugged. "Probably."

"Excuse me for one moment, then." He stood and ducked out the back entrance. Less than a minute later he returned. "Problem solved. The cavalry is on their way."

"What?"

"Thomas. He and Detective Kerry are on their way."

"I thought they were processing Henry's arrest."

"Must have gone smoothly. He said they're at headquarters across the street and will be here in a flash."

Sure enough, before our turkey platter arrived Thomas and Detective Kerry made their way into the pub. Thomas wore his standard police uniform with dark navy shorts and a matching short-sleeved shirt. Kerry was still dressed for undercover work. Lance noted her wardrobe change immediately.

"My, my, Detective Kerry, you're quite fetching in that sundress. If I didn't know better, I would think you were one of the coeds."

She shot me a dirty look. I could tell she thought I had shared her secret.

I shook my head in response. I had kept my promise, and never made mention of her assignment to Lance.

"It's the weekend," she said, trying to sound nonchalant.

Lance looked skeptical, but he changed the subject. "Since Juliet and I consulted on this case, will you please share what you've learned from Henry and put Juliet—and subsequently me—out of her misery?"

Consulting on the case? I watched Thomas and Detective Kerry for their reaction. They ignored Lance.

Thomas leaned forward. "What do you want to know? We'll tell you what we can. Which may not be much."

"Did Henry admit to killing Edgar?" I asked.

"No. Not to us." Thomas frowned. "We have substantial evidence linking him to the crime. We're fairly confident that we have enough for a conviction."

"What about George Mill?" I wasn't even trying to mask my desperation.

Detective Kerry answered. "We're working on it. We have a witness to the crime who is reluctant but we think will be forthcoming with more information as time goes on."

"Anna Mill?"

"I'm not at liberty to answer that." She pursed her lips.

The waiter delivered our turkey leg. He asked if Thomas or Kerry wanted a drink. They declined. Thomas flashed his badge. "On duty."

"Soda's on the house, then," the waiter offered, and

returned with extra plates and silverware and two sodas in pewter steins for Thomas and Kerry.

"Are you working under the assumption that Henry killed George Mill and Edgar knew, but stayed silent for some reason? That's what Henry told us. We can testify if you need us to, right, Lance?" I helped myself to a slice of sharp Irish cheddar and a few black olives.

Lance gave them a salute. "At your service."

"We don't work under assumptions. We work with facts and evidence." Kerry plunged a straw into her root beer. "But, yes, you may be called to testify."

"Oh, don't give Juliet the company line," Lance scolded. "It's *us* you're talking to. You don't have to spill all the gory details, but you must have a working theory. Do you think that Edgar was a conspirator or a poor, lonely victim?"

Kerry sipped her soda. I caught the slightest glance between her and Thomas. Whatever code they had communicated, it must have given him the green light to share.

"We're building our case for the DA. Like I mentioned there's substantial, credible evidence against Henry. We don't yet have confirmation as to why Edgar didn't alert the authorities. Hopefully as we scour financial records and interview witnesses a clearer picture of what happened in the 1960s will emerge. The Professor has been sifting through old articles and paperwork. He has two thoughts."

"Which are?" I interrupted.

Thomas took a drink of soda. "Basically what you told us. If he was involved—directly or indirectly—maybe the discovery of George's remains made him have a change of heart. Edgar was nearing the end of his life. Maybe he wanted a clear conscience before meeting his maker. It's been known to happen. If that's the case, it's likely that he told Henry that he was going to come forward with a confession. That was his mistake. Henry couldn't let the truth come out, so he killed him before Edgar had a chance to contact us."

Lance shaved a piece of turkey off the leg with his knife. "Tragic."

"What's the other theory?" I asked.

Detective Kerry answered. "It's also possible that Edgar never knew that Henry was the killer. Perhaps he wondered but chose to believe that George disappeared."

"And finding the skull changed that?"

She nodded. "Or Edgar suspected Henry and confronted him. In return Henry bribed him or paid him off to keep quiet. Edgar went along with it because he never had proof, but the discovery of George's body changed that."

"Either way you think Edgar was involved?" I asked, taking a sip of my beer.

"I'd say that your instinct is probably right," Kerry replied. "However, if Edgar had been bribed for his silence, we'll find a record of money somewhere."

"That's the spirit." Lance applauded her. "I knew it was only a matter of time before the four of us would get along swimmingly."

Kerry gave him a hard stare.

"Too soon?" Lance teased.

I kicked him under the table. "The Professor mentioned something about George Mill staying put when the lake was expanded. That one of the theories surrounding his disappearance was that he had refused to leave his property, but that he had listed it for sale. Could the sale of his property be tied to Henry? Does any of this ring a bell?"

Kerry tapped her fingers on the edge of her pewter stein. "Like I said, Doug has been in contact with the historical society and has spent hours reviewing old notes from when the missing persons case was first filed in the 1960s. He never found any evidence of a sale, or of any witnesses other than Henry and Edgar, claiming George was going to stay on the family homestead no matter what. The land would have been worthless, since it now sits underwater. That was obviously a rumor started by Henry; as for tracking the sale of the property, I don't have answers yet."

Another wave of sadness came over me. "It's bizarre that no one ever searched further for George."

"I wouldn't say that," Kerry replied. "The lead detective back in the day was convinced that there was more involved in George's disappearance. This was the sixties though here in remote southern Oregon. They conducted a search of the lake and never found anything. He brought Edgar, Henry, and Anna in multiple times for questioning. Considered all of them persons of interest in the case. They were brought in for further questioning on two occasions. Once in the early eighties and once in the late nineties. Both times when new detectives reviewed the cold case. Indictment for murder without a body is tough. Historically it has been done a few times, but it's extremely difficult."

"Yeah, no body and no modern technology." Thomas

clicked on his phone. "Now we have apps, modern science, and a forensic team." He polished off his drink and stood. "We should probably head out. We have other duties, right?"

They shared another veiled look, then Kerry nodded. "Yes."

"Thanks for the update. I really appreciate it," I said as they started to leave.

"Don't spread it around." Kerry smiled.

"She's becoming most interesting," Lance said after they made their exit. "I do believe she likes us."

I had to agree. Detective Kerry was definitely warming up. We finished our dinner. A wave of relief came over me. There were still questions that I was hoping we might eventually have answered, but for tonight I could sleep peacefully knowing that my beloved Ashland was safe.

Chapter Twenty-seven

Sunday dawned bright the next morning. I woke refreshed from a decent night's sleep, and eager to reinstate our Sunday Supper. When I arrived at Torte, I was surprised to find Mom already in the kitchen kneading bread dough.

"What are you doing here?" I called over the sound of Bach playing overhead. Mom's hearing had diminished from years of exposure to industrial mixers and the constant noise of customers and clattering plates and cups.

She pointed to the speakers and then to her ears.

I turned down the music. "What are you doing here?" I repeated.

"Some greeting. I thought you would be happy to see me."

"I am. I am." I wrapped her in a hug.

She pretended that she was going to touch me with her flour-coated hands. "I needed some time alone with the dough. I couldn't sleep last night. And I was in the mood for brioche. It's the perfect slow Sunday bread, don't you think?"

"You had me at brioche," I said, walking to the sink to wash my hands with rosemary-lemon soap.

"You heard the news about Henry, right?" Mom painted the yeast loaves with melted butter, and then slid them into the ovens.

"Yeah. Thomas and Detective Kerry filled me and Lance in last night. Such a sad outcome." I grabbed an apron from a hook.

Mom brushed flour from her apron. "Long-held secrets do the most destruction."

"I'm sorry you couldn't sleep. Was the Professor upset?"

"No. I think he feels relieved knowing that there's finality and he can offer some closure to Anna Mill and everyone involved. I couldn't sleep because I have some big news." A smile burst across her face.

"The house?"

She nodded enthusiastically. "We got it!"

"Mom, that's so great." I wrapped her in another hug, not caring if she got flour all over me. "What's the next step? When will you move in?"

"There are a few things that have to happen first, the inspection and appraisal. If everything goes according to plan we should take possession early next month."

"Just in time to sit in your new dining room and watch the leaves shift to fall." I squeezed her shoulders. "I'm so happy for you. Is the Professor excited?"

"He's over the moon. I don't know how I'm going to keep him occupied for the next month. We went for a late-night drive after he finished processing the necessary paperwork to see it by the light of a half-moon."

I could picture the Professor doing just that.

"You know our offer still stands. The house is yours if you want it. I won't pressure you, but if you don't want it we'll plan to put it on the market after we get everything moved out. Maybe in late September. Doug and I also discussed renting it if you don't want it."

"I want it!" I couldn't believe those words had escaped my mouth. Hearing them aloud confirmed it. I did want the house. I was ready for permanent roots. And there was the added bonus of space. If Carlos and Ramiro ended up in Ashland they couldn't stay in my tiny apartment.

"You do?" Mom's mouth hung wide open. "Are you sure? Honey, my feelings will not be hurt. Promise me you're not doing this for me."

"I'm not. Honestly. Until this very moment I wasn't sure. I've been thinking about it, but it's kind of fallen to the back of my mind. Hearing that you and the Professor have found your dream house and knowing that I can continue our family legacy in the house is almost too good to be true."

"This means we both have some packing to do." Mom stood on her tiptoes to kiss my cheek. "I can't wait to tell Doug. He's going to be thrilled."

"We'll have to spend some time going through the old house. I'm not taking all of the furniture. Doug and I have doubles of so many things. You can keep whatever you want."

"Thanks. I'll definitely take you up on that." When I had returned to Ashland, Mom had helped me find a temporary rental. I hadn't needed much—a bed, small kitchen, bathroom, and living room. My apartment had come furnished and since I'd been home I had acquired very little in the way of material goods. I spent so much time at Torte that I hadn't spent much time decorating my place. For my entire career on the ship, I'd been able to fit everything I owned in a couple suitcases. That hadn't really changed in Ashland. Packing for me would involve my clothes, my collection of cookbooks, and a few special mementos that I had acquired over my years of travel.

"Excellent." Mom put a finger to her lips, leaving a smudge of flour on her chin. "We're going to need to do some shopping for you. How fun."

Her enthusiasm was contagious. The smell of the buttery sweet bread perked up my senses. While we molded more loaves of bread dough together we discussed house plans.

When I removed the first batch of brioche from the oven, I knew right away what I wanted to bake for our Sunday brunch menu. Sundays in the bakeshop held an unhurried pace. Sure, there were the occasional customers who raced in for a latte to go, but most Sunday guests lingered over pots of French press and our rotating brunch items. Some weeks we served egg frittatas, other times we served chicken and waffles, or a crowd-favorite biscuits and gravy. This morning I would use Mom's brioche as the base for a decadent breakfast sandwich—the fluffernutter.

The fluffernutter consists of peanut butter and marshmallow fluff smeared in gooey layers between white bread. I would take our own spin on the retro sandwich with a sweet and a savory option. I started by grabbing peanut butter and Nutella from the pantry. I mixed them together on medium speed until they had whipped into a creamy chocolaty goodness. I dipped my pinkie into the airy mixture and swooned at the nutty-chocolate flavor.

Next, I followed suit, blending cream cheese, marshmallow fluff, and vanilla bean. The creamy mixture reminded me of pillowy white clouds. For the sweet option, I sliced bananas in half and soaked them in bourbon syrup. For the savory option, Mom fried bacon on the stove and set it aside to cool.

It had been a while since Mom and I had worked alone in the kitchen.

"This is like old times, honey," she said, breaking off a piece of the salty maple-cured bacon and offering it to me. "We should make this our new tradition. Sunday-morning baking sessions. Just the two of us. Before everyone else arrives. What do you say?'

"Count me in." I savored the morsel of crispy bacon. It was the perfect accompaniment for the sweet fluffernutter sandwich.

With the bananas, bacon, and fillings ready to go it was time to begin assembling the sandwiches. I sliced thick pieces of the brioche and Mom submerged them in an egg mixture with a touch of cinnamon and nutmeg. Then I melted butter in a sauté pan on the stove. I browned each side of the eggy bread and removed it from the heat. Mom slathered the peanut butter and Nutella mixture on one slice while I coated another slice with the marshmallow cream. We made a few of each version of the fluffernutters to share with the team when they arrived.

"Juliet, can I ask you something?" Mom said, stacking a sandwich on a plate.

"Yeah, anything." I stared at her.

She hesitated for a moment.

"Is it about the house?" I turned the burner to low to allow the fluffernutter to crisp.

"No. Not exactly." Her face clouded. "It's about you. I'm worried about you, honey."

I started to protest.

She held out her arms. "I know. I know what you're going to say. You're fine. But I can see it in your eyes. You're conflicted. About Carlos, aren't you?"

How did she always know exactly the thing to say to cut through to my core?

"Mom, I feel like I've been conflicted forever. Since I left the ship." I sighed.

"That could be true, but you haven't been home for that long. In the scheme of your life, your time here in Ashland again has been a tiny blip on the radar."

"Yes, but this entire time I've been back and forth and back and forth about what to do. Not knowing what's next for us is making me crazy." I flipped the sandwich.

She buttered a slice of brioche. "What if you gave yourself a break? What if you tried to embrace the not knowing?"

I made a grunting sound. "Embrace the not knowing? That's exactly what I've been doing."

"You haven't embraced it. You've fought it. Fought for *the* answer. Sometimes there isn't one answer. There are many." She locked her warm, walnut eyes on me. "You know, losing your father brought me an unexpected gift. The gift of uncertainty. After he died I had no idea what would be next for us. I didn't know if I could keep the bakeshop. If I could run it alone. I didn't know how you would fare in the face of grief. Many nights I cried myself to sleep after you went to bed from the weight of it all."

I reached for her hand. "I didn't know that."

Her eyes were moist. "I didn't want you to know. It was my job as your mother to spare you from the burden of my own grief. That wasn't for you to carry. You had enough of your own, and you were learning how to become an independent young woman at the time."

I swallowed twice.

"One night about a year after he died, I was up late. It was after two o'clock in the morning and I was missing him desperately. I was at the end of my rope. There were so many choices I had to make—whether to hire help, if I should keep the house or have you and me move into something smaller. We had had so many plans for Torte and suddenly none of them made sense." She paused and handed me a stack of buttered brioche. "I was worried about you too. You were so focused on school and Thomas that I was afraid you were shoving your grief inside. In any event, I got up and went into the kitchen to make myself a cup of tea. While I was waiting for the water to boil, I had the strongest moment of clarity that I've ever had in my life. I heard your dad's voice in my head, saying, 'Helen, "All other doubts, by time let them be clear'd: Fortune brings in some boats that are not steer'd."' His voice was so real. I never finished making the tea. I had to go look up the quote to see if it was real or if I was imagining things. It's Shakespeare. What did it mean? I was furious that night. If he had come to comfort me, why do it with Shakespeare?"

"Because that's so Dad," I said, brushing away a tear as I smiled.

"Exactly." She threw her arms up in surrender. "That's exactly how your dad would have come to comfort me. The next morning it was as if everything appeared different. I repeated the words again and again, and suddenly I had a new understanding. My plans were just that—plans. They weren't etched in stone or promised to me. There was something so freeing about knowing that. In the years since I've never had another experience like that night. Maybe because I never needed it. Your father, in my darkest moment, brought me the gift of understanding that sometimes the best—and worst—moments in our lives can come to us without planning, without direction, without even trying. Sometimes it's up to fate."

"Wow." I removed the pan from the stove and placed the first sandwich on a cooking rack. "Why haven't you ever told me this before?"

"I never thought you needed to hear it until now."

"So, are you trying to tell me that I should let Carlos come?"

She placed her hand over her heart. "I didn't say that, honey. That's up to you, but what I'm trying to say is that there are no wrong choices. That it's okay not knowing. Be gentle with yourself, and let things unfold."

"I'll try."

She kissed my cheek. "Good." Then she brushed her hands together. "Now, it looks like we have a serious stack of fluffernutters that we've been neglecting."

We returned to grilling the whimsical sandwiches. Mom's story rang in my head. Should I allow Carlos to steer his ship to my harbor and release my worries about our future to the sea?

Chapter Twenty-eight

Within minutes of everyone's arrival they sniffed out the ambrosial smells coming from the kitchen. Marty was the first to arrive. He took one look at the plate of fluff-ernutter sandwiches and pretended to faint. "Those sweet babies make my teeth itch. Watch out or that plate might disappear."

The group consensus was that the fluffernutters were a slice of nostalgic, gooey heaven on a plate and should be served with a pile of napkins and a fork. Mom and I asked for feedback on whether everyone preferred the bananas or bacon.

"Both," Andy and Bethany shouted in unison.

We opted to give our customers three choices. The classic fluffernutter with bananas, a bacon-nutter, and the double dare with layers of both smashed together with oozing marshmallow cream and melting peanut butter sauce.

As the team scarfed down every last crumb we went over the schedule for the day and Mom shared her house news. Everyone was equally excited about Mom's news, which offered a buffer for Andy to come clean with her about his decision to drop out of school.

"Hey, Mrs. C. Wait, I mean Mrs. The Professor. Do you have a minute?" He had come downstairs to grab extra bags of coffee beans. "There's something I need to talk to you about."

"Of course." Mom untied her apron. "Shall we go talk in the office?"

"That would be great." Andy caught my eye and crossed his fingers. I gave him an encouraging nod.

Meanwhile, Sterling, Marty, and I began preparations for the evening meal. Marty diced bulbs of garlic and chopped bundles of fresh rosemary for the focaccia bread we would serve with the chicken cacciatore. "If anyone had fears of vampires running free there's no need to worry now," Marty joked. "I think there's enough garlic here to ward off an army of vampires."

"You never know when an angry mob of vampires will descend on Torte," I bantered back.

"Isn't that every teenager with a cell phone these days?" Sterling asked.

"Touché."

He had assembled the ingredients for the cacciatore. "You're sure you're cool with trying to re-create my mom's recipe? It's not exactly a traditional version."

"Absolutely. That's what makes it even better."

Marty agreed. "Put us to work. We're at your bidding."

Sterling took quiet command of the kitchen. He assigned Marty to searing the chicken breasts in olive oil and garlic. "I'm going off memory, Jules," he said, opening cans of black olives. "I definitely remember olives, crushed tomatoes, sweet peppers, and lots of Italian spices, but I'm not sure what else. I pulled up a few traditional cacciatore recipes to use as a starting point."

"Perfect. Trust your instincts." I paused and chuckled internally at my own advice. Trusting my instincts had been the theme of the past days, weeks. I hoped that I could learn to continue to trust myself more when it came to my future.

Sterling jotted a couple of notes on the recipe. "And taste as I go, right?"

"And the apprentice becomes the master," I teased.

Marty passed by us with an armful of baguettes. "Master chef in the house, high five." He paused to give Sterling a high five.

Sterling returned the gesture.

"The kid has got the chops," Marty said to me. Then he ran one finger along his handlebar mustache. "And that's high praise from me."

I laughed.

"He's going to be one to watch. We're going to be able to say we knew him when. I see a James Beard award in his future, don't you think?"

"Absolutely."

Marty continued on with his crusty stack of bread. Sterling ran his fingers through his dark hair.

"See, I'm not the only one who thinks you're a natural talent."

He rolled his eyes. "We'll see, Jules. I have a lot to learn."

"So do I, but that's what makes this business fun."

Marty and Sterling cranked out dozens of fluffernutters. The double dare was by far the most popular. As the morning gave way to afternoon we shifted gears from sweet sandwiches to our Sunday Supper. Soon the smell of charred sweet peppers and caramelized onions wafted from the stove. Sterling added crushed tomatoes, olives, Italian parsley, basil, salt and pepper, and a touch of lemon juice to the sauce. "Taste it." He held out a spoon for me. "It needs something else."

I took a bite of the tangy sauce. It needed time to simmer in order for the flavors to marry and deepen, but from the first taste I could tell that we were on the right track. "What about a splash of white wine and balsamic vinegar?"

"Good suggestion." Sterling poured chilled wine and dark fig-infused balsamic vinegar into the bubbling sauce.

We tasted it again.

"That's it." He took another taste with his pinkie. "It's just like I remember."

His eyes became dewy. That was the ultimate gift of food. Its ability to transport us to another place or time. To evoke powerful memories with a simple bite.

"It will be even better once it simmers for a few hours," Marty said, poking holes in the focaccia dough. "Did you know that 'cacciatore' translates to 'hunter' in Italian?"

"No," Sterling and I said in unison.

"Yes, it's an old hunter's recipe. A hearty, rustic dish created with ingredients hunters would forage in the forests and then set to rest for an afternoon."

"We'll have to share that tidbit of history with our

guests tonight," I said. Then I glanced around the kitchen. The focaccia was ready to brush with olive oil, garlic, rosemary, and sea salt. We would bake it in the wood-fired oven to give it a smoky finish. The cacciatore would simmer for the next few hours. Right before dinner service we would boil spaghetti noodles, grate fresh Parmesan and Romano cheeses, and assemble the salad.

Marty and Sterling shifted gears to dessert. Bethany was tasked with baking more cookies to pair with the frozen custards.

"Everything is running like a well-oiled machine. I'm going to get started with setting up the dining room. Steph, can you help?"

She had finished the final custom cake order for the day. It was boxed and ready for pickup with the customer's name and order tag. I couldn't get over how smoothly things were running again after the renovation.

"Yeah." She didn't sound enthused but trudged after me.

The day had flown by. I hadn't had a chance to talk to Mom about her conversation with Andy.

"Did he tell you?" Steph jumped on her, the minute she spotted Mom.

"Yes." Mom kept her expression neutral. "I know you're upset, but Andy will be fine."

Steph grunted. The last lingering customers gathered their dishes and shut down their laptops when I flipped the sign on the front door to CLOSED.

"You don't need to hurry out," Mom assured a young woman who was still eating. "We're going to be rearranging furniture, but you're welcome to stay as long as you like."

The woman looked up and smiled. It was Gretchen. I excused myself from the preparations for a moment to go check in with her. She was finishing my Sunday-morning special—the fluffernutter sandwich.

"How is it?" I asked, pointing to the sandwich.

She tried to answer with a mouthful of thick brioche and peanut butter. I waited for her to swallow and wash the bite down with an iced latte. "This is the best thing I've eaten in my entire life. Who knew that bacon and bananas went together so well? If I could I would eat this every day."

"That's high praise." I grinned. "But I'm guessing your stomach might revolt at some point. These aren't exactly low-cal, low-sugar sandwiches."

Gretchen cut the sandwich with a fork. "It would be worth it." She dabbed peanut butter from the corner of her mouth. "I can see that you're setting up for something, so I won't keep you, but I did want to stop by to say thank you."

"Thank me for what?"

Gretchen licked gooey marshmallow from her fork. "For everything. If it weren't for you, we might not be about ready to make an announcement about our plans for the homeless village."

"What?" I was confused.

"Yeah. It was a strange twist of fate. I found a new partner. Thanks to you." Gretchen took a last bite of the melty masterpiece and then wiped her fingers on a napkin.

Note to self, the fluffernutter was a two-napkin sandwich.

"I don't understand."

Gretchen folded her napkin on the empty plate. "You see, when you told me about Edgar, I lost it. I've put every ounce of my soul into the plans for the village, and knowing that Edgar was dead meant that my plans would likely die with him. But then I bumped into Stella. I couldn't believe it, but she told me that she had a space on the south end of town that would be perfect for the village. She offered to work pro bono for us. It was like a gift from the gods."

"That's amazing." I was stunned by Gretchen's news. "What does that have to do with me though?"

"Stella overheard me talking to one of our donors about how wonderful Torte has been to us. I was sharing a story, like the one I shared with you, about how it's the small things that can make the biggest difference. Stella told me that her family struggled financially when she was younger. She was on free or reduced-price lunch at school and would receive a grocery bag with peanut butter and bread on the weekends. The Torte donations reminded her of a time when she received a pink box with chocolate cupcakes for her sister's birthday in the weekend lunch bags. She never knew who added the cupcakes, but the memory stuck with her."

"I had no idea."

"Neither did I. I thought Stella had a singular focus on money when we first met. To be honest I didn't like her much, so it was a complete shock when she showed up at my office and said she had a proposition for me." Gretchen tried to tame her wild curls. "Like I said, you never know what kind of lasting gift your pastries might give." She stood. "You'll have to come see the location.

We should be breaking ground within the next few weeks."

She gave me a genuine hug before she left. I couldn't believe that Stella Pryor had had a one-hundred-eighty-degree shift. Nonetheless it was great news for Gretchen and the transient community. The fact that Torte had been even a tiny piece of Stella's decision to partner with the homeless council left me on the verge of grateful tears.

Chapter Twenty-nine

After Gretchen left, I returned to helping Mom and Steph. We pushed chairs to the edge of the room and moved the two- and four-person tables together in the center to form one long communal table.

"Did you tell him it's a terrible idea?" Stephanie asked Mom. It was clear she wasn't going to let the subject go.

Mom wiped the table with a wet cloth. "No."

Stephanie scowled. She looked to the espresso bar, where Andy and Sequoia were cleaning and taking inventory for tomorrow's morning rush. "Why is everyone so chill about this?"

Mom's voice was soothing. "Because we're all afforded our own choices. We are the makers of our own destiny."

"Even if you're throwing your destiny away?"

"Even if." Mom walked over to Stephanie and placed her hand on her wrist. "You are a good friend to care this much about Andy, but he'll find his own way."

Stephanie didn't look convinced, but she dropped the

subject. We strung twinkle lights from the ceiling. Mom covered the table with a crisp white linen tablecloth.

A knock sounded at the door. I looked up to see Thomas waiting with a box of flowers.

"Are you going to let me in, or are you going make me stand here all day? These things are heavy, Jules." He flexed his toned arms as I opened the door for him.

"It's a good workout, right?"

"Where do you want these?" he asked.

The delicate, sweet scent of the flowers hit my nose. "Just put them on the counter for now. We're still setting up."

"I can see that." Thomas placed the box of flowers on the counter and then inhaled deeply. "What's on the menu tonight? Something smells amazing."

"Chicken cacciatore, rosemary and garlic focaccia, salad, and our new line of concretes and cookies."

Thomas pretended to stab himself. Then he tapped his badge. "Too bad I'm on duty tonight. Otherwise I'd beg my oldest friend for a seat at the table."

"You wouldn't have to beg. You know you're always welcome here."

"But begging is much more fun." He winked.

"Where's Detective Kerry?" I asked. Lately Thomas and Kerry had appeared glued at the hip. It had been a while since I'd seen one without the other. "Is she still working undercover?"

Thomas cleared his throat. "I'm not at liberty to comment on any open investigations."

"Got it."

"I do have some news though," Thomas started to

say. A buzzing sound originated from his chest. He removed his mini iPad from his pocket and clicked it on. "Just got a notification through the new app. Can you believe this? The app has generated over one hundred community responses since we made it live. We've had reports of missing cats, panhandling on the bricks, and of a suspicious van casing the Railroad District."

"A suspicious van?"

He flipped through the app. "Turned out to be a grandpa who was surprising his grandkids with a swing set he brought up from California. He got turned around thanks to the new construction in the Railroad District and couldn't find their house. A neighbor used the app to report that they kept seeing a van rolling up and down the street. We were able to respond within minutes and help deliver a brand-new swing set to some happy kids."

"That's great news."

He typed something on the iPad and then returned it to his pocket. "That's not my news. What I was going to tell you is that the Professor made it official. Kerry is no longer on a trial period. She's Ashland newest detective."

"Excellent. That really is great news." I meant it too. Detective Kerry had grown on me in recent weeks. "I like Detective Kerry."

"Me too, Jules." Thomas's voice caught for a brief second. "Me too." He glanced toward the dining room where Mom and Steph were dragging tables together. "Looks like you have work to do. I'll let you get to it."

"Thanks for the flowers." I walked him to the door. "Tell Detective Kerry congratulations from me. We'll have to have a celebratory drink soon."

He gave me a half salute. "Will do. And, yes, I know she would like that."

"It's a date," I called as he headed for the police station.

Detective Kerry was here to stay. I wondered if that meant the Professor was speeding up his retirement plans. I also wondered what she was working on at Southern Oregon University. Why the secrecy? There was no need to dwell on it tonight. I'd had enough secrecy and lies with Edgar's and George's murders to last me for a while.

I helped Mom and Steph finish assembling the tables and then placed the abundant centerpieces from A Rose by Any Other Name in the center. The red roses with touches of greenery gave the dining room a subtle elegance. Mom set out flatware, plates, and red napkins. Steph lit votive candles.

For a final touch, I opened bottles of red wine to let breathe and brought out two buckets of ice to chill the white wine.

We stood back and surveyed our work.

"Breathtaking," Mom said.

"Now we need the guests," I said.

"And food." Mom winked.

There was just enough time for us to run home to change and freshen up before the dinner. I hurried to my apartment. The tapestry that Mom and the Professor had bought for me in Greece sat wrapped in its original box. There was no need to unpack it now. I decided that it should be the first thing to adorn my new walls.

I ditched my baking clothes and pulled on a pleated sundress with spaghetti straps and a low, square neckline.

It fell to my ankles and its Turkish blue cotton fabric made my eyes look almost silvery. I paired the simple dress with strappy sandals and my favorite sapphire earrings. Then I twisted my hair into a messy bun. I dusted my cheeks with blush, added a touch of shimmering pink lip gloss, and finished my transformation with pale blue eye shadow and mascara.

I stood back and appraised myself in the mirror. Not bad, Jules.

Lance caught up with me as I made my way back to Torte.

"Darling, you look absolutely ravishing." He kissed the top of my hand. "It's a shame that you and I are destined to be nothing more than besties. We would make a devastatingly handsome couple, don't you think?" He twirled on the sidewalk. Then he swept his arm over his tailored suit with taped slacks and pin-striped tie.

"Such a shame," I joked. We linked arms and walked to Torte together.

The bakeshop glowed with happy warmth. A line queued outside. Mom opened the doors to the eager crowd. There were many familiar faces. Lance as always played the role of Ashland's regal set, moving with flourish and regaling his captive audience with tales of our recent discovery.

I circulated the table with bottles of wine. Stella, Malcolm, and Pam were seated together at the far end of the table.

"White or red?" I held up each bottle, and then filled their glasses.

"You've heard the news, haven't you?" Pam asked as I poured a lovely red Chianti into her glass.

"Heard the news? She broke the news." Malcolm sounded impressed. "Although she thought I did it."

I gave him a sheepish smile. "I was so sure that Edgar's death was connected to the sale of the lot. I got that totally wrong."

"We all did," Pam agreed.

Stella swirled her wine. I was glad that she had come to the dinner. Stella had puzzled me. Her actions didn't add up. She had wanted the lot for her own development, but then ended up selling it to Malcolm. I decided there was no time like the present to ask.

"To be honest, I thought you might have been involved at one point too, Stella. You never showed an ounce of emotion about Edgar's death and I couldn't figure out what your motive was with the property."

"Ha!" Malcom threw his head back. "Stella is a killer in the business."

She glared. "Because I had to be. I didn't have a choice. I started out in commercial real estate when I was the only woman in the entire Rogue Valley working in the field. I had to develop a steel exterior as a lone woman in an industry dominated by men."

Pam reached out her arm. Her red and teal bracelets jingled together. She was dressed for the evening in Torte colors with doughnut earrings. "You are a trailblazer, Stella."

Stella and Pam were about the same age, but that was where their similarities ended. Pam's cute style and warm personality were the opposite of Stella's, who as usual was dressed in black from head to toe and had mastered the art of keeping her face in a neutral, disinterested stare.

"I never asked to be a trailblazer. Like I said, I didn't have a choice." She addressed me. "As to your question about the lot. I'm always on the hunt for a new project, but when Malcolm came to me with the proposition that I could develop the parcel for OSF, I decided it was a win-win. It would be a good coup for my career to partner with OSF on the project, and I have bids on a number of other properties around town. Actually I've got my sights set on Talent and Phoenix right now. Anything on the outskirts of Ashland is booming. Costs are lower and there aren't the same city restrictions. If anyone is looking to invest, I would suggest heading north."

"What happens to the lot now?" I asked.

"It'll get turned over to the courts," Stella replied. "It's going to be a nightmare. Edgar signed contracts with multiple parties. I have no idea why, but it's going to be a mess."

"And Gretchen was telling the truth too?" I topped off Stella's wineglass. "Edgar signed a contract with the homeless council in addition to OSF?"

Stella's brows arched. "Terrible business decision, but yes. It appears that he did. I have a sense that Gretchen and the homeless council will land somewhere else soon. The city is definitely invested in finding a permanent solution to the housing crisis." I knew she was referring to her partnership with Gretchen, but she didn't expand. It wasn't my story to share. Assuming the homeless-village development proceeded as planned, news of Stella's generosity would spread soon. Until then I would keep quiet.

She swirled her wineglass. "The authorities will have to scour his estate, see if they can find any living relatives, and then the negotiations can begin. I would put good money on the fact that the lot will sit empty for another five years."

"That's a shame."

Malcolm looked thoughtful for a moment. "Unless there's a way we can compromise. Lance suggested scheduling a meeting to brainstorm alternative outcomes."

"Like what?" Pam asked.

"Shared use. Henry's property is likely to sell as well. Maybe there's a way to develop both lots to accommodate everyone's needs."

That sounded more like the Ashland spirit. I was glad that everyone was at least willing to broach the idea of compromise.

Sterling and Marty brought up steaming bowls of pasta, chicken cacciatore, rosemary and garlic focaccia bread, and green salad. Cheers erupted from the dining room. The Professor snuck in just as dinner was about to be served. He greeted Mom with a kiss. They looked like they had coordinated their outfits for the evening. The Professor wore a pair of white shorts and a navy-and-white-checkered dress shirt with a solid fire-engine-red tie. Mom wore a navy checkered sundress with lace trim. She accentuated her narrow waist with a red sash. Her skin glowed with happiness in the candlelight.

She stood on her tiptoes to whisper something in his ear. He nodded. Then he stepped to the front of the table and dinged a fork on an empty wineglass.

"Ladies and gentlemen, friends and neighbors, I have been asked to give a toast this evening by my beautiful bride." He raised his glass to Mom. "Let me veer away from the Bard this evening and offer you these words by the great mythologist Joseph Campbell. 'Find a place inside where there's joy; and the joy will burn out the pain.' To Torte, a place where there is only joy."

"To Torte." Everyone raised their glasses.

Dinner was a merry affair. Laughter filled Torte's walls. I wanted to pinch myself. Sometimes it was hard to believe that this was my life. I was beyond lucky. My staff was growing and changing, the space was complete, Mom and the Professor were heading for a new adventure and I was too. The last few days and weeks had had the past and present clashing together. Not only because of Edgar's murder, but because of my choices. I thought of Andy. My decisions had led me here. Now they were leading me to a home in familiar territory with the promise of grand new adventures on the horizon. I couldn't wait to see what would come next.

Recipes

Cherry Almond Hand Pies

Ingredients:

1 package puffed pastry (thawed)
1 pound fresh cherries sliced in half and pitted
½ cup sugar
1 can of almond paste
1 cup of sliced almonds
1 egg yolk
Turbinado sugar

Directions:

Preheat oven to 400 degrees. Thaw puff pastry. While the pastry is thawing wash cherries, slice into halves, and discard pits. Place in a bowl and mix in ½ cup sugar. Once the pastry is to room temperature, roll out both sheets and cut into quarters to create 8 square pieces. Spread a thin layer of almond paste on a square. Then add heaping scoops of cherries and sprinkle with almonds. Carefully fold the pastry into a "V" and press edges together to seal. Whisk egg yolk and brush on the top of the pastry. Sprinkle with turbinado sugar. Repeat steps for remaining squares. Line 2 cookie sheets with parchment paper. Place hand pies 1-inch apart and bake for 15–20 minutes or until golden brown.

Fluffernutter Sandwiches

Ingredients:

1 loaf brioche or Hawaiian sweet bread
Bacon (optional)
2 eggs
½ cup milk or heavy cream
1 teaspoon cinnamon
1 teaspoon vanilla
½ cup peanut butter
½ cup Nutella
1 jar marshmallow cream
4 bananas
Butter

Directions:

Preheat oven to 350. Cut brioche into two-inch thick slices. Fry bacon (if adding bacon) and set aside to cool. Whisk eggs, milk, cinnamon and vanilla together. Dredge slices of brioche in egg mixture and grill on both sides of bread until each side is slightly golden brown and crisp. Once each slice of bread has been grilled begin assembling the sandwiches.

Spread peanut butter on one slice and Nutella on the other. Then spread a layer of marshmallow cream on both slices. Cut banana length-wise into four slices and place on top of bread. If desired add bacon. Sandwich slices together and place on a cookie sheet. Bake for ten minutes or until the fluffernutters are oozing with deliciousness. Jules recommends eating with a fork!

Chicken Cacciatore

Ingredients:

2 tablespoons olive oil
4 chicken breasts
1 onion
2 carrots
2 stalks of celery
4 cloves of garlic
1 cup dry white wine
2 15-ounce cans of diced tomatoes
1 cup chicken stock
2 tablespoons balsamic vinegar
1 teaspoon brown sugar
2 springs chopped rosemary
3 bay leaves
1 15-ounce can black olives
1 jar pitted Kalamata olives

Directions:

Add olive oil to Dutch oven or large stock pot and heat to medium. Cut chicken into one-inch strips. Once oil is heated, add chicken and brown on both sides. Remove from heat and set aside. Dice onion, carrots, and celery and cook over low heat for ten minutes. Chop garlic and add to veggies. Allow to cook for one minute. Return chicken to pan and cover it with white wine. Simmer for five minutes.

Add tomatoes, chicken stock, balsamic vinegar, brown sugar, rosemary, and bay leaves. Bring to a slow boil, turn heat to low, cover, and simmer for thirty minutes.

Remove lid and stir in black and Kalamata olives. Simmer for another fifteen minutes. Serve hot over pasta and garnish with fresh grated parmesan cheese.

Raspberry Bars

Ingredients:

- 1 ¼ cups flour
- 1 ½ teaspoon baking powder
- ½ teaspoon salt
- ¼ cup butter
- 1 ½ cups brown sugar
- 1 tablespoon lemon juice
- 2 eggs beaten
- ¼ cup flour
- 1 teaspoon vanilla
- 1 cup chopped nuts
- 1 ⅓ cup coconut
- 1 package frozen raspberries (thawed and drained) If fresh raspberries are in season Jules highly recommends using them!

Directions:

Preheat oven to 350 degrees. Sift flour, baking powder, and salt. Cream butter and ½ cup of brown sugar. Stir in lemon juice. Add to flour and mix until it resembles coarse cornmeal. Press into a 7 × 11 greased baking pan. Bake for fifteen minutes. Allow to cool.

In a new mixing bowl, combine eggs, 1 cup brown sugar, flour, and vanilla. Stir in nuts and coconut. Spread raspberries over cooled crust and then pour the mixture over the raspberries. Bake for another 30 minutes. Cool and cut into bars.

Summer Minestrone Vegetable Soup

Ingredients:

1 white onion
4 carrots
4 stalks celery
2 tablespoons olive oil
2 cloves of garlic
4 Yukon gold potatoes
A bunch of fresh herbs—Sterling used rosemary, parsley, oregano, and basil, but anything you have in your garden is fine.
3 cups homemade chicken stock or vegetable
1 15-ounce can crushed tomatoes
Salt and pepper

Directions:

Chop onion, carrots, and celery. Add olive oil to a stock pot and sauté veggies on medium heat. Once they have begun to sweat and become tender add chopped garlic. Peel and cut potatoes into cubes. Add them along with chopped fresh herbs to the veggie mixture. Cover with chicken or vegetable stock and tomatoes. Bring to a boil and then turn heat to low. Cover and simmer for an hour. Serve with a hunk of crusty bread for dipping.

Andy's Affogato

Ingredients:

1 pint vanilla bean ice cream
Espresso
Dark chocolate shavings
Chopped hazelnuts

Directions:

Fill 8-ounce glass with a generous scoop of vanilla bean ice cream. If using an espresso machine, pull a shot of espresso. If using a coffee pot, brew a half pot of strong coffee. Pour shot of espresso or 4–5 tablespoons of brewed coffee over the ice cream. Dust with chocolate shavings and chopped hazelnuts. Serve immediately. As Andy would say, "It's like dessert in a glass."

Don't miss these other Bakeshop mysteries!

MEET YOUR BAKER

A BATTER OF LIFE AND DEATH

ON THIN ICING

CAUGHT BREAD HANDED

FUDGE AND JURY

A CRIME OF PASSION FRUIT

ANOTHER ONE BITES THE CRUST

TILL DEATH DO US TART

. . . and look for the first two books in Ellie Alexander's intoxicating new series

DEATH ON TAP

THE PINT OF NO RETURN
Coming in July 2019

From St. Martin's Paperbacks